MY HOPE
NEXT DOOR

OTHER WORKS BY TAMMY L. GRAY

Sell Out
Waves of Summer
Mercy's Fight

Winsor Series

Shattered Rose
Shackled Lily
Splintered Oak

MY HOPE NEXT DOOR

TAMMY L. GRAY

Waterfall
PRESS

To my wonderful brother, Josh.
For loving us all unconditionally, for being a Godly
husband and father in your home, for teaching me the
power of compassion, and for being one of my best friends.
I'm so honored to call you family.

CHAPTER 1

The Fairfield water tower loomed over Katie's regrets like a guard she had to sneak past. She was almost home. Eight point two miles away, to be exact. Two of those miles stretched through the heart of downtown, where her past sins were as vast as the Atlantic Ocean.

She wished it were true that time healed all wounds. But time held no real power. If absolution were that simple, she'd have come back to Georgia long ago and not waited until her father's plea had forced her out of hiding.

Katie swung her car into the parking lot of her old haunt, the service station on the corner of Main and the highway. She needed a hit of caffeine and chocolate before facing her hometown, and it was now or never.

A bell dinged as she entered, but no one acknowledged her, not even the store clerk who talked on her cell with her back to the door. Relief stretched through Katie's stiff, car-trapped muscles, even though she knew her anonymity would be short-lived. Eventually, everyone in Fairfield would know she'd come home. They'd dissect why, add their own dose of juicy gossip, and discuss her return until they had an explanation as monstrous as Katie's reputation. But this time there was no power play or grand finale planned. She simply wanted to do the right thing for once in her life.

A deep voice said hello from the other side of the snack aisle. Katie wandered along, her eyes lingering on a chocolate bar and pretzels before glancing up. To her relief, she didn't recognize the middle-aged trucker who was grabbing two bags of chips. She returned his greeting with a nod and went back to her browsing.

Another *ding* ushered her trembling legs along, away from the next customer. Soon she was nicely hidden in back, where three large coolers held everything from beer to bottled coffee. This place was busier than she remembered. But that didn't surprise her. A lot changed in four years.

Two more patrons entered, the bell reverberating twice as they came in one after the other. She inhaled deeply to calm her sudden nervous adrenaline and focused on choosing a drink she could actually swallow. Returning home suddenly felt much easier in theory than in practice. There was too much history here. Too many loose ends.

The decision that had felt so concrete just four days ago now faltered in her mind. She'd thought one selfless act would allow her to heal. That maybe coming here, helping her parents, would somehow diminish the growing mountain of guilt. But even these faded walls and archaic fuel pumps held reminders of the girl she used to be. The girl she'd spent the last several years trying to forget.

"Well, look at this. My Firecracker has finally found her way home."

Katie gripped the edge of the chilly refrigerator door and focused on not letting her legs buckle. Cooper Myles's presence here was a cruel, sick, horrible joke. Of course he'd be the first one in town she talked to; that was her luck. Or maybe her deserved penance for daring to start over.

She shut the cooler and held the Dr Pepper bottle like a shield in front of her chest, knowing the coming confrontation was inevitable. Cooper wasn't the kind of guy who would be dismissed.

"Hey, it's been a while." The words were acid on her tongue. Four years hadn't lessened the animosity she felt toward him, nor had they erased her memories of their life together. The dysfunction. The brutality. The poor choices. And ultimately the weekend that sent her fleeing from Fairfield in the first place.

She tucked her free hand into the back pocket of her shorts and met his familiar dark eyes. Most men would have taken a second to peruse her body, examine how much it had changed since they'd last seen her. But Cooper was too calculated for such a cliché move. He kept his gaze steady, a laser into hers.

He hadn't changed much. His hair was still in need of a good cut, and his mouth still wore that infuriating smirk that attempted to be both condescending and charming. But he'd aged. Lines cut around his eyes, and his skin had a weathered look from his working outside in the hot Georgia sun.

She eyed the distance between his massive body and the edge of the narrow aisle he blocked.

As if he could read her mind, he broadened his stance and cut off the little space that remained. "'A while'? It's been years, Katie. I almost didn't recognize you."

Of course he didn't. She'd stopped dyeing her hair jet black and had cut at least five inches off the length. She also wasn't wearing frayed booty shorts and a ticked-off expression. Well, she hadn't been scowling, not until Cooper cornered her.

He reached out to touch her natural, more traditional locks of hair, and she flinched. Physically, he'd never hurt her, but the man knew how to throw an emotional right hook that could knock a person down for days.

He dropped his hand. "Where have you been?" The chill in his voice came after a jump in his jaw.

"I went to Jacksonville for a while. Then Tallahassee."

"You should have called."

"I had nothing to say to you." She took a breath. Her face felt hot, the skin beneath her bra straps damp and itchy. Standing there, Katie felt twenty-two and stupid all over again. Condensation from her drink dripped down over her fingers. She switched hands and wiped the water off on her clothes.

"Maybe I had things to say to you. Maybe all of us did."

When she refused to respond, he relaxed his voice. "So, what brings you home after all this time?" His disingenuous attempt to sound concerned made the hairs on the back of her neck bristle.

"Just visiting my parents."

He tugged on the edge of his T-shirt as if he needed to do something with his hands. The front was splotched with dirt and he reeked of sweat and wood shavings, echoes from a day spent at the fencing factory where he worked with her father. At least, that's where he used to work, before she left him.

"So that's it? You just walk back into town like you hadn't run off in the middle of the night? No one's seen or heard from you in four years. You didn't even have the courtesy to tell me good-bye."

Done with niceties, Katie met his eyes with a cold stare. "Don't rewrite history. You and I both know it was over."

"It was a fight."

No. It was an apocalypse.

Familiar rage grew in her belly. She needed space. Needed to get away from everything this man represented in her life. She inched forward. "Can you move? I'd like to pay for this now."

He didn't budge, and she wasn't surprised. Cooper was two hundred pounds of stubbornness and had controlled her for most of their two-year relationship. But she wasn't that messed-up girl anymore.

Frustration touched his eyes. "We all did things we regret that night." His chin dipped, and even though she sensed his simmering temper, he kept his voice mild. "I see no reason we can't talk about it like mature adults."

She could give him a million reasons, one being that his proximity was making her nauseated. "I've changed, Cooper. I'm not the same girl you remember."

"Nobody really changes. They just adapt." He took another suffocating step toward her and placed a hand at the top of the metal shelf above her shoulder. "I know you, better than you know yourself. You need a rush. You need an outlet for all that pent-up aggression you have inside. That fire is what sucked me in all those years ago."

Bile crept up her throat as she remembered the "rush" that blew up her old life. "I told you I'm different now. Please, get out of my way."

Katie immediately regretted her words. Cooper loved a challenge, and his slow smile proved she'd just issued one. He stepped aside, but it didn't feel like a victory.

"I'll see you soon, Firecracker. I bet you get bored before the end of the week. We both know you don't have it in you to play the good girl."

She somehow made it past him without slamming her fist into his gut and tried to ignore the name she hadn't heard in forever.

He was right. She'd been wild. The first to try anything, go anywhere, and do whatever made her forget her loneliness. But no matter how far she chased that elusive peace, she never found it. Not until four months ago when she stepped into a church next to Tallahassee's women's shelter and Reverend Snow told her it wasn't too late. Even for someone like her.

Still clutching her drink, Katie walked past the chips and the candy bar she'd originally considered but now couldn't stomach the thought of eating. She'd have kept going past the red exit light if it weren't for the soda in her hand and her sheer determination not to let Cooper know he bothered her.

At the counter, she cursed her nonexistent luck. Did she have to know everyone in this town? Missy Baker snapped her gum with disinterest until she recognized the new, milder Katie, then hung her mouth open, exposing the pink blob.

"OMG! Katie Stone. How are you?" Missy squealed and ran around the counter to give Katie a bone-crushing hug. Missy was the youngest of three girls. Katie had gone to high school with her eldest sister, Maebry, and the two of them had spent many days together in detention.

"I'm good. How are you? You're graduating this year, right?"

Missy slumped before her. "Ugh. Yes. Don't know how I'll ever make it."

"You will. It's only a month away." Katie handed Missy the drink, wishing the girl would move faster. She could practically feel Cooper staring at her.

"I guess. You were so smart to get out of this town, but I swear, with you gone, it's been all kinds of boring. Course, now that you're home, I'm guessing things are going to get much more colorful." Missy continued to chat as she rang up the soft drink, but Katie stopped listening.

Beyond the windows, the sky darkened to dusk, just like her hope of things being different this time around. There was way too much history in this little town, and her younger self had left a black mark, not easily erased. TP-ing the mayor's house, getting high right before her senior presentation, skinny-dipping in the lake, protesting at city hall when they proposed making Fairfield a dry city. She'd always found some way to buck the system or cause a scene.

"How long you stayin'?"

Katie snapped her attention back to Missy and handed her a five-dollar bill. "Not sure yet." At the rate things were going, she'd be high-tailing it out of there tomorrow.

A big tan hand slapped a twenty on the counter, and Cooper's chest pressed against her arm. "I think Katie needs a reminder of life in Fairfield, starting tonight at Joe's Bar." His eyes drilled hers. "Think how surprised Laila's going to be when I give her the news that our girl has come home."

Missy giggled and nodded like a bobblehead doll. "Laila and Katie together again. I can't wait to call Maebry. She's going to die when I tell her."

Katie shifted left until her elbow bumped a tower of Budweiser cases, her former best friend's name lingering in the air like a phantom. She'd tucked Laila's memory away, kept it locked inside the dusty corners of her mind.

Cooper hadn't changed. His words were still harsh and calculated. He wanted her to remember. Wanted her to hurt.

Without taking his eyes off Katie, he slid the money to Missy. "Pump six, dollface."

Katie looked away, not bothering to mention he'd cut in line.

Or that he'd ripped the scab off her greatest emotional wound.

Hot breath touched her ear, and her skin went cold. "Your key still works, Firecracker. I'll be home all night." He strolled out the door, a victorious beat to his stride, as if running into her were the spark of a new beginning.

But leaving Fairfield was supposed to be the end, a closed chapter she never intended to reopen. She'd left home a broken, bitter girl, searching for answers, and finally, over the last few months, had become someone she was actually starting to like.

Defeated, Katie pushed open the glass doors and walked to her rusty old Toyota in the parking lot. She hadn't even crossed the city line and already the positive transformation she'd worked so hard to make was unraveling. She had thought she was ready. But she'd only been high on wishful thinking.

It would take a miracle for her to get a second chance in her hometown.

CHAPTER 2

Asher leaned against the porch post of his Victorian-style home and watched as his mother's small sedan eased down the gravel driveway. Her car was definitely not made for the country, but she came anyway. Three times a week. Just to make sure he didn't die from bachelorhood.

The wood creaked and rattled against his weight, and he mentally added the porch to the growing list of things he needed to repair on his hundred-year-old fixer-upper. But that was what he'd signed up for when he bought the place from Dr. Mills two years ago. The former owner had spent forty-five years in this house, raised two sons, and buried his soul mate, and he only agreed to sell because Asher's dad had been his pastor for twenty-five of those years. Well, that and the fact that he knew Asher loved his home almost as much as he did.

His mom emerged from her car, balancing a plate in the same hand that held her keys.

He hopped down the steps. "Please tell me that's food. I swear I'm wasting away."

She hugged him with her free arm, her hold tight despite her tiny frame. Asher towered over her, his rangy build a gift from his dad, who also stood over six feet. But height was one of the few traits he'd inherited from his father. The blond hair, brown eyes, easygoing nature—those all came from his mother's side of the family.

She patted his back. "Of course I brought you food. I always bring you food. But it comes at a price today."

"I'll pay anything." He took the large plate out of her hands and reveled in the glorious smell of red meat. "Is this brisket?" He lifted the foil completely off the mound of savory goodness. "And homemade potato salad? Have I told you how much I love you?"

His mom waved off his affectionate words, but her eyes glistened. She was the sensitive type, always one word away from a flood of happy tears. But he loved that about her. Laura Powell was revered in Fairfield, not just for being the best cook in the county, but also because she was perpetually optimistic and graciously forgiving.

He followed her into the house, sneaking a few pieces of meat along the way. She went straight to his new stainless fridge, poured him a tall glass of lemonade, and sat on the barstool adjacent to his. "So, to discuss my payment."

"Take the house. It's yours," he said with his mouth still full.

Handing him a napkin, his mom shot him a glare that scolded without a word. Poor table manners were a pet peeve of hers, but in his defense, he hadn't eaten a real meal in two days.

"My cooking isn't that good. Besides, you'd be heartbroken."

True. The property had become more than just a dream realized; it'd become his refuge.

He took another heaping bite of potato salad. "So, what do you need me to do this time? Leaky sink? Clogged gutters? Maybe a good wax on that new car of yours?"

She placed a hand on his forearm. "Come to church with me this Sunday."

His fork froze midbite. At least she'd let him get through half the meal before souring his stomach. He closed his eyes and set the utensil down slowly.

"Asher, please. I'm asking for one Sunday." She said it like it was no big deal. Like he hadn't been absent from church for almost a year. "Susan and Tom are in town, and I don't want to explain all the drama that happened last summer."

"Drama isn't the right word." His voice was sharper than he intended. "More like judgment, legalism, and hypocrisy. Bob Murray should be kicked out of the church, not hold the position of elder."

"He was protecting his daughter."

The muscles in his neck tightened. "She was twenty-four, not fourteen."

Asher had given his life to that church. Half the people in it had known him since he was a baby. Yet one lapse in judgment, and they crucified him. Demanded he step down as media director and made his father's life miserable until Asher finally resigned.

His mom rubbed her hands up and down her arms. She hated this conversation as much as he did.

The house suddenly felt too small and too hot. He pushed aside his half-eaten dinner and left her sitting in the kitchen.

"Asher." Her call was lost in the slam of the screen door. He closed his eyes and sucked in the humid air to keep his stomach from trying to jump into his throat. This degree of bitterness was new to him, and for the millionth time he prayed for it to go away.

The hissing of springs said his mom had followed him. He didn't turn. "You have no idea how sick I am of hearing those words."

"I know. And they're not an excuse. Just an explanation. He's apologized to your dad several times. Bob knows he acted unjustly."

Asher let out a grunt. Unjust? More like irrational and cruel. The man's daughter had gone to him crying, spewing lies about her and Asher's relationship, and his first response was to stage a political coup in the church. Asher wasn't even a staff member. Just a volunteer who'd devoted late nights and early mornings to making sure the church had an online presence. His thanks? A swift kick out the door.

His mom touched the sleeve of his shirt, sending a bolt of regret through him. He wrapped an arm around her shoulders. It wasn't her fault. None of this was her doing. "I'm sorry, but I'm still angry."

"I know. And I understood that you needed a break from the church, but it's been months. When do you plan to come back?"

Never. "When they stop attending."

"You know that's not going to happen. Bob's granddaddy donated the land the sanctuary is built on." She paused, her sigh as heavy as the wet air. "When you told your dad and me that you needed time away, we didn't like it, but we trusted you would know when your heart was ready to return. But I'm starting to worry you may never see beyond the hurt."

"It's not hurt that's keeping me away."

"Then help me understand. Jillian's dating again, and Alice swears her daughter wants to put all this ugliness behind her. They feel terrible about what happened."

"Not terrible enough to apologize to me. They dragged my name through the mud, insulted my integrity, all because a pastor's kid isn't allowed to be human." He wondered when it would ever stop, the town constantly watching and waiting for him to mess up. The sad thing was, he really had tried to be perfect. At least that was over. He was done with all the pretense.

"I'm sure they're too embarrassed to say anything to you," she said.

"They should be. She lied to them."

"They know that."

He peeked at her from his peripheral vision. "They do?"

"Well, they haven't said so outright, but I got the sense that Jillian had come clean to Alice. The woman's been bringing me baked goods every week for two months." Her smile lasted long enough to chase away the tension in his shoulders. He wasn't at a place where he could joke about Jillian or her parents, but maybe he could honor his mom and attend one Sunday.

"Can I think about it?"

His mom practically leapt with joy and hugged him. She knew him well enough to know that his "thinking about it" was the same as saying yes. "Thank you, sweetheart. This means so much to me."

He knew it did. Nothing about Sundays had been the same since Bob's vendetta started, and his mom wasn't the only one who missed the way things used to be.

"Well, I'd better go. Your daddy wanted me to watch some documentary with him when I got back."

"You're just afraid I'll change my mind if you stay."

Her eyes crinkled with her smile. "Well, that too. I'll see you Sunday." She leaned up and kissed his cheek. Within minutes, she was pulling away from his house, leaving him to come to terms with what he'd just agreed to do.

A strip of orange cut the sky, making it just bright enough to see his mom turn off his street and onto the highway. This was his favorite time of day. It was no longer a million degrees outside, and the breeze shifted from the south to the north, lifting the hair off his forehead. The chirping of cicadas echoed through the air as calm rolled through his body.

His mom was right: ten months should be enough time for him to heal and to forgive. So why did it feel like his stomach lining was getting scraped out every time Sunday showed up on the calendar? He wasn't in love with Jillian anymore. Hadn't been since even before the explosive breakup. But seeing Christians behave like bullies had shaken his faith in the church, and he didn't know how to get it back.

The crunch of gravel drew his attention back to the road and to the battered car pulling up to the house next door.

He should go inside. His neighbors had made it more than clear they didn't want to be friendly, and Dr. Mills had labeled them "the heathens who can't seem to cut their grass but once a year." Asher had thought he was exaggerating, but when Asher rolled his own mower over to their neglected plot of land, Mr. Stone told him he didn't want any handouts, especially from the preacher's kid.

A girl with straight shoulder-length hair emerged from the car as the trunk popped open. She walked around to the back, reached down, and tugged at something, but managed only to lose her footing.

Asher hesitated, but when the girl stumbled for a second time, he jogged across the yard.

"Hey, let me help you with that," he called when he was close enough for her to hear him.

The girl looked up, half startled and very familiar. Asher wondered how rude it'd be to turn around and jog right back home. Katie Stone. He'd recognize her anywhere. She was the only person he'd ever met with eyes so pale blue they looked like crushed silver.

Forcing himself to do the right thing despite their history, Asher freed the bag from her strained grip. It was one of those massive green duffels with "U.S. Army" stamped on the side, and it was packed so full even the zipper looked ready to burst.

"Thank you," she said in a tone that surprised him. It was soft and gentle, lacking the crass attitude he remembered from high school. "I was beginning to think I'd have to roll it inside."

"Well, that's what neighbors are here for. Rescuing damsels from overstuffed luggage." Asher had to work to keep his voice steady. He could tell she didn't recognize him, and he preferred to keep it that way. Their interactions in high school had been less than friendly.

"Oh? You're our neighbor?" She pulled a second, smaller bag from the trunk before shutting it. "Are you staying with Dr. Mills?"

"Nope. I bought the place from him two years ago."

Her mouth dropped open as he set the bag down. Despite the forty pounds of muscle he'd packed on since high school, he questioned the wisdom of throwing out his shoulder for a girl who used to call him Holy String Bean.

"Dr. Mills sold the place?" She stared at his house as if she were seeing it for the first time. "Wow. I truly thought he'd die right there, scowling at us from his front porch."

Asher sucked in a laugh until he realized he'd been doing the same thing not five minutes earlier. Great. He'd officially turned into a crotchety old man.

Katie's face fell when he didn't respond. "I'm sorry. That was terribly rude. I really didn't mean it how it sounded. I just sometimes let words fly out of my mouth before I consider the impact. It's something I've really been working on. Honest."

Now it was Asher's turn to be surprised. Katie Stone had just apologized. Not only that, but she'd strung two sentences together that didn't have a cuss word in either one. "It's fine. You're actually not too far off base with the scowl thing."

Their eyes met for a moment, and heat crawled along his neck. The years had been good to her. No, they'd worshiped her. The girlish chubbiness in her face had thinned, leaving cheekbones and a jawline so prominent an artist would get on his knees just for a chance to paint her.

He needed a distraction. Now. He lifted the hundred-pound bag and started toward her house. "This doesn't feel like an overnight stay," he said, no longer willing to look at her. It was the hair that was confusing him. The caramel color softened her olive skin and made her appear sweet and kind. Neither of which was possible.

"It's not. Well, at least I thought I'd be here a while. Not so sure now."

He sensed sadness in her tone but kept walking until the bag was firmly planted on the edge of the cracking wood porch outside her front door. "Do you need me to take it inside for you?"

"No. I'm not really sure what I'll find in there." She slowly climbed the three steps up to the sagging entry and stared at the door for so long, the silence turned awkward.

The shadows on her face pulled at something deep inside and made him almost forget he was talking to the girl who slugged the homecoming queen. "Okay then, I guess I'll see you around."

He made it three paces away from her house before she called after him.

"Wait. You didn't tell me your name."

He hesitated, but turned around. "Asher. Asher Powell." And there it was. The reaction that came with the Powell name: wide eyes, hitched breath; the uncomfortable pause while the person hurried to remember if they'd said anything offensive.

Her cheeks turned pink, and suddenly her shoes became her singular focus.

Yep. She remembered him now.

"Welcome back, Katie."

CHAPTER 3

Katie stood in stunned silence as she watched Asher jog across the field that separated their houses. She'd certainly jumped into the fire drenched in gasoline. Just twenty minutes back in town and her past offenses were already wrapped around her like garland on a Christmas tree.

She hadn't seen Asher since graduation, and although the skinny boy with glasses had disappeared, his chivalrous heart obviously had not. In high school she'd found it revolting, his kindness, the way he watched her with eyes that promised understanding. Even when she'd flung stinging commentary his way, that look had never faltered.

Blood pounded against her temples. Another person she'd wronged. The list was endless.

Refusing to slide down into a sea of regret, she turned back to her parents' front door and tried to regain the little bit of bravery she'd lost when Asher told her his name. But the house wasn't any more welcoming than Cooper's sneering innuendos. Everything felt off. Decayed somehow. As if time had cruelly attacked her childhood home.

Paint curled and separated from the door and yellow siding in long, ugly streaks. The porch was barely functional, its rotting wood sagging toward the ground. Had it always been this way, or did her memory recall only what it wanted to?

The door was unlocked, so Katie let herself in without a knock—and immediately recoiled from the smell. It was the stench of filth: urine, cat litter, old chicken stock, soiled laundry. All magnified by hot, humid air.

Choking back the urge to gag, she covered her nose and concentrated on breathing through her mouth, only now fully understanding why her father had broken down and made the phone call. He was a proud man, and Katie knew that asking his wayward daughter for help meant he was desperate.

A floral bedsheet hung in the doorway to her left. Her parents' old parlor. She tiptoed closer and peeked behind the barrier. The room had been converted to a bedroom, and her mom lay asleep, still fully clothed, on a twin mattress. A wooden cane stood propped against the footboard.

Katie pressed a hand to her stomach. She'd been in such a hurry to come home, she hadn't had time to fully process what it meant to do so. She and her mom hadn't seen each other in four years and had spoken only twice on the phone. Once on Katie's birthday and once at Christmas. All other communications had been conducted through polite voicemails that kept them both off the hook until the next mandatory call.

Not wanting to disturb her, Katie pulled the sheet back into place and headed farther down the hallway. The lights were off, but the last bit of setting sun cast a glow through the house that felt both eerie and oppressive. The dining room was stuffed full with its old furniture plus the rejects from the parlor. Boxes were stacked to the ceiling in columns, rendering the space virtually unusable. She shuddered, the smell getting worse as she approached the kitchen.

This house had never felt especially warm or inviting—that wasn't the Stone way—but even Katie could see the deterioration went well beyond some ignored maintenance. Something dark and ominous had settled over their lives, and for maybe the first time, Katie knew she would sacrifice whatever she needed to in order to fix it.

A low voice hummed from the television in the living room, and Katie followed the sound. She found her father sitting in his recliner, holding the remote in one hand and a can of Miller in the other. A sense of familiarity swept over her and she clung to it, needing something in the house to feel unchanged. For a decade now, her father would come home from work, eat dinner, watch the news, and drink two cans of beer. No more. No less. An hour later, he'd go outside, have a cigarette, and then tell the family good night.

"Dad?" Katie took another step into the room, keeping her eyes focused on her father and not on the stack of newspapers shoved into the corner.

The TV went silent. "Katiebug. You're here." He lowered his feet until the chair snapped upright, and then he stood.

She crossed the space between them and fell into his open arms. He smelled like nicotine and welded metal, and she realized how much she'd missed his embrace.

"I thought you quit smoking," she teased.

"I'm working on it. Still." He'd been working on it for seventeen years now.

He released her and stepped back, pinching his brows as he took in her new style. "You cut your hair. Changed the color too."

Her father was a man of few words and even fewer compliments, so she didn't have a clue if he hated it or not. "Yeah. It was time for a change. You look the same."

He grunted. "I'm fatter and older." And way more tired, although neither of them said it. Instead they just stood there until the silence became uncomfortable.

"Your ma went to lay down. This medicine kinda makes her feel like she has the flu. Doc said that should go away in a few weeks." He settled back in his chair and kicked up his feet.

"Should I let her know I'm here?"

"Nah. I'll help her get showered and changed later. She'll want to see you in the morning when she's fresher. You know your ma."

That she did, and fresher meant fully engaged with a semiautomatic of disappointment, judgment, and guilt.

Suddenly Katie was glad she'd have another twelve hours to prepare for their reunion.

Her father pointed to a couch covered in unfolded laundry. "Well, sit down. Unless you plan on leaving again already."

Katie pushed aside the pile of clothes and jumped a foot when the mound trembled and hissed. She placed a hand over her beating heart and tried not to imagine the type of vermin their house was likely to attract in this condition.

To her relief, a very fat cat emerged from beneath the linen, walked along the edge of the couch like a gymnast, and jumped off the other side.

Her father laughed. "Don't mind Agatha. She's a snobby one."

Katie forced herself to sit, but a part of her expected another animal to pop out. "I didn't think Mom liked cats."

"She doesn't, but the thing just kept showing up and eventually wormed its way inside."

"That's nice."

A blanket of awkwardness fell over them. Katie could tell her dad was itching to turn the sound back on, and she was quickly running out of small talk.

She cleared her throat. "What are the doctors saying?" Her parents had gotten the diagnosis a month ago, although Katie's father had informed her only last week. Multiple sclerosis. Reportedly, her mother had been having symptoms for almost a year but finally went to see a neurologist when she suddenly couldn't stand without falling.

"Just to wait it out. The medicine has helped. Doc says it can even reverse some of the damage if she takes it long enough." He rubbed his forehead. "Good thing, too, 'cause that stuff ain't cheap."

Katie's stomach ached as if she'd been elbowed there. She hadn't even considered the financial ramifications. Her mom's condition had forced her to quit her job at the bank, and her dad's had never paid that well, not even after twenty-three years of employment.

"Well, I'm going to get unpacked. Should I use my old room?"

"Yeah." Her father grabbed at the back of his neck, an old habit he fell into whenever he felt uncomfortable. "But you may have to move some stuff around." He stood and stretched his back. "Come on, I'll help. Things have gotten so crowded, I think the only floor space we have left is in the bathroom."

Katie and her dad each took an end of her duffel and carried it up the stairs. Her muscles burned with every step. A large painting of a lighthouse hung where her graduation picture used to be, and Katie concentrated on not hitting it with her shoulder.

"Never knew one lousy bag could be this heavy." Her father took two more steps backward toward the upper floor. A bead of sweat fell from his brow.

Katie remembered the easy way Asher had hiked the bag up on his shoulder. "So, Dr. Mills sold his house?" She was sweating too, but not from the load. The upstairs was at least ten degrees warmer than the downstairs had been. But, thankfully, it smelled better. Which was sad, because it still reeked of mildew and wet cardboard.

"Yeah. To the preacher's kid, of all people. I think Dr. Mills did that on purpose as a final middle finger. Now I have to keep my blinds closed and pretend to be friendly every time I take a smoke. The kid's always outside working on something. Waves at me too."

"Waves, huh? What a jerk."

He snorted. "Figures you'd change the hair, but not your lip. Those people are all the same. They pretend to be nice just so they can suck you into their cult and take all your hard-earned cash. Not gonna happen."

A weighted sigh fell from her lips. She knew her father's stance on religion. She'd shared it most of her life. But she'd come to take a different view. She'd seen believers sacrifice for her and care about her. She'd experienced something beautiful.

Problem was, she didn't have a clue as to how to explain the difference to him, or whether she even wanted to. Her parents represented one world; her new faith, another. And if Katie had learned one thing about survival, it was to keep her life divided—the good and the bad clearly marked and separated. She'd broken that rule only one time, and it'd been enough to destroy her life.

They deposited the bag in the hallway outside her old bedroom, and Katie wanted nothing more than to click her heels together and make the room disappear. It had been gutted of everything Katie had once cherished and filled with four years' worth of bills, magazines, advertisements, and junk. Not even one picture remained.

"Where's all my stuff?" Her antique queen bed had been replaced with a cheap twin trundle covered in boxes.

"Your ma donated most of it and put the personal stuff in the attic."

Katie knew what he wasn't saying. That she'd abandoned them. That leaving without a word had hurt her mother enough to make her want to erase Katie from their lives.

Her dad slid one stack of boxes away from the door and then did so with two other stacks, giving them a two-foot pathway to the bed. He scratched his head. "Couple of years ago, your ma had this harebrained idea about making money off eBay. Bought a whole bunch of wholesale stock but never really got around to sellin' it. Being home from the bank means more buyin', but the sellin' stuff hasn't really picked up."

Hearing the fatigue in his voice, she laid a hand on his arm. "It's fine, Dad. This will work for tonight, and tomorrow I'll get a plan together on how to start decluttering. Believe it or not, organizing is one of the few things I'm good at." And she was. Cleaning and organizing houses had paid her bills since high school.

Her dad studied the overstuffed room as if seeing it for the first time. He gripped the back of his neck. "Well, I guess I'll let you get settled. I should probably go check on your ma anyway." He shuffled back to the door, where he paused and placed a hand on the doorframe. Worried, tired eyes met hers. "I'm glad you're home, Katiebug."

She could have sworn there was a slight catch in his voice, but she would never know. The Stones didn't show emotion. And they certainly didn't shed tears over sentimental nonsense.

Katie sat on her duffel and eyed the stacks and stacks of junk. Her father was probably the only person in town, including her, who was happy she'd returned.

Thomas Wolfe believed you could never go home again.

Maybe he was right.

CHAPTER 4

It was ten o'clock by the time Katie had made her room livable. She'd stacked half of the boxes in the hall and the other half against her dresser. She wouldn't be using the drawers anytime soon, anyway. Every one of them was stuffed with bills, receipts, and other papers too important to simply throw away.

Her dad had gone to bed an hour ago, after getting her mom settled. She'd heard their muffled conversation drift up the stairs, and her mom's sour tone confirmed he'd been right about waiting until morning.

Katie ran a hand over the new curtains. Everything in her room was different. The walls were bare. Her stuffed animals and childhood treasures were only a memory. She should have felt upset by her mom's drastic response to her leaving, but in a way she was relieved. It made forgetting easier.

Floodlights from outside drew Katie closer to the window. She could see the pitched roof and wraparound porch of Dr. Mills's house. She'd always coveted that porch. To her, it embodied peace and comfort, things she'd never felt in her own home. Dr. Mills would sit there for hours just rocking and rocking, sometimes reading but mostly just staring off into nowhere. She still couldn't believe he'd sold the place.

Asher hadn't kept the wooden rockers. A love seat with cushions stood there instead, along with a two-person swing and three wicker club chairs.

A strange curiosity pulled at her. What else had he changed about the place?

She quietly tiptoed down the stairs, carefully avoiding the spots that creaked. She'd made a mental map as a teenager and could slip in and out of the house without making a sound.

A warm breeze lifted her hair as soon she shut the back door. Sneaking out brought on an assault of memories. Laila giggling so loudly that Katie had to put a hand over her mouth. Chad telling her *Come on, come on, you're going to get caught* in a whisper that was louder than Laila's giggles. They'd been only thirteen. Innocent still, all of them.

Katie squeezed her eyes tight and forced down the creeping sting in her esophagus. The deed was done. She couldn't take back her choices. Another deep breath and the sting disappeared. She was in control once more, the past locked up again, where it belonged.

The back steps were steeper than the ones in front, and two of them were cracked in the middle. She skipped down the stable ones and started toward her neighbor's house. Her parents' lawn was as neglected as their home. More weeds than grass, and the sharp contrast of Asher's lush green Bermuda made the two plots look like a before-and-after advertisement for a lawn maintenance company.

Seven wood posts marked the property line, with ten more lying on the ground at equal increments. She wondered if the fence was Asher's idea or a rude suggestion from her father. Katie guessed the latter. Asher had always been warm and friendly. It used to make her uncomfortable, which is why she'd been especially cruel. His presence had provoked guilt and shame, even when he hadn't said a word.

She walked toward one of the posts sticking up from the ground, hoping to subtly get a better peek. Light spilled from several places around Asher's roof, illuminating a half-finished deck off the back.

The new addition was beautiful and grand enough to entertain at least thirty people. She stepped closer. Rounded corners, a vaulted roof, a decorative rail that ran horizontal to the ground. Spectacular.

A rhythmic scraping sound from the corner of the structure halted her steps, as did the sight of the man on all fours, sliding his arm back and forth over the wood. He wore no shirt, and his back pulsed with a row of muscles that seemed impossible for a kid who couldn't gain an ounce of weight in high school, no matter how many cheeseburgers he stuffed down at lunch.

He sat back on his heels and ran a towel over his face and neck. His blond hair, now wet around his temples, was darker than she remembered. He set down the towel and stood, stretching his arms behind his back. Broad through the shoulders. Flat across the stomach. Asher Powell had turned into a very handsome man, and Katie's treacherous eyes soaked in every single inch.

"Did my sanding bother you?" His voice snapped her eyes back where they belonged. On his.

"Um, no. Not at all."

His light-brown eyes had an I-can-see-deep-into-your-soul quality as they wandered over her. It made her skin tingle. Made her pull on the edge of her shirt and think about the state of her hair for the first time all night.

"Okay, good." He pulled a T-shirt over his head. It didn't help. The fabric clung to every hard line, and there were many.

She inched closer, even as her mind told her she shouldn't. This was the preacher's kid. She'd called him names, laughed at his clothes, told dirty jokes in front of him just to see his cheeks turn red.

"You've changed a lot," she blurted out.

His brows pinched together.

"I mean, the house. You've changed a lot about the house. Since Dr. Mills lived here." She pointed in the direction of the porch. "The rocking chairs are gone."

"Yeah, he wanted to take them with him. They reminded him of his wife."

She could sense Asher's discomfort. But being the nice guy he was, he continued to stand there, waiting for her next awkward statement.

She was at the edge of the deck now and needed only to walk up two steps to be level with him. "I didn't recognize you."

"I figured."

His body language practically begged her to leave, but for some reason she kept moving closer. It was as if her soul sensed a kindred spirit. As if the changes she'd gone through in Florida put them on common ground. The old feeling of unrest had turned to comfort and safety. It didn't make logical sense, this connection she felt to a practical stranger.

"I never saw you after graduation," she said.

"I went to Georgia Tech. Worked in Atlanta for a while."

Wow. He'd gone to college. A hard college, too. She'd dropped out of community college after one semester. "Your parents must have been proud."

"They were, I guess." He tilted his head as if trying to decipher hidden code. Like the rest of this town, he probably still remembered her as the girl who was more likely to pull a prank than actually have a meaningful conversation. "Listen, I stop the power tools at nine so I don't disturb your folks, but if you need the light off, too, I can call it a night."

In other words, *I'm not interested in talking with the girl voted Most Likely to Become a Felon.*

Anxiety crept up her spine. She was going to need to do something more than throw out one-liners if she hoped to ever change his opinion of her. Katie had spent a lifetime mastering an I-don't-care-what-anyone-thinks attitude, yet this moment with Asher felt important, as if it were the first step to the new beginning she so desperately craved.

"I guess it's time to quit stalling." She cleared her throat, wishing she'd grabbed a water bottle on her way out of the house. "I didn't come out here to ask you a bunch of dumb questions. I, um . . ."

Katie took a deep breath before spitting her words out in a rush.

"I came out here to apologize."

CHAPTER 5

Apologize.

Typically a positive word. But from Katie Stone, it could mean a million things, not all of them good or even legal.

"For what?" This new, vulnerable Katie had him feeling wary. He'd made the mistake of thinking she was soft one time their freshman year. He'd seen her boyfriend hit her, but when he'd gone to intervene, she'd already clocked the jerk. She'd warned she'd punch Asher too, if he ever told. He hadn't, but she'd hated him all the same.

Katie stood a couple of feet away, wringing her hands and sliding her slippered toe across his freshly cut grass. She wore SpongeBob SquarePants boxers and a yellow T-shirt that said "One in a Minion" on it. Her hair was pulled up into a high ponytail, and she looked way younger now than she ever had their senior year.

"For all of it. I was terrible to you in high school. For reasons that had nothing to do with you. I'm sorry." Her voice was hesitant, her eyes sparking with an unmet demand. And maybe that's what she was doing. Demanding forgiveness. Redemption. He wasn't in a position to give either, but at least he could ease her obvious discomfort.

"That was eight years go. I haven't really thought about it." Well, he hadn't until she showed up next door. Now he couldn't get her out of his head.

The sides of her mouth tilted up into a teeth-exposing smile. She looked gentle when she smiled. Almost friendly. Not remotely like the girl who used to kick his chair in class if he dared to make eye contact.

"Really?" She let out a huge breath and climbed the last few steps to join him on the deck. Her gaze drifted to the roof he'd finished just last weekend. "And here I was sure you dreaded the idea of me being next door."

Maybe a little.

A flurry of gnats bounced around the porch light while she trailed one hand along the rail. "This is really amazing. Did you do all the work yourself?" She leaned over, inspected the underside of the rail, then stood back up.

"The hands-on stuff, yes. But my dad designed it."

She continued her walk around the edge of the deck, stepping over the electric sander he'd turned off an hour ago. Frogs croaked in a nearby pond, and crickets responded with echoes of excitement. He couldn't share their sentiments. Katie was the first besides his parents to see his handiwork, and here she was, absorbing every inch with her touch. It felt too intimate.

"It's so different. Is it shaped like a . . ." She bit her lip while she studied the structure.

"Turret," he finished for her. "I'm following the same lines that are on the front of the house."

"'Turret.' Hmmm. I guess that's better than the 'tower thingy' I was going to say." She met his gaze with a smile that was both teasing and warm, and Asher's skin suddenly felt too tight for his body. He rotated his shoulders to ease the sensation.

"So what were you doing before I interrupted you?" She walked over to the area he'd been working on and picked up a scrap of sandpaper. "You sand all this by hand?"

"I do after nine p.m." Because the last thing Asher wanted was to give Mr. Stone more ammunition for his rude commentary.

"That's really thoughtful of you." She ran her fingers over the fine grain. "Maybe I could help. I hear four hands are better than two." She raised one hand and wiggled her fingers.

Asher hadn't moved since she had stepped onto the deck. Maybe it was the shock of seeing her so exposed. No deep line of makeup around her eyes. No mane of black hair covering half her face. No snarled lip hurling insults at him.

Or maybe it was just her presence in the only place that held any joy for him. He'd spent months bleeding into this structure. It was more than a project. It was his escape, the source of his stillness. Hours spent here were the only time his heart didn't ache with bitterness.

Her company felt a little like an ambush.

"I was just about to pack up and hit the shower." As if to prove this true, he lifted the electric sander and began rolling up the cord in a tight loop.

Katie dropped the scrap of sandpaper she'd been caressing. "Yeah, of course. It's late. I'm sure you have to get up early for work and all that."

He didn't correct her or admit he worked from home and had a mostly flexible schedule. Right then all he wanted was for Katie to disappear back into her house and take with her whatever voodoo magic was making him notice how ethereal she looked in the moonlight.

Katie put a hand on one of the columns and spun around it like a seven-year-old. "Well, if you decide you want some help, I'm trainable." She stared at the dimly lit house next door. "Besides, it's ten times nicer out here than it is in there."

He thought that was her good-bye, but instead she sat down on the edge of the wood as if she couldn't force herself to go back.

His instinct said to let it go. Her issues were her own. Not his.

But Asher found himself moving in her direction, then sitting down and scooting her way, until they were side by side, their thighs almost touching. "So, what did you do after high school?"

"Nothing, really. I tried college. It wasn't for me."

"Why's that?"

She shrugged. "I don't know. I guess I'm not good at the committing-to-something-long-term thing."

He thought of Jillian. "Or maybe you just haven't found the right thing to commit to."

She tilted her head as if she knew he was talking about himself too. "Maybe." She went back to staring at the house next door. Her movements and voice seemed free enough, but a haunted sadness kept returning to her face, despite the plastered-on smile.

"I heard about your mom," he said.

"Yeah, most people have. It's a small town."

"Is that why you came back?" Asher reached down and pulled out a lone weed that was coming up through the wood.

"Yes . . . maybe." She lifted her gaze toward the sky. He followed her lead, and they both stared at the stars scattered across the darkness. "I came to help her. But I'm also hoping this illness will be a way for us to heal. Our relationship has never been . . . well, stable."

A feeling like being sucked into a storm washed over him. He didn't know Katie or the Stones. They'd made a point of pushing him as far away as possible. But here she was, extending an olive branch. Offering him the kind of honesty he hadn't seen in far too long.

"Do you think people really get second chances?" she asked into the silence.

Asher studied her profile, the slight slope of her nose, the elegant line of her neck, the shadow of pain in the tilt of her eyes, and he wanted nothing more than to believe she could. "I hope so."

She leaned back on her elbows and straightened her legs out in front of her. They were long and tan and legendary in Fairfield. Yet it wasn't her beauty that struck him now, it was her uncharacteristic vulnerability. Tough, no-nonsense, wild-hearted Katie Stone. It was how he'd always known her. But that wasn't the girl next to him.

A sudden giggle pulled him from his musing.

"What?"

"The laundry moved."

"The laundry?"

Her giggles grew until they were gut-deep hysterics that made him smile for some reason.

"I'm telling you, it's so messy in there, I might be better off sleeping outdoors." Her laughter faded to a sigh that was anything but humorous. "What's something you tell yourself when a task feels too great? Too overwhelming?"

Her attention was back to him, as if he were a fortune cookie that held winning lottery numbers. But he had no clue how to answer, because he'd felt overwhelmed for months. He knew what his dad would say. He'd quote 1 Peter and tell her to pray. But that advice had barely resonated in his own life; he certainly couldn't expect it to resonate with someone who'd spent her adolescence bashing organized religion.

He thought again of the Jillian mess. "I guess I would take it one day at a time. One project at a time, and try to find purpose in each one." At least that was what he was trying to do.

She sat up and furrowed her brow like she was memorizing his words. "Find purpose in every task. One box at a time. One square inch and then another." Her voice grew stronger with each line, but he had no idea what she was talking about.

"Sure. Something like that."

"Okay." She gave a determined nod and stood. "Thank you." The way she said the words made him believe she was talking about more than his simple advice. Her fingers lovingly stroked the design etched in the wood column. "This really is beautiful, Asher."

She patted the surface twice and then took off back to her house, swatting away invisible insects as soon as she crossed into her family's knee-high field.

Asher suddenly felt as if the air had been knocked out of him. Or maybe all those stars had collided overhead. He'd been ambushed, all right. But for some reason, her coming over didn't feel like such a bad thing anymore. In fact, he felt strangely relieved.

For the first time in ten miserable months, someone understood.

CHAPTER 6

K atie woke up to a massive fur ball crushing her sternum.
"Get off." She shoved Agatha to the floor and frantically tried
to remove the mound of hair deposited on her shirt. The gray beast
popped her tail in the air, and Katie could have sworn the cat smirked
at her.

When she'd made the decision to come home, she'd planned on staying only long enough to get her parents back on their feet. A week . . .
two weeks, maybe. But she had never imagined they were this bad off.
Her timeline would undoubtedly be stretched from weeks to months,
and still she wondered if it would be long enough to accomplish the task.

Covered in sweat thanks to the pitiful AC, Katie made the trek to the
bathroom, having to slide her body between stacks of boxes to get there.

She'd sprayed the mildew-infested room with half a bottle of tile
cleaner the night before, and to her relief, several of the black stains had
disappeared. Still, she wore flip-flops when she stepped into the tub and
closed the curtain with two fingers, barely touching the plastic.

One task at a time.

Talking with Asher had left her feeling empowered, almost super-
human. But the reality that came with sunlight was worse than the
night before. This house was too much for her parents. Too big. Too
many small rooms and doorways. A staircase so steep her father would
be first-floor-bound like her mother in only a few years.

She had to convince them to sell. But who in their right mind would buy a house in this condition? No one. And her parents needed more than what an investor would pay. They needed money for retirement, medical expenses, and paid help.

Worry pounded in her temples. She was only twenty-six. Too young for such a monumental responsibility. But there was no one else. Her half-brother was ten years older and refused to speak to their father. Her mom had a sister who lived somewhere in California, but Katie had never even met her.

Panic shook her chest, pain pressing against her lungs. She closed her eyes, spoke words to a God she'd only just met, and waited until the anxiety went away. She'd been in a more desperate situation than this before, and it had led to a new beginning. Asher was right. There had to be a purpose for her being here.

With damp hair and wearing a wrinkled set of athletic clothes, she navigated the creaking stairs back to the main floor. The hallway actually felt cool this morning. Maybe the air conditioner wasn't completely worthless.

Her mom's curtain was pulled to the side, and to Katie's surprise the bed was made. In fact, it was the only space in the house that lacked any clutter or dirt. Katie quietly poked her head into the attached bathroom, and relief rolled through her. Spotless, although a lingering odor of urine burned her nostrils. A portable handicap commode with a plastic pan had been mounted above the real toilet.

"Katie? Is that you?" Her mother's sharp voice carried through the hallway and made her heart pound in quick, nervous beats. A face-to-face conversation was unavoidable, and she knew the last four years had undoubtedly worsened their hostile relationship.

She followed the sound to the kitchen. The smell was better. Last night she'd run the dishwasher and taken out two loads of trash.

"Hey, Mom," she said as soon as she made eye contact with her mother.

Maureen Stone sat at the kitchen table, surrounded by plastic bags filled with who-knows-what and drinking a cup of coffee. She pushed down on her cane and very slowly stood. Katie waited, knowing her mother wouldn't want any coddling. "Well, come here. Give me a hug."

She obeyed. Her mom had gained some weight since Katie had left, but it worked for her. Made her face softer, despite the dark circles and permanent scowl.

"It's good to be home," Katie said. And it really was. Even if her home felt like an indoor trash compactor, at least it wasn't some jerk's apartment or worse, the women's shelter.

Her mom trembled in Katie's arms, so she let go and eased away while her mother found the safety of her chair again. There was despondency about her, a depression trapping her like cling wrap.

She gave Katie a quick once-over. "You're prettier without all that black. It made you look like a streetwalker."

A wave of defiance tightened in Katie's muscles, but she forced a smile. "Thanks, Momma. You look good too."

Those words brought a glare that could level a building. "No I don't. I look crippled, and don't go acting like I don't. I'm stuck here in this hell of a house with no help. No daughter. Although I don't know what I expected. Even when you did live in town, you were unreliable. Carrying on with Cooper, Chad, and Laila like you didn't have a family."

And so it began: the verbal list of everything she had done wrong and couldn't change.

Katie pulled out a chair and sat. "I'm here now." She took her mother's hand. "I want to help you."

Her mom looked away. "For the record, I didn't want him to call you."

Swallowing the lump in her throat, Katie stood up and walked to the coffeepot. Her mom didn't trust her, but she'd prove this time was different. A carton of half-and-half stood open on the counter, and she smell-checked it before adding a splash to her mug. "So, what is your routine like? I'm going to clear out some of this stuff, and I need to know which room I should start in."

"This is my home business. I have a plan for every little thing. Just need to get a system together."

Katie bit her lip and prayed for patience. There were enough knick-knacks, clothing, random kitchenware, yard tools, and costume jewelry to fill a warehouse.

"A business is good, Mom. But . . ." She hunted for the right words. "Maybe I can help reduce your inventory a little." She couldn't believe she was calling this filth inventory, but she knew exactly from whom she'd inherited her stubborn streak. One wrong word, and her mother would shut down her plan completely. "We can donate the stuff that won't bring much money and focus on the items that will. We can clear out the dining room and set up your office down here."

Her mom's coffee mug clattered against the saucer while she tried to get her hand steady. Katie ached to help, but stood silent until her mom was able to get the cup settled. "Who decides what's important?"

"I'll separate them into piles, and you can have the final say."

Her mom snorted. "Like you've ever given me a say. Not when you quit community college. Nor when you took off like a rodent on fire four years ago. Ain't that our pattern? I give you advice and you do the exact opposite?"

Katie gripped her mug tighter. "Yes, but I've grown up a lot since then."

Her mother made a *harrumph* sound, likely surprised that Katie had agreed with her so easily. "Cooper and Laila know you're back in town?"

Katie's stomach sank, and she examined the contents of her coffee cup. She didn't want to answer that question. It would only lead to a conversation she had no intention of having.

Her mom raised a quick eyebrow. She knew Katie's silence spoke volumes. "He's gonna come looking for you, you know. The boy asks about you every time he sees me."

Katie's eyes snapped to her mother's, and she knew her mom was right. When she'd met Cooper, she'd been attracted to his conquer-and-win personality. He'd spent his childhood drifting from place to place, yet still managed to get his GED and worked harder than most to earn a paycheck. But together they'd been a hazardous train wreck: Katie always searching for the next high, Cooper believing the world owed him some kind of debt.

She took a deep breath, trying to uncoil the tightness in her chest. "I ran into him yesterday at the Stop and Go. He knows it's over between us."

Her mom stood and held on to the table as she took her first step. "Knowing and doing are two different things, and we both know you aren't one to stick to your guns very long." Another arduous step, and then she grasped the chair Katie had vacated. "You can start in the dining room, but nothing goes until I see it. I'm gonna go poke myself with a needle now and try not to crash on my way back to my room."

"I can walk with you," Katie offered, though she already knew the answer.

"Do and I'll knock you out with this cane. I ain't no invalid. And we both know you care more for yourself than you ever did for anyone else, so just stop pretending otherwise. I don't know what finally made you come home, but it ain't me." She paused, and identical blue eyes met Katie's. "I can tell you got secrets. Deep ones." With one last painfully slow step, her mom disappeared into the hallway.

Katie sagged against the sink and covered her stomach with one hand. This was one of those times when doing the right thing made her want to puke. Her mother was right about her having secrets. But nothing in Katie's past had brought her home. Just the opposite.

Every horrific memory made her want to run far, far away.

CHAPTER 7

Asher hadn't spoken to Katie in four days, although he'd watched her endlessly from his office window. Every morning she'd pull out three big tarps and lay them across the grass. Then, without fail, she'd spend the next four hours unpacking boxes and sorting everything from clothing to hardware onto one of the squares. Her mom would join her in the afternoons, and they'd argue for another hour over the three piles.

When the volatile negotiations subsided, Katie would disappear for twenty minutes. Sometimes she'd go for a walk. Other times she'd go inside the house. But eventually, she'd return and pack everything up. The stuff on two of the tarps was bagged and tossed into the back of a rusty old Chevy. Asher always knew when she left because the ancient truck required three tries to start and blasted smoke from its muffler.

Today was different, though, and not just because he'd be going to his dad's church for the first time in months. Katie still hadn't emerged, and it was well past her usual starting time.

Asher stood in front of the mirror and tightened his tie. He shouldn't care. He shouldn't know her schedule down to the time she took a break for lunch. They weren't even really friends. Just two people who'd shared a moment under the stars. Yet Asher couldn't shake the memory of how she'd clung to his every word. How her eyes had conveyed vulnerability and desperation.

His phone buzzed from the dresser, his mom's text not at all unexpected.

Mom: *You're still coming today, right?*

Asher: *Yes. Leaving now.*

A small part of him had considered backing out. Dread inched up his spine, and he reminded himself that church service lasted only an hour. He'd walk into the building, shake a few hands, fake a few smiles, and try not to make eye contact with anyone from the Murray family.

Yet his anxiety grew with every mile he drove, and it skyrocketed the minute he pulled into Fairfield Fellowship. This wasn't the first time he'd been to the building since his firing. He'd come here to take his dad to lunch a few times and had even helped his replacement learn how to update the website. But Sundays were different. They brought crowds of people. People who had judged and betrayed him.

Fellowship's campus sat off the main highway on an acre of land. The new sanctuary loomed two stories in the air, and both the Georgia state and American flags waved from almost as high. Two more buildings had been added in the last five years: a two-story children's center and a gym. Every dream his father had envisioned for the church was now realized.

With a quick check of his watch, Asher confirmed he'd stalled enough to avoid pre-service small talk, and he walked toward the wide glass doors.

Barry and Linda Ferguson were the greeters for the day, and their surprise when he entered was palpable and immediate.

"Asher?" Linda's mouth fell open an inch. She moved more quickly than he, and soon he was enfolded in her embrace. She'd been his Sunday school teacher when he was in the fourth grade. "It's so good to see you."

He patted her back twice, feeling his gut tighten. "You too."

Barry put out his hand and slapped his arm. "Been a while, son. Glad you came back."

He wanted to say "just for today" but instead muttered a thanks and detangled himself from the gushing couple. One hour. He'd played the part for twenty-six years; this should be easy.

But it wasn't. Everything about being at church hurt. The smell of wood paneling, the new carpet he'd heard his mother talk about but hadn't seen, the two rows of teenagers that used to be just one. Fellowship had changed, grown, and he hadn't been a part of any of it.

Careful not to glance toward the left side of the sanctuary, where the Murrays generally sat, Asher found his mother standing front and center like always. His dad said it helped his confidence to be able to see her, so she always sat in the first row where the stage lights didn't blind his view.

Asher walked up behind her, placed his hands on her shoulders, and squeezed. "I made it, with three whole minutes to spare."

She turned immediately and hugged him. "It could be three seconds and I wouldn't care. You're here." She pulled back and laid her palms on his cheeks, her eyes glassy and illuminating a happiness he wished he shared.

His mom stepped aside so he could shake hands with her guests, Susan and Tom. They were related to them somehow. Second or third cousins or somewhere down the family tree. Asher had given up trying to keep track of his mother's extended family.

The older couple smiled and asked questions about his job and house, completely unaware Asher was sweating profusely underneath his tie.

He'd caught a glimpse. Just one small glimpse of long platinum blonde hair, and his lungs practically collapsed. It wasn't even Jillian, but the thought that she might be near destroyed his weakening resolve. They'd stolen more than just his ministry. They'd stolen part of his soul.

He prayed for the music to start, but time seemed to stand still. Coming back had been a mistake. He wasn't ready. Not when all he could feel was a deep, pulsing hostility.

Katie waited until the glass doors were shut and the greeters had vanished before getting out of her car. She was known for boldness, for fearing nothing, for barreling toward the fiercest opponent without slowing down. Yet none of her old courage was surfacing today.

Fairfield Fellowship.

She'd vandalized their sign the night of graduation and egged the youth pastor's car on Halloween. She didn't deserve to be there. Didn't deserve the grace she'd received months ago. But when they'd said good-bye in Tallahassee, Reverend Snow had made her promise to find a church home, even if it was temporary. Asher's easy forgiveness the other day made her think maybe others here would act the same.

Katie slid into the back row, near the sound booth, and kept her head bowed. The house lights were dim, and a song about mercy echoed off the walls. She took a minute to just breathe and listen to the powerful lyrics. When the soloist finished, applause filled the room, as did light. What had been unrecognizable silhouettes were now people Katie remembered.

The principal from her high school sat in the section to her right, his face drawn in like he'd aged thirty years since retiring. He leaned over to whisper something to his wife, and she shook her head. Katie let her hair fall like a curtain over her profile. She'd probably caused at least half the gray hairs on the man's head.

She spotted Asher in the front row, next to his mother. He shifted nearly every minute and kept stretching his neck as if it hurt to sit there.

Periodically, he glanced at the side doors and then turned sharply back around to face the front.

She wouldn't say his behavior distracted her, but it certainly surprised her. Shouldn't this place be like a second home to him? Yet he seemed even more uncomfortable than she was.

Pastor Powell took the stage and, after leading a prayer, asked the congregation to stand while he read the text. A movement to her left caught her eye, and despite her inner warning to keep her head down, she glanced that way. Mary Blanchard was struggling to stand, using her walker for support and stability. A young woman held her elbow and patted her wrinkled hand.

Pain seared Katie like a branding iron. Mary hadn't changed at all. Bluish-white hair was still teased into a puff around her face. Mounds of dangling jewelry hung from her neck, and as always, she wore a silky pantsuit—the kind that could rival even those worn by the richest socialites. Katie inhaled, the memory of Chanel No. 5 so powerful she could almost smell it from across the room.

Pulse racing, she fell into her seat when the scripture reading ended. Every street in Fairfield held a measure of shame, but nothing compared to what she'd done that weekend she'd fled from town.

Pastor Powell was speaking now, but she couldn't hear anything but the cries of her own guilt. Mary had relied on Katie, trusted her, even defended her when people said the benevolent widow was out of her mind for hiring such a troublemaker.

Katie had loved her for it, too, though not enough to do the right thing. And that one transgression had been the unraveling of her life.

She stood, no longer caring about remaining invisible. It wasn't supposed to be like this. She'd spent four years locking that night away. Four years trying to forget.

She was supposed to get a second chance. A clean slate. A new life. "Beauty from ashes" is what Reverend Snow had said. And she'd tried. She'd buried those ashes deep in her mind, ready to cast away everything she had been before she found peace. But starting over was a lie. Her past was standing right in the middle of her future.

Katie rushed to the exit.

It didn't matter that Asher turned around just as she bolted. It didn't matter that his eyes widened, or that he smiled as if her being there brought him some sense of relief.

None of it mattered. Because deep down, she knew her mistakes were much too big to ever be forgiven.

CHAPTER 8

From her seat on top of the picnic table, Katie spooned another mound of flavored ice into her mouth. The sno-cones at Fairfield Park had been the go-to solution in many of her crises, and today was no different.

She'd fled from church thirty minutes ago, and only now had her hands stopped trembling. She'd never been one to cry. In her family tears meant weakness and were regarded as manipulation. Instead, when she got too emotional, her stomach would curl in on itself and her body would shake like a petrified puppy. For some reason, sugar was the quickest remedy.

The park was mostly vacant. Just a few children laughed nearby as they navigated the massive jungle gym. By two o'clock, the place would be swarming with after-church crowds, barbecue groups, and clusters of families who didn't spend their life trapped by dysfunction.

In the distance, Katie could see the cars emptying Fellowship's parking lot. She shoved in another bite of cherry goodness and tried to forget that she'd left right in the middle of Pastor Powell's sermon. Word had probably already spread through half the town, and given her reputation, people would think she'd intended to make a scene. They'd never guess that Katie Stone had gone to church because she actually wanted to be there.

An SUV pulled into the parking lot near her, and darn if the shaking didn't start back up. Asher emerged a second later, tall and blond and much too determined. She'd been dying to talk to him for days, and now she couldn't even think of a single word.

He looked different all dressed up. His hair was combed instead of spiked in a wet tangle of sweat. His jeans had been replaced by black slacks and a belt. She knew it was at least eighty degrees already, yet he wore a long-sleeved shirt and a red-striped tie. She couldn't decide which style suited him best, or if he was just one of those men who looked good in anything.

He passed by the green sno-cone hut and walked right up to her isolated table. "I see I'm not the only one addicted to sugar."

She raised her cup an inch, hoping she didn't look as completely uncomfortable as she felt. "It's one of the few things I missed in this town. That and the train parking on the tracks during rush hour."

His chuckle seemed forced, and she couldn't blame him. Nothing about the two of them being friendly made sense. He was the golden boy who did no wrong. She was the wild child who left havoc in her wake. He'd grown up in church. She grew up thinking Sundays were meant for beer drinking and football.

The sun blazed overhead, yet Asher hadn't moved.

"Aren't you going to get one?" She pointed to the sno-cone hut and raised an eyebrow. The line was starting to grow.

He shifted his weight and tucked both hands into his pockets. "The truth? I saw you sitting here and wanted to say hi. You left church before I could talk to you."

Katie hung her head, embarrassed. "Yeah, about that. Please tell your dad I'm sorry if I distracted him. I wasn't feeling well."

"It's fine. He can't even see past the first few rows when the lights are on him." Asher motioned to the space next to her, a silent request for permission.

She sighed and patted the tabletop—partially glad and equally terrified that he hadn't just scolded her and walked away.

He sat and leaned his elbows on his knees. She took another bite, but even the ice dissolving in her mouth couldn't take away her resurged nervousness.

"I was surprised to see you there." He stared aimlessly at the church across the street.

"I bet."

"I was also glad."

They turned to face each other at the same time. She was sure she'd heard him wrong, but his pressed lips and weighty stare told her she hadn't. "Why?"

He shrugged. "I don't know. I was antsy and irritable, and then I saw you." His laugh was tight, but genuine this time. "Pale as a ghost and completely mortified. And I thought, *finally*, there's someone in this building who's being real."

Katie's next bite missed her mouth, and she quickly put her cup under her chin to catch the runoff. Asher handed her a napkin.

"Thanks." After she'd wiped off the red goo, she set down the nearly empty Styrofoam cup.

He eyed her jerky movements. "I take it you weren't expecting that response."

"Um . . . no. You're the heir to the pulpit. You're supposed to sing 'Amazing Grace' and tell me how wonderful everyone is."

Asher's shoulders dropped. "If you're expecting me to spew rainbows and sunshine every time I speak, then you picked the wrong person. That's not who I am." He stood abruptly.

She knew unspoken disappointment. She'd seen it in people's eyes her whole life. But somehow, seeing it in Asher's made her want to erase every word she'd just said.

"Wait." She grabbed his hand before he could walk away. "I went there today because you were kind enough not to treat me like a stereotype. I'm sorry I didn't give you the same courtesy. You can be as gloomy as you want to be. I promise."

A stream of laughter echoed from the nearby swings while Katie waited for absolution.

It came with a squeeze to her fingers. "Don't mind me. I'm extra sensitive today."

Katie let go of his hand, feeling strangely flushed by the simple touch, and scooted over so he could sit back down.

"So what's with the truckloads of stuff I see you hauling away every afternoon?"

Her groan could probably be heard a mile away. "My mom became a hoarder while I was gone. Three days"—she put up a corresponding number of fingers—"*three days*, and I only made it through half the dining room. And I need to figure out how to move a couch that weighs more than an elephant. My dad said he'd do it, but he practically threw out his back just helping me with my luggage."

The corner of his mouth quirked up. "I can help you get rid of it. Just text me when you're ready." He pulled out a cell phone, and she wondered again if there was an end to his kindness.

"That's okay. I don't want to put you out."

"We're neighbors." He set the phone in her hand. "That means we take care of each other."

She doubted her dad shared his opinion, but she punched her number into Asher's phone all the same. Only three people in town had it: her parents, and now him. "Thanks. I know my folks haven't exactly been the friendliest, so if you change your mind, I get it."

He slipped his phone back into his pocket. "I won't change my mind."

She could feel his conviction, the finality of each word, and wondered what it must be like to know yourself so well. She had yet to finish anything she'd started, and here Asher was the same age but a college graduate who owned his home and built an outdoor area that could be featured in a magazine. And she knew if he said he'd move the couch, he would move the couch.

"So why were you at church today?" Curiosity laced his voice, but she also sensed a deeper motive. Like he truly wanted to understand her.

Katie kept her hands in her lap and stared at them. Nothing had gone right that morning, and she wasn't entirely sure she was ready to spill her guts to her next-door neighbor. But at the same time, she wanted him to know that she was no longer that girl he'd known in high school. "I started going to church in Florida. There was a minister there who helped me understand it all, or at least understand enough to know I wanted a new beginning. He taught me to pray and then held my hand when I did for the first time." She snuck a peek at him. "I know it's impossible to believe, but I really have changed."

Asher's eyes locked on to hers. His were light brown, only a shade darker than gold, and while they didn't betray a thing about what he was thinking, a world of experience radiated through them. How had she never noticed the depth of this man?

"It's not impossible to believe," he finally said. "In fact, now everything makes sense."

Maybe to him. She still felt as if she were swimming through molasses.

A caravan of cars flew through the parking lot, and seconds later the noise at the park had doubled. Katie combed her fingers through her hair and pretended to be interested in the strands. He was still staring at her in that unnerving way of his. Unlike other men, Asher's gaze went much deeper than her bare skin. It penetrated places she wasn't even willing to examine herself.

He slapped his hand on the table and stood. "I think this calls for a celebration."

"What?" Her eyes widened. "Why would we celebrate?"

"Because we both went to church today, and I don't think it's a coincidence." Victory rang through his tone, leaving Katie even more confused.

"I didn't even make it through half the service," she reminded him.

Asher leaned in, and she caught the slight scent of his cologne. Spicy and dark. A complete contradiction to the man in front of her. She swallowed when he inched closer.

"Katie. You walked in the door. That makes you braver than most of the people in this town."

"I'm not brave," she whispered, her throat constricting to the point of hurting. She pushed down the sadness and let practiced mischief seep back into her voice. "I'm a risk taker, remember?" She slid away from him. "Reckless."

"Reckless or courageous? There is a difference." The wind ruffled his hair, and a strand freed itself from its styling. It drew her gaze to his face. A mistake, because she could now see his smile, playful and challenging, and for some insane reason it made her smile back.

"Definitely reckless."

"We'll see. You never know what God will do with that firecracker spirit of yours."

Her throat flushed hot. *You only have to pretend for a few months, Firecracker. Do this and we're set for years.*

She squeezed her eyes shut, pushed Cooper's voice from her head, and practically fell as she attempted to get off the table. "I should go."

Asher steadied her. "You okay?"

No, she wasn't okay at all. But her demons weren't something he could help her with. "I'm fine. Just hot. Besides, don't you church-going types always have some kind of potluck thing you do on Sundays?"

He let go and laughed. "You know, I'd love to say that stereotype isn't true, but I can't. And honestly, I kind of like it." He patted his stomach and his eyes sparkled.

She could picture it: Asher mingling with a crowd of people, making each one feel special and important. He was like that in high school too. Outgoing and friendly. Back then, she'd thought it was an act. After all, that was what she had done all through high school: put on a show.

They fell in step together, passing a large family eagerly rolling two coolers toward the picnic table they had abandoned.

"You could come with me today. My mom loves extra people around the table."

Katie practically choked. "You may think I'm fearless. But there's no way I'm eating lunch at the pastor's house. I'd have to bathe in holy water for, like, three weeks first."

He quit walking. "That is by far the most ridiculous thing you've ever said." Shaking his head, he resumed his long strides. "My dad is seriously the most down-to-earth person I know. He's no different than you or me."

When they got to her car, Katie crossed her arms. "Really? Prove it. What books sit on his coffee table?"

"His coffee table?"

"Yes. You find out a lot about a person by the books they display. So what are they?"

Asher's brows pinched as he tried to recall, and she knew the minute he remembered because his lips pursed.

"Ha!" she said and pointed at him. "I'm totally right. What are they?"

He shook his head, but he was also grinning now. "Doesn't mean a thing." He backed away toward his car. "You're just looking for excuses."

"Ten bucks says you'll switch them out today," she shouted across the lot.

"Hope you like that couch. Don't see it moving by itself anytime soon," he yelled back.

Katie fumbled with her keys, feeling an unfamiliar joy bubble in her gut.

For a few minutes, she almost forgot who she used to be.

CHAPTER 9

Even the familiar car parked in front of his parents' house wasn't enough to ruin Asher's mood or wipe away the ridiculous grin he'd been wearing since he left the park.

He'd laughed. For the first time in months, he'd laughed and actually meant it.

"Asher? Is that you?" his mom called when he shut the front door. She quickly appeared in the hallway, wiping her hands on a dish towel. "What took so long? Your father actually beat you home."

"I swung by the park on my way."

She lifted a brow and tossed the towel onto her shoulder. "Should I ask how you went from brooding to cheerful, or should I just enjoy it?"

He leaned down and kissed her cheek. "Just enjoy it." Because they both knew an hour spent with Darrell Wheeler would drive off whatever joy he'd managed to find.

Voices echoed from the kitchen, the bellow of Mr. Wheeler's carrying farther than the others.

She exhaled, a long whoosh of air. "I should have warned you he was the deacon this week."

"It's fine." Not really, but he could fake niceties with the best of them. Besides, if Katie could muster the courage to walk into Fellowship, he could certainly sit through lunch with the man who'd sided with Jillian's father.

The kitchen was in full chaos by the time Asher and his mom entered. Little voices begged for drinks, chairs scraped against the floor, and a long line of people wove around the island in the center. At a quick glance, he counted fourteen, not including him or his parents.

His mom gave him a slight shove. "Go get in line before it's all gone."

Not possible. There was enough pot roast, potatoes, green beans, and coleslaw to feed an army, but he was more than ready to help polish it off. He fell in line behind Ms. Ferris, a widow of five years and his mom's focus for April. Every month, she'd pick an elderly person in their church and would help them with household chores or rides to the doctor.

"Afternoon, Asher." Ms. Ferris's words weren't accompanied with a smile, but he wasn't surprised. Frown lines were etched deep in her face and had been as long as he could remember. "Great service today."

"Yes, ma'am." He didn't confess he'd been far too distracted to pay attention, or that once he'd caught sight of Katie leaving, he'd abandoned the pretense of trying to listen.

"It's been a while since I've seen you there." She took a few pieces of meat and continued down the line.

"Yes, ma'am."

"Is that new job making you work Sundays now? 'Cause I hear they are doing that type of stuff, and it's just shameful. When I was a girl, every store in town shut down on the Lord's Day. Now, you can shop at all hours of the night, every day of the week. Ridiculous. Kids these days have too much stuff as it is. Can't hardly pull their eyes from those minicomputers either."

Asher piled meat on his plate and threw a *help me* glare at his mom. She immediately came to his rescue.

"Barbara, let me take your plate." His mom lifted the paper ware from the old woman's hands and ushered her to an empty seat.

He trailed along behind. Most people knew why he'd stopped going to church and had the courtesy not to rub salt in the wound. He'd bet his lunch Ms. Ferris knew too.

The volume of the conversation rose as seats were grabbed and glasses were filled. Asher eyed the available spots and squeezed into the one farthest away from the Wheelers, who'd avoided eye contact since he walked in. A much-too-familiar burn ignited in his stomach, but he wouldn't allow them to destroy the warm relief talking with Katie had brought, even if he could hear bits and pieces of Darrell's conversation across the table.

". . . and I told him those chairs were not be moved . . ."

". . . it's just not right. Our class purchased them, and I don't care if the choir is short . . ."

". . . that's what Henry said too. Anyway, it's all been settled . . ."

Asher clutched his napkin, set it carefully on his lap, and began to silently count to a hundred, throwing the *one thousand* in between, to make it last longer. When he'd reached twenty-eight, his father strolled into the room.

At six foot two, Brian Powell owned every step he took. His dark suit had been replaced by jeans and a polo shirt, and the atmosphere immediately lifted when he smiled at his guests. He pulled Asher's mom close and kissed her head. "Laura, thank you for this lovely meal. Let me say the blessing and we can all dig in."

Asher bowed his head, wondering if he'd ever be as gracious as his father. Through the entire mess with Bob Murray, his dad had never once questioned his word. Their strong relationship was the one positive thing that came from Jillian's lies. He and his dad were closer now than ever before in his life.

His dad said "amen," and chatter erupted around his mom's eighteen-person farm table. It had been a gift from Tim Morris, a master craftsman and longtime church member. Asher had watched every step of the process, asking a million questions that Tim had been patient enough to answer. One day he would make a replica, right down to the two benches that ran the length of the table. Though he'd probably scale it down to seat twelve.

He passed the salt to a little girl with ringlet curls and an obvious distaste for red meat. Her family had visited the church, and his mom always asked new guests to lunch, though they rarely accepted the invitation.

"Push the meat around your plate a little. Your mom will think you ate some of it," Asher whispered.

The girl giggled and he winked. He remembered these meals as a kid. They seemed forever long and torturous back then. He swallowed a mouthful of potatoes. Not much had changed. At least not today.

"You will never guess who came to church this morning." A pause for effect, and then a lengthened "Katie Stone."

Asher lifted his head, interested for the first time in the surrounding conversation. Miranda Wheeler mirrored an eager salesperson as she expectantly waited for his dad's reaction. Being the first to drop that nugget of gossip would likely give her a ten-day buzz.

His mom answered instead. "Really? Well, that's wonderful. I didn't realize she was back in town."

The woman scowled, obviously not satisfied with this reaction. "I'm not so sure it *is* wonderful. She left during the sermon. Was quite a distraction for the rest of us."

His dad wiped his mouth. "Well, I guess I'd better make sure my sermon is more interesting next week."

"Oh no, I didn't mean it like that." Miranda's cheeks flushed red, and Asher had to duck his head to hide his snickering. "It's just that Katie Stone likes to make waves everywhere she goes, and I think we need to be careful. This could all be part of some elaborate scheme."

"I wouldn't put it past her. She's been plenty vocal about her disdain for the church," Darrell added, his double chin bobbing as he finished chewing.

"People can change," Asher's mom reminded him.

"Not often."

Asher watched his dad, who had yet to weigh in. While he knew his father was genuine in his love for people, no matter their background, his stomach still knotted. Katie *was* different. She *had* changed. And she deserved more than to be some punch line. But he wasn't about to get into an argument with the Wheelers. They'd only use it against his dad later, or worse, run back to the Murrays and give Jillian more firepower to use against him.

"If Katie was there, I'm thrilled." His dad's gaze bounced around the full table. "No matter what her motivation is, our response should be the same. We welcome her, and we treat her like we would any other guest. What an opportunity for our congregation to show the love of Christ to someone who has maybe never felt it before." He directed his attention to his deacon. "I hope every one of you makes her feel wanted and cared for."

"Her parents too," his mom added. "The whole family needs our prayers right now."

Miranda lowered her head, her brown curls hiding a portion of her face. *Good.* Asher hoped she was embarrassed. Hoped they both were.

He sat back in his chair as he witnessed the remarkable shift in conversation. There was no more talk of Katie coming to church or biting commentary about her sins. Yes, one day he'd be like his father. One day he'd be that kind of leader.

His dad winked from across the table, and Asher suddenly couldn't wait for his new neighbor to meet his parents. He eyed the coffee table in the living room. A hardback photo book of Israel and his dad's leather-bound Greek Bible lay next to a bowl of potpourri. She'd nailed it, without ever setting foot into their home.

He shook his head, hid a smile, and wondered what books were displayed in her living room.

Asher finished loading the last dish while his parents said good-bye to their final guest. Since leaving the church, he'd only come to lunch sporadically and was usually gone before dessert. Today felt like a turning point. It was the first time in months he wasn't the first to leave.

His father shut the front door and went to stretch out in his favorite leather recliner. The hinges protested and the armrests were faded, but he insisted the chair would outlive him. Doubtful.

Asher pressed Start on the dishwasher and joined his dad in the living room.

"Well, son, how was it today? Honestly."

Propping his feet on the coffee table, he pressed the balls of his hands to his eyes. "Hard, but I knew it would be. I didn't see them, so that helped." Only the ghost of them. The ghost of sitting next to her, hand in hand. The ghost of Bob Murray calling him "son" and her mom secretly picking out china. The ghost of a future that would never be.

"You were wiggling around like your seat was full of fire ants. I swore I'd gone back in time and you were my squirmy five-year-old all over again." His grin was teasing, but it was still true. Church used to be a resting place, a relief after a week out in the world. But no more.

"So was this a one-time deal you made with your mother, or will I see you squirming next week too?"

"I don't know. Do you ever feel like everybody in the room is watching you?"

His dad nodded. "Yep. Every Sunday."

"Not the same." He didn't need his dad's humor. He needed someone to understand. "I can feel their judgment. People watch me and I know all they see are the lies the Murrays told about the breakup." And some embarrassing truths too. He sighed. That was the hardest part. His sins were practically plastered on the sanctuary walls. He had probably even been the topic of someone's lunch conversation, as Katie had been.

"Maybe they're staring because they're happy to see you. I know I was. Seems to me the only one still passing judgment is you." The subsequent pause was an uncomfortable one. "The church isn't your enemy."

Asher didn't want to talk about it anymore. They'd gone around this circle of logic more times than he could count and rarely made any headway. He leaned over and picked up the three-inch-thick Bible. "Why don't you put out that architecture book I gave you for Christmas?" His dad loved building design. Studied the historical context, the innovators, the scale and space down to the finest detail. Family vacations were planned around landmarks, and the little free time he had was spent drafting for fun on his computer.

"I don't know. Ask your mother. She slaps my hand every time I move something." His dad shut his eyes, recognizing Asher had tabled the "coming back to church" talk once again. "So how's that deck coming along?"

"Really good." Asher eyed his father's lethargic position and smiled. He was the only man Asher knew who could nap and engage in conversation at the same time. "I only have about ten more planks to lay down and sand. Then I'll stain it all."

"What about the fence? I'm free on Tuesday. I can come dig those last postholes with you."

Never. Never again. His dad's "help" had been a disaster. Besides, when Asher thought of his spunky neighbor, the fence suddenly felt like a bad idea. "You know, I may wait on those. Get started on my bathroom next."

His father popped open an eye. "I thought that fence was your number one priority."

It had been . . . before. "I just think maybe it's a good thing for me to run into the Stones right now. Especially now that their daughter's back." He set down the Bible. "She's changed. I'm pretty sure something big happened in Florida."

His dad sat up, and the back of the recliner followed suit. "Really? So you don't think today was a stunt."

"No. In fact, she asked me to apologize to you for walking out. I think she was nervous about being there. And honestly, after hearing the Wheelers, can you blame her?"

"Who was nervous about being there?" His mom tapped Asher's legs, and he dropped them to let her by.

"Katie Stone," his dad answered.

"That poor girl. She's been the gossip in this town for years now. The rumors after she disappeared." His mom shook her head. "They were just terrible."

A new rush of anger hit him. No wonder she'd been trembling on that picnic table. He'd spent most of the last eight years away from Fairfield and its incessant chatter. First at college, then in a small cubicle at Synco Intelligence. He'd met Jillian three months after returning home, and they'd been too wrapped in each other to bother with the rumor mill.

He moved a throw pillow so his mother could sit on the couch beside him. "What were they saying?"

She frowned deeply. "Nothing I care to repeat. But I know this much for sure: that child needs all the kindness we can offer her."

CHAPTER 10

Katie tugged on the back of the couch, maneuvering it another six inches from the wall. She'd gone back and forth between pushing and pulling and finally had it positioned so it could be picked up.

"There's no way you and I can get this thing to the truck," her dad said, staring at the sleeper sofa with as much disgust for it as she had. "Why do you think it's still here? It was my granddad's, and back then they made things out of steel."

She didn't doubt it. The cushions were marred with multiple tears and cigarette stains. Not to mention the embedded cat hair and an odor that reminded her of sweaty feet. She didn't care if they had to take a chainsaw to the frame, they were moving the couch *today*.

"Let me call some guys from work," he offered.

What he meant was *Let me call Cooper*. Her father's hints about her ex-boyfriend had been anything but subtle. Apparently, the manipulative jerk had wormed his way into her dad's good graces while she was gone. Well, her opinion wasn't nearly as pliable. The answer wasn't just no, but H-E-double-hockey-sticks *no*.

"I already called for reinforcements."

"Who?"

"Our neighbor."

Her dad kicked an empty cardboard box, and it bounced off the wall. "I told you I don't want him sniffing around here."

She threw up her hands. "Well, I don't want Cooper here, so it looks like we're at an impasse."

"Except it's *my* house."

That was true, but Katie had spent a week sweating and sorting and cleaning. She had a right to expect a little understanding. "It's just a couch, Dad. He won't even go down the hallway. Ten minutes. That's it."

He tightened and released his fist like he was trying to control himself. "Katie, I'm glad you're home. I wanted you here, but there are boundaries I do not want crossed. You know my limits, and between the fighting with your ma and you turning my house upside down, you're getting very close to pushing too far."

The doorbell rang, and he made a grumbling sound in his throat. "Don't invite him over again."

"Fine," she said with an edge honed by years of arguments.

Her dad marched toward the door and swung it open with annoyance. "Hope you ate some spinach this morning," he said without a hint of humor.

Asher's brow pinched together as he tried to come up with an acceptable response, but her dad didn't give him time.

"Whatever. You're too young to know what I'm talking about anyway. It's in the dining room. Just follow the sound of Katie huffing and puffing."

She'd seen her dad be rude, but never like this. Every word was stretched and harsh, like he thought Asher had personally wronged him in some way. Only she knew he hadn't. His only crime was that he'd been born to the town's pastor.

Asher's attempted smile communicated something between complete discomfort and mild defensiveness as he stepped over the threshold. Her dad shoved a piece of cardboard under the door to prop it open, still grumbling under his breath.

"So this is where you've been hiding for the last few days." Asher examined the partially cleared space that had stolen a week of her life. "It looks good."

"Hardly." There were still two columns of boxes and half-built metal shelves in the room, now shoved to the side so they could move the eyesore beneath her hands. She leaned in and whispered, "Sorry about my dad."

"No worries. I'm used to it." He circled the couch and settled at the other end. "How do you want to do this?"

"Personally, I want to burn it, but I've been told I'm being rash."

"Trying to move this thing last-minute and without proper manpower is what's rash," her dad griped, joining them in the room. If the aggravated energy between her and her father bothered Asher, he gave no sign of it. His face was a mask of concentration as he measured the couch and then the doorway.

"I think it will fit through the opening with just a slight tilt. I guess we can try to carry it. Mr. Stone, can you and Katie take that side?"

The older man nodded.

Asher squatted down to get a grip. Katie and her dad did the same, each taking one corner. After the count of three, they all lifted. Heat ripped through Katie's fingers and up her arms, but together they got the monstrosity airborne.

After fifteen grueling minutes, multiple readjustments of the upholstered beast, countless bursts of angry commands from her dad, and various strained muscles among them, they finally closed the truck bed behind the couch, each of them gasping for air. Her father was wheezing so badly she had to bite her tongue not to remind him that smoking tends to wreak havoc on one's lungs. But even she knew when her old man had reached the breaking point, and he was there.

"That's the last time I cater to your stubborn, stupid pride. Next time, we get more help," he announced between puffs. Without even a *thank-you* to their guest, he stomped up the rotted front steps and slammed the door.

Asher jumped from the bed of the truck, and Katie fought the urge to kick the tires repeatedly. Buried rage swelled in her belly, reminding her why she'd spent most of her adolescence either gone or locked in her room with Laila.

"I'm so sorry. I had no idea he was in such a mood." She closed her eyes, humiliated by her family. It wasn't worth it. Here she was sacrificing and suffering for them, and yet they both seemed to resent her all the more for it.

"Is it always like that between you and your dad?"

She pulled at a hangnail until the sting forced her to stop. "No, sometimes we throw in awkward silence and uncomfortable small talk."

"And your mom?"

"The same. Just add in a dose of sarcasm and a heaping spoonful of bitterness."

Her body sagged against the truck. "I had hoped it would be different than before." Though she didn't know why. Nothing had changed. If anything, her inability to connect with her parents had only worsened.

"Are they the reason you left town?"

She wished it were that simple. "No. I left town because I couldn't breathe here anymore."

And suddenly, that feeling returned. The constricting regret, the ache of knowing she'd hurt so many. She tried to focus on Asher. His long legs, the way his elbow barely touched her arm, the careful way he asked just enough to know her but never pushed too hard.

"I've felt that way before too. Like I couldn't breathe," he said.

Her pulse settled, and she studied his profile. "What did you do?"

"The same thing you did. I left." He shifted his body so that he faced her direction. "How did you know it was time to come back?"

"I can't really explain it. My dad called to tell me about my mom's diagnosis, and I just knew. Even before he asked me, I knew it was time.

Like something deep inside was pushing me, telling me to go." She'd fought with herself about it too. Her life had finally become stable. She had a new apartment and a job, and yet she'd packed up and left it all behind. Because she still believed that if she could do one good deed, maybe all the bad ones would stop haunting her.

"Were you happy in Florida?"

"Not at first." Not even close. Her first two years had been spent flitting between boyfriends, crashing apartments, and so entrenched in darkness that it was a wonder she ever broke free. "But later I was." After that wonderful night when she'd surrendered her life to Christ.

"Like I said before, I think you're incredibly brave."

She shrugged, uncomfortable with his compliment. He didn't know her. He didn't know everything she was hiding from. "It's just a few months, right? I'll get them settled and then go back to my life in Tallahassee. I lived with them for twenty-two years. I can certainly last a summer."

"And you have your friends, right? I remember a certain blonde who stayed permanently attached to your hip in high school."

A gust of wind spun through the air, making the trees rustle and the birds chirp, but all she could feel was grief. And it hurt. Deep inside her, under her rib cage, beneath her lungs, the memories pulsed with never-ending shame. "I don't have anyone. Not anymore."

His hand brushed hers. "You have me. I'm right next door, and I'm kinda short on friends right now too."

She cleared her throat, managing to banish the worst of the pain. "Be careful what you offer. At this rate, I may end up moving in."

He pushed himself off the truck but didn't argue with her exaggeration. It almost made her think he wouldn't mind the idea so much. But that was crazy.

"I guess I should get home. I'll be working on the deck later if you still want to help." He walked backward, keeping his gaze focused on her.

"I guess it is different this time," she said.

"How so?"

"Dr. Mills never knew when I used his power tools."

Asher's face lit up with a smile so bright it warmed all the parts of her that had gone cold. "Not a chance. Sandpaper only."

"We'll see about that. I told you. Be careful what you offer."

He threw his head back and laughed, then gave her a quick wave before starting the trek back to his place.

Somehow, the whole world felt lighter as Katie walked up the steps.

Friends with Asher Powell? Her?

Yes, she could certainly get used to that idea.

CHAPTER 11

Goose bumps covered Katie's arms as she turned the corner for the deli case. She'd managed to avoid Fairfield's only grocery store since arriving ten days ago, but after she'd tossed out three trash bags full of expired food from her parents' kitchen, her mom demanded she go shopping. Whatever. She was done arguing, especially since her dad was still barely talking to her.

She kept her focus on the shelves of turkey, ham, and salami, ignoring that prickling sense that someone was watching her. She was being stupid. It was midmorning on a Thursday. Half the town was at work.

"Excuse me," she called to the woman working behind the meat counter. Katie wanted to move, to get in and out of the store and back to the relatively safe haven her house had become, but the girl simply pointed to the phone she was chatting on and shifted her body so all Katie could see was her back.

Fine. She'd get prepackaged meat today.

Turning away in frustration, she shoved her cart forward, only to have it collide with another one and elicit her worst-case scenario.

Cooper.

Her former boyfriend studied her with dark eyes that seemed to soak in every inch, from her still-damp hair down to the flip-flops she'd thrown on in a rush to escape her mother's fiery words.

Within seconds, he had navigated around their locked carts and moved right into her personal space. "You never came by." It wasn't a statement but an accusation.

His scruffy chin obviously hadn't seen a razor in a few days, but as always, his faded blue uniform lacked even a wrinkle. The memory of his meticulous ironing brought a shiver to her spine.

"I told you I wouldn't." She tried unsuccessfully to pull her cart free from his grip.

"You've told me a lot of things—including that you loved me."

She couldn't look at him. "That was a long time ago."

"Not for me, Firecracker." The warning in his voice forced Katie's attention back to him. "I deserve more than a casual hello. I put up with it at the Stop and Go because you surprised me, but I've been stewing on it for over a week."

Her mom had been right. The confrontation in the gas station was only the beginning. She'd been lying to herself, believing that he'd let her start over.

His hand slid up the edge of the metal cart until it landed on hers. Her fingers trembled beneath his hold. "Why are you scared of me? I've never laid a hand on you."

No, but he had a temper. She'd seen it, had felt it rumble through her body. Had experienced the rippling effects of his vicious words.

She tugged her hand free. "I'm not scared. I'm just finished."

He stepped forward until her retreat pinned her up against the meat display case, his arm resting casually beside her as if he were simply perusing the selection.

A mom with two kids who were arguing over cereal pushed past them. Cooper nodded a hello and with his free hand pulled their carts out of the aisle. He still didn't touch her, but he was much closer than necessary. His chest rose and fell in rapid succession, the telltale sign that he was fighting every instinct to lose control. She felt her courage shrink within. Cooper intimidated her. He always had, and this physical display of dominance was all too familiar.

"May I help you?" A woman in a hairnet and red apron—not the woman who'd ignored Katie but an older, friendlier one—appeared on the other side of the meat counter.

Cooper didn't miss a beat. "Hey, Sally. I need a pound of turkey and some salami. Maybe just a quarter."

Her smile broadened. "You got it, Coop." She busied herself with his order.

Cooper's demeanor morphed from flirtatious back to resolute. His hand encircled Katie's arm and pulled her away from Sally's eavesdropping. She went willingly, grateful for the escape, even if it was short-lived.

They stopped near the ATM nestled back in the corner for privacy. The loudspeaker announced a sale on cookies, and Cooper shoved her arm away as if it singed him.

His jaw was tight, and a line formed between his eyebrows. "Your dad asked me to give it some time, and out of respect for him, I waited. But I'm done. You owe me a conversation."

"I don't owe you a thing. We ended it." It was her turn to get heated. He was doing what he always did. Demanding, controlling, pushing until she exploded.

He ran a hand through his hair and took a deep breath. "We were angry. Messed up. But we would have fixed things if you hadn't left."

"There was no fixing what happened that night."

An immediate ripple of tension made every part of his body turn hard and furious. "You don't get to make that call. Not when the rest of us were stuck here wondering what the hell happened to you. The rest of us didn't get to run away."

Katie tried to return to her cart, but Cooper blocked her path. Her head ached and her throat cracked from all the repressed aggression.

"I'm sorry, okay?" *Let it go, please.*

"Sorry's not good enough."

"Then what do you want from me?" She was going to lose it. Right there in front of a market full of witnesses. "I'm not staying, Cooper. I'm here to help my parents, and then I'm moving right back to Florida."

"I want a conversation."

"We're having one."

"No, not like this." Cooper paced back and forth. Glanced at the counter where his order waited for pickup. And finally fixated on a blue diamond painted on the floor. "Meet me tonight at The Point."

Her body went cold. "No." He was trying to force her back to the past. To rip open the box she'd carefully sealed shut.

"I never told Laila." He looked at her, a hint of remorse slipping past the drawn eyebrows. "Not any of it."

Of course he hadn't. It was his fault too. "I'm not meeting you at The Point."

Anything resembling concern disappeared, and his eyes went blank. A scary kind of opaque she couldn't read. "You'll be there, or I'm gonna start talking, and I won't stop until this whole town knows what you did."

Katie stumbled back, tripping over herself. Keys slid through her fingers and clattered on the floor. "You wouldn't."

"Don't test me, babe."

Silence spun out, muffling the ding of the cashiers, the wails of a hungry baby, and the slamming of Katie's heart against her rib cage.

He picked up her keys, dropped them into her clammy hand. "I'll be there at seven. Waiting for you."

Cooper was a con artist. A master of the bluff. He wouldn't tell. Would he?

She couldn't think. Breathing was all she could handle. Breathing and watching him walk away, once again, with the victory.

CHAPTER 12

Asher stepped out onto his back deck and studied his workman-ship. The stain he'd sprayed on the railings that morning had soaked in nicely. Tomorrow he'd do one more coat and then finally place the order for the outdoor furniture set he'd had bookmarked on his computer for over a year.

Only a hint of sadness came now when he thought of Jillian. She had helped him choose each piece. They'd daydreamed of a wedding outdoors. Imagined kids running along the grass in their bare feet. It was a dream he'd held on to for way too long.

"You finished." Katie bounced up the steps and then spun around while staring at the wood slats. "Great color choice."

Asher had gone with a dark mahogany stain to match the trim around the house's windows.

"Thanks. How about you? That dining room finally cleared?"

"Almost." She pulled out her phone, glanced at the screen, and slid it back into her pocket. "I have six more boxes to go through, and then I'll have to figure out a way to organize the stuff we kept so my mom can sell it."

He opened up two folding chairs and dropped into one of them. Since he'd helped her move the couch, she'd come over twice, both times after her parents had gone to sleep. She'd ask to be put to work, but in the end they'd spent more time talking than being productive.

Their conversations never went too deep, but what they did talk about lingered long after she'd left for the night.

Asher stared beyond the trees. The sky had dulled into a gray blue, and soon reds and oranges would split the clouds, unencumbered by artificial lights. His favorite thing about living in the country.

"Is your mom still badgering you about the work space?" He motioned for Katie to sit, but she paced the perimeter of the deck instead.

He'd wanted to show Katie this beautiful phenomenon from his back porch, wanted to ask her opinion on the furniture. He'd even wanted to tell her just how much her friendship mattered. But something stopped him. Tonight felt different. Her entire countenance was off.

"You okay?"

She checked her phone again. "What? Oh, yeah, I'm fine. I was just supposed to meet someone and I didn't go." She strolled over to him and sat as if she was forcing herself to. Her knee bounced and her heel tapped the metal leg of the chair.

"Why didn't you go?" He didn't know if that was crossing some imaginary line they'd drawn, but he pressed anyway.

Katie shot to her feet and found a stretch of woodwork to admire. "I didn't want to."

"That's a fair reason, I guess. Who were you supposed to meet?"

She glanced at him but didn't answer his question. "Why did you come back to Fairfield? You got out. You went off to college. Nobody ever comes back here after they go away to school."

Asher rose to his feet. He hated sitting while she stood. He hated everything about their interaction tonight. She was edgy and distracted. "I grew up here. I wanted my kids to grow up here." He crossed the deck, leaned a hip against the rail, and studied her. It wasn't just the scattered thoughts or skittishness. She looked lost, defeated, tired. He should comfort her, wrap her up and chase the sadness away, but that wasn't their relationship. So he just stood there, next to her, hoping his proximity was enough. "What happened today?"

She hung her head. "I swore I'd never come back here."

"Famous last words. Seems like God always changes the game when we do that."

She covered her face with both hands. "I can't do this. I can't be different and be in this town. There are too many ghosts. Too many memories. Too many people I've hurt."

The earlier pain in his chest returned. Two years ago he wouldn't have understood, but now he did. The church, Jillian, his own failures. It had all ripped apart the fabric of his plan. "I wish I could offer you some advice, but I don't have any."

Katie lowered her hands. "You say that like you've been there."

"I'm living it." He scanned the yard and the thick surrounding woods, not offering more. He wasn't sure he was ready to blur the lines around . . . well, whatever they were doing. But, he also refused to pretend anymore. A year with Jillian had cured him of that particular ailment.

The first hint of pink shot out in rays from the thinning clouds.

Katie didn't pry, like he had. She just watched the sun dip lower in the sky. When the ball of orange had disappeared beyond the horizon, she pointed to one of the fence posts.

"Is this your next project?"

He sensed disappointment behind her question. "Nah. I'm gonna wait. I still have to build some benches and the countertops around my grill. I want the outdoor kitchen done before we start hitting three digits."

Katie pushed off from the railing and walked toward the side of the deck where the kitchen equipment and countertop would go. He'd built out areas for the mini fridge, a stainless sink, and the industrial-sized grill he planned to install. Right now, though, the wood framing had more holes than appliances.

"Where did you learn how to build this stuff? Your dad?"

Asher's snort made him feel a little guilty. His father really did try. "No, my dad should never be given a power tool. See those three posts over there?" He pointed to the area his father had helped with. The posts all leaned several degrees to the left, and while it wouldn't ruin the fence line, it would forever bug him. "He was supposed to use a level after pouring the concrete. He eyeballed it instead. My dad is gifted with big-picture vision, but the minute details? Well, they tend to annoy him."

Katie grinned and tilted her head to study the posts. Even in shorts, a faded T-shirt, and hair that encircled her head like a mane, she had a presence. An aura, almost, that in one sense screamed *back off* and in another begged to be rescued.

"It's still weird for me to think of Pastor Powell as having flaws. My whole life he's been this beacon for goodness. Even people who hate religion seem to respect your dad."

He cleared his throat. Her comment had slipped under his skin, even though he doubted that was her intention. "There are no perfect people, Katie. Just some who try harder than others to do the right thing."

She circled back to him and stopped a foot away. "And what is 'the right thing'?" She made furious quotation marks in the air, her hands trembling.

"What do you mean?"

Her entire demeanor had changed. Or maybe it hadn't. Maybe all that pacing and fidgeting had simply distracted him from the blaze of exasperation in her eyes.

"How does one define 'right' when everyone is raised with a different standard? 'Cause I'm trying to do the right thing. And yet I keep hitting this wall. So maybe I don't know what the right thing is. Maybe because I didn't get the memo early, like you, I'm doomed. Trapped by a lifetime of making choices I can't take back."

The accusation filled the void between them, heightening his senses, and wrapped chains of defensiveness around their standoff. This was the battle he'd always fought. This idea that being a pastor's kid made him immune to sin.

He laid hands on her shoulders and resisted the urge to shake her. "You're not being fair. I struggle just like you do. I face the worst parts of myself every day." His voice felt full of gravel, and a rising ache brought with it every failure. "Growing up in church doesn't give me a magic cloak that protects me from mistakes. I make them all the time."

Katie blinked as if he had pulled her out of a haze, then returned her focus to the west, where the sun had long ago disappeared. A break from the tension. Or maybe just from him.

He dropped his hands and rubbed one over his face, wishing the motion would ease his frustration. If this was where a friendship with her would take him, he wasn't sure he wanted to go. Despite everything, all they'd shared, she still saw him as a stereotype.

"We may be from different worlds, Katie, but that doesn't mean I don't have things I wish I could take back. It doesn't mean I'm without my own share of demons."

Her head dropped and her shoulders slumped. "I'm sorry. I don't mean to take this out on you. I'm just so tired. I'm so incredibly tired, I don't even know what it feels like not to want to run away."

He thought of the months he'd spent hiding. Spent licking the wounds inflicted by people he'd trusted. But none of it had helped; it just made returning so much harder.

He backed away from her, feeling an alarming urge to pull her into his arms. He wanted her to understand, to know that sometimes life is a hard-fought battle, no matter what weapons you've been given. "A little over ten months ago, my life shattered. And even with my faith and my family supporting me, I haven't been able to get past the hurt. Sometimes it's worse when you know what to do. When you know that you have all the power inside you to experience peace, and yet still feel nothing but shame."

"But what if you didn't feel anything at all? Wouldn't that be better? What if you could simply pack away the past and focus only on what's ahead?" Her wistful eyes seemed to beg for a yes.

But he wouldn't lie to her. "Nobody can do that long term."

"I can." The words seemed to drop on the ground in front of them, and she watched them as if they'd exposed her soul. "I have to."

"Do you?"

She finally stopped staring at those words, but even when she looked at him, he couldn't find the woman he knew in that face. She'd retreated, closed herself off.

Asher dared to touch her, just a slight brush of his fingertips against her skin. "I know you think hiding is your best option. But trust me, you have to feel something in order to heal. Ignoring pain only makes it worse."

CHAPTER 13

I'm not getting rid of any of those, so just stop pushing."
Katie rubbed her throbbing head. "Mom, you have six more boxes
of costume jewelry in my room. I'd like to actually unpack my duffel
bag at some point." Right now, she couldn't even get to the dresser to
start cleaning it out.

"I paid good money for this stuff."

"And you'll never make any of it back until I can sort through it and
find what's valuable." They sat on the porch despite the hot breeze. Katie
had carried out a couple of dining chairs, making sure to bring one with
armrests for her mother to lower herself into. There was a ceiling fan
erratically spinning from the gable, and outdoor furniture pushed off to
their left, but the aluminum chairs had long ago been rendered useless
by flowerpots, piles of water hoses, and bags of seed and soil that were
leaking out of their containers and onto the cushions and concrete.

Her mom picked through each of the boxes, alternately grabbing a
handful of mangled necklaces and then dropping them. She'd attempt
to detangle a few until her trembling fingers forced her to give up with
a curse. This was her mother's typical reaction when her body didn't
obey her mind.

The side effects of the medicine had eased off a little, but the symptoms were getting worse. Two days ago, her mom's vision had blurred
so badly, her dad was forced to call her doctor. He said the flare-up

was normal and caused by an inflammation in her nervous system. He assured them that the attack would eventually subside. The night before, her vision had returned to normal, to the relief of all three of them. Permanent blindness was still a real possibility, and her mother's greatest fear.

Even more reason for Katie to get the house in working order.

"Why don't you go check on your listings? That way I can take a trip to the post office and Goodwill at the same time."

Her mom would never say so, but she'd been noticeably happier since they'd created the work space downstairs. Aluminum cases lined the walls of the old dining room and were filled with inventory to sell. Katie had given her labels for tagging items once they were listed on eBay. The process was slow, but her mom had emptied two full shelves. A victory both of them needed.

"Don't patronize me. I'm not a kid who needs a task thrust at her. And I don't want this stuff going to Goodwill. There's a new shopping center out toward your dad's factory. The right end has a thrift store that sends all the proceeds to help pregnant women who don't have support. If we're giving this stuff away, I want it to at least go to them."

Warmth seeped into Katie's chest. "I think that's a great idea."

"Don't be so surprised." Her mother's lips hardened into a line. "Your fancy new church friends aren't the only ones who help people."

Once. She'd gone to Fellowship that one time only, yet her parents had been relentless with their comments. "I never thought they were."

"Well, the way you're fawning all over that Powell boy says otherwise. You can give up whatever fantasies you have. I've seen his type. She was tall, blonde, innocent as a daisy, and practically wore a halo." She eyed Katie up and down. "We both know you ain't seen a halo since your third birthday."

"Thanks for the reminder. But Asher and I are just friends." Although a stirring in her gut argued this point.

It wasn't jealousy. No, it was deeper. He'd become a lifeline of sorts. Her place to fall when all her strength had dried up. He kept her focused, grounded, and encouraged. Kept her from losing her mind while she waited to see if Cooper would follow through on his threats. It'd been five days since she stood him up, and there'd been no sign of retaliation.

"Friends, huh? I guess I shouldn't worry about him sticking around, then. We both know how well you treat the people you supposedly care about."

"Don't." She'd warned her mom not to ask about Laila. Told her flat out that if she did, she would leave and never come back.

"I'm not. That's your own guilty conscience tugging at your strings." Her mom slowly rose to her feet, her face dotted with sweat. She could only bear the heat for so long. The fatigue was bad enough on its own. But on days when she came outside, it seemed to hit with even more ferocity. "I'll check the sales and print out what needs shipping."

Good riddance.

Working the tension from her shoulders with one hand, Katie stretched her neck and waited for the sick churning in her stomach to subside. Asher's advice continued to buzz in her ear, but she wasn't ready to open herself up to more pain. She wanted to pack things away. Keep the good. Trash the bad.

It didn't take long to calm herself. She was a pro at pushing aside emotions. She'd been taught by two of the best.

Katie moved the boxes out to her three tarps: one for selling, one for giveaway, and one for the dump, because broken items always seemed to end up in each box.

The sun blazed overhead, sending ribbons of sweat down her neck. She twisted her hair into a high bun. It was only May, and it was already miserable outside. Rumor had it they were in for a record-breaking summer in Georgia. *Great. Just great.* The air conditioner barely kept the house below eighty.

She'd never understand how her father had let things get so bad. It was as if he put on blinders every time he walked through the front door. All the sinks were leaking—the one in the master bathroom so badly, Katie had to bleach away the mold. Worse, since the couch incident, she'd lost any influence over him, getting only an "I'll take care of it" response every time she mentioned a repair. Yet in two weeks, he hadn't taken care of one single thing.

One task at a time.

She examined a handful of necklaces. All but two were cheap and belonged on the giveaway tarp. She found matching earrings for one set and a "gold" bracelet that would probably turn someone's arm green.

Halfway through the second container, her heart fluttered. A jewelry box. She quickly pulled it free of the tangle of chains, her pulse beating wildly when she confirmed it was real. She touched every centimeter of the ornate pewter trinket. It was a rectangle, with decorated Queen Anne feet, just like the one she'd held that night. Hope rose up within her. Maybe this was her miracle.

Her hands shook as she lifted the lid. *Maybe . . .*

An empty red velvet liner. No ring.

A clanking sound and subsequent thud broke Katie out of her free-fall of emotions. Asher stood across the tarp, a long cloth bag at his feet.

"That's pretty," he said with a smile she was starting to crave. "You were stroking it like a genie's lamp. Any chance we'll get three wishes?"

"No. Unfortunately not." Katie quickly lowered the jewelry box to the "keep" tarp and stood. "What's up?"

"Well, I saw you from my nice cool office and decided you needed some shade. It's supposed to hit ninety today." He crouched next to the bag and unzipped it. "We use these for picnics at the church. Cuts the heat significantly."

Asher pulled out a portable shelter and began to set it up on the ground. He was dressed the same as he always was during the week.

Tennis shoes, gym shorts, and a white T-shirt he sometimes covered with a button-up if he had an online meeting.

"Thank you for doing this." She didn't add that no one had ever been so considerate to her, or that she'd already sweat through two shirts. "I really appreciate it."

"Here. Take this end and walk backward. Watch your fingers; the top slides up."

She walked around the tarp and took the end he offered. Seconds later, they were extending poles and positioning the tent over her work space.

"Just hold it steady while I put the stakes in."

Katie kept her post and watched as Asher pounded metal rods into the ground. His muscles tightened with each strike, and she found herself mesmerized by the movement. So much so that Asher had to repeat himself twice when he told her to come around to his side.

Her cheeks flared. "Sorry."

Asher pounded until the next stake was in the ground. "You weren't at church Sunday."

A wave of tension washed through her. She'd felt guilty all day about not going, yet couldn't make herself do it. "You noticed?"

"Of course I noticed. You're one of the few reasons I went. I couldn't have you tearing out during another one of Dad's sermons. You might give him a complex."

Katie knew he was teasing, but she still sensed an underlying disappointment. They'd spent enough time together that she was beginning to detect his actual mood, buried under the one he worked to portray.

She considered making excuses. Telling him she'd been too busy, or was needed at home. But the truth was, she lacked the courage to go back.

"I wasn't quite ready to try again."

"I understand," he said, and went back to his hammering.

Once the shelter was in place, the temperature beneath it felt ten degrees cooler. Katie pulled her shirt away from her body, in and out, creating a breeze along her damp skin. "I owe you big-time. Wow."

He chuckled. "Nah. It felt wrong to watch you sweat while I sipped iced tea and played on my computer."

"Play? Somehow, I doubt that's what you're doing." He ran some kind of complicated computer system that went over her head every time he tried to explain it. She put her hands on her hips. "In fact, all I've seen you do is work."

"I enjoy my job and love fixing up the house. My work is my hobby." He shrugged. "It's the perfect life."

She didn't believe him. Not when every stroke, hammer, or brush over his outdoor kitchen seemed to her like a therapy session. She would bet that he used construction the way she used organizing, as an escape.

Unfortunately, her "escape" was beginning to feel stifling. "We should get you out. Go do something fun." Her offer wasn't just for his benefit. She needed a night away from her parents. They'd all been one step from igniting a bomb all week.

"Fun, huh? What did you have in mind?"

"I don't know. What do sober people do around here?"

"Well, there's bowling."

"No." Just the thought made her cringe.

"Feller's Gym has a climbing wall that's pretty sweet."

Katie's mouth twitched sarcastically. "Any idea that doesn't involve strenuous activity or ugly shoes?"

His laugh confirmed he was messing with her. "Personally, I love the drive-in. It's one of the last working outdoor theaters in the nation."

"Sold. How does Friday sound?"

He tilted his head and she made the grave mistake of looking at his mouth, the shape of his lips, the straight line of his teeth. He said something, but she forgot to listen to his answer.

"I'm sorry." She shook herself out of her daze for the second time. "What did you say?"

His smile was indulgent. "I said Friday sounds perfect."

Katie told herself this wasn't a date. They were just two friends who were planning to go see a movie together. Yet the pounding of her heart made the lie nearly impossible to believe. She felt a rush. A high she recognized and still often craved.

She was getting too used to Asher being around. Too dependent on him. And that never led to anything good. *He's not like the other ones,* she told herself. He wasn't the type of man to yell or punch or throw things. He was calm, steady, kind.

And above everything else, he made her believe in second chances.

CHAPTER 14

Asher peeked out the window for the third time. Katie had asked him to drive and politely implied it'd be better if they met at his house. He knew it was because of her folks. He'd seen her mom watching them through the side window the last time Katie came over to chat.

His phone buzzed on the counter. Dylan.

Asher smiled as he answered. "What's up, brother?" He and Dylan had met in college. Both had been paired with miserable roommates their first year, and they had ended up sharing an apartment for the last three.

"On my way to pick up Marissa. I wanted to see if you were still game for our October trip. Our OCD buddy is driving me crazy, trying to get us all locked down."

Will was a year younger than both Asher and Dylan, yet he still served as the father figure in their trio. He and Dylan had known each other since birth.

"I already told him I was a yes."

"Yeah, but you bailed on us last year."

Asher sighed. Heavily. "You wouldn't have wanted to be around me then. Trust me, I did you both a favor." He'd just resigned from the church and was in full self-pity mode. Wallowing didn't go well with primitive camping.

"I know. Just wanted to check your current state of mind."

An image of Katie flashed through his head. He'd be lying if he said he was back to his old self, but he felt hope that he'd get there soon. He looked forward to her late-evening visits, had even noticed a new urgency to get his work done so they could just sit and talk.

"My current state of mind is that camping sounds awesome. I can now be trusted with sharp objects and annoying friends."

Dylan laughed. "Good, because Will brought this guy from work last year and I swear he whined the whole time."

"Not everyone is cut out for Will's definition of fun."

"Very true. Anyway, I'm at Marissa's now. I'll call when I have more details."

Asher heard Katie knock. "You mean: when Will sends our four-page itinerary."

"Exactly."

"Lord help us both. Tell Marissa I said hi."

"Will do."

He ended the call right as he opened the door, and had to actively concentrate on not allowing his phone to slip through his fingers.

Katie stood opposite him wearing a short black-and-white striped dress with a red belt. Her usually ponytailed hair was down and super straight.

"I know I'm way too dressy for the movies, but I found this outfit in my mom's stuff, and I was dying to wear something other than my grungy work clothes."

His gaze lingered longer than was polite. Her transformation had created this contradiction of edgy and sweet that was not only fascinating but also striking.

"You look great." Asher stepped aside to let Katie into his house, a moment he'd anticipated since their first real conversation. As soon as he shut the door, the molecules in the air shifted. He'd expected her careful observation, expected her endless questions. But never this *atmosphere*. It had to be her, as if she was making the atmosphere by just being there.

For months, his home had served as a kind of a security blanket. A place free from anyone who could hurt him. But here Katie was, filling the space with a presence much too large for her small frame, and he welcomed it. Enjoyed it, even.

Maybe his ability to trust hadn't been forever severed.

"Wow. It's so different than my parents'. I just expected the layout would be the same." She walked around the open foyer in awe, running her hands over the new drywall.

"It used to be." He'd torn out two walls on the first floor to open up the living room more.

She continued her silent perusal, periodically stopping to peek in a doorway or touch his new woodwork. At the fireplace, she spun around, the motion lifting her skirt up an extra inch. As if he needed something else to distract him. The way that dress draped over her curves had been plenty enticing.

Asher adjusted his collar. "We should go or we're not going to get a decent spot."

"Oh, okay." Katie strolled out the door and leaned against the porch rail while he locked up. "So, I checked the movie listing, and it's basically sci-fi action thriller, cartoons, or really bad chick flicks."

"Sci-fi."

"My thought exactly." She hopped down the steps. "You know, I've never actually gone there before."

He clicked his key fob to unlock his SUV. "What? You're kidding."

"Nope. By the time I could drive, the last thing I was interested in was hanging at the movie theater."

"So what kind of stuff did you do while the rest of us were gorging on popcorn?" He shouldn't have asked. He wouldn't like any of her answers, but he wanted to know her. Really know her. And her careful avoidance of any conversation regarding her life before coming home only added to his curiosity.

She stood in front of him and fiddled with her belt buckle. "I'm sure you've heard all the rumors. Pick and choose."

He hated that answer more than any other she could have given. "Rumors are nothing more than fabricated lies that give people an excuse to ignore their own misery. I was asking *you*. You know, since it's your life I'm talking about."

"My old life. And I don't want to dwell on it." A wave of annoyance rolled off her. "Tonight's supposed to be fun, remember?"

He was smart enough to know when to back off. She may have changed her hair and attitude, but Katie had always been able to slay a person when provoked. "Okay, fun it is. And since you are a drive-in newbie and I am a pro, get ready to be hooked. I have a system so solid, you'll want to go back every weekend."

Katie didn't move and the intensity in her blue-gray stare made him wonder if he'd once again said the wrong thing.

"Thank you," she finally said.

"For what?"

"For treating me like I'm a good person." She tucked a piece of hair behind her ear, and Asher had to ball up his fingers to keep them from reaching out and touching the soft skin her quick sweep had exposed.

"Katie, I would have treated you this way always. You just never let me."

There was a beat of silence, and then she stepped close. Close enough that heat sparked up his spine. Close enough that when he took a breath, their bodies touched. Slender arms weaved around his torso, and before he could process what she was doing, Katie hugged him, pressing her head against his chest.

Asher closed his eyes, felt the silky touch of her hair on his chin. He tried to define her smell, like citrus and flowers and delicate beauty. Intoxicating.

It should have been a platonic hug. A simple gesture of appreciation from a person who was searching for answers. Only nothing about her embrace felt platonic.

His hands followed the line of her waist and touched the rope leather of her belt. He could feel the heat of her skin, her chest rising and falling rapidly. He wanted to caress her face and graze her lips. The impulse was more than just physical. More than a fleeting moment.

He wanted the freedom to love someone again.

She pulled away, her smile self-conscious, as if she too felt the gravity of what had passed between them. "So, um, we should go, right?"

Go. Leave. Yes. They definitely needed to do something. "Here. I'll get the door." He quickly slid past her and opened the passenger side, allowing her to step up and into the vehicle.

"Why, thank you, sir." Her voice was just airy enough to make him believe their hug hadn't tilted his world. "You are such a gentleman."

"Nah, I'm just trying to impress the girl next door."

Her gaze pulsed with emotion. "Don't worry. You've already done that. Many, many times."

Katie fought with herself all the way to the theater. She shouldn't have hugged him. Shouldn't have allowed her guard to be so completely annihilated. Whatever she thought she was feeling, it had to stop.

Asher paid the attendant through his window and chatted with him for a few moments before driving up to screen number four. He maneuvered a three-point turn and backed into an empty slot with speakers on each side. Only one car stood between them and the massive movie screen.

"Now it gets fun." He opened his door and hopped out of the SUV. The theater's radio station played filler music while he lifted the tailgate and adjusted blankets over the lowered backseats.

"Can I help you with something?"

"Nope. It's all ready." He climbed into the back and motioned for her to join him.

She crawled through the seats and past the cooler he'd brought. Two big bags of red licorice sat on top.

He was already seated, legs crossed, eager and excited as a seven-year-old. It was endearing, the way he wanted to share his joy for this dilapidated spot in the country. As if he didn't even notice the speakers were rusty or the screen was slightly torn on the right side.

He popped open the lid to his cooler. "Thirsty?"

"Always." She sat opposite him and matched his pretzeled position.

The ice swooshed when he pulled out two twenty-ounce plastic bottles . . . of soda. She almost laughed at the absurdity of it all. Katie Stone at the drive-in, sober.

"What?" Of course he noticed her amusement. He noticed everything.

"Nothing. How did you know I'm a sucker for licorice?"

"I assumed you had good taste." He pulled the candy bag open, tearing it at the seam, and offered her one. She took two.

"So, what's your all-time favorite movie?" She swung her licorice in a circle before biting into it.

"The Lord of the Rings movies, but the Star Wars series is a close second."

Katie lowered her head into her palms and shook it back and forth. "Oh no. You're one of *those*."

"Come on, those are epic movies."

"Yes, but totally unoriginal. Ask a hundred people on the street, and I guarantee at least forty percent will pick one of those."

"Different doesn't always make things better," he said.

"Whatever you say . . ."

"Okay, Miss Judgment, what's yours?" His smile was back. The one that pushed the storms from his eyes and made their banter easy.

"Good Will Hunting."

"Interesting. What makes it rise to the top?"

She shrugged even though she knew exactly why. In the movie, Will had overcome injustice, chosen love, escaped his ghosts. Everything Katie was still afraid to do. "Robin Williams, of course."

"Of course."

She brushed off her hands, grabbed another twisted vine. "Favorite food combination, and don't say something easy like hot dogs and mac and cheese."

"Gross. Who likes that?"

Katie slapped his knee. "I was practically raised on hot dogs and mac and cheese. Sheesh."

"Sorry, didn't mean to offend." Asher lifted his hands in mock surrender.

She waved an imaginary wand, tapped it twice. "You're exonerated. Now go."

"I'm not so sure I want to after you dismissed my movie. Besides, I plan to introduce you to it firsthand, after the first feature is over."

"No, you can't hold out on me. I'll never enjoy the show. I hate, hate, hate waiting."

"Really? I can't tell." He laughed, and she felt the sound move through her.

She leaned over and tickled his side. "Come on. Tell me."

"It's a secret." He pushed her hand away, and the tingling contact with his fingers was enough to make her pause for a second to make sure he wasn't going to fall back into awkwardness.

His piercing smile said no, so she relaxed.

"I can make you talk. I have many, many ways."

"That may be true, but I'm stubborn."

"Not as stubborn as I am. In fact, no one is as stubborn as I am." She said it proudly, although that trait had been a thorn to her many times before.

He lazily shrugged one shoulder. "We'll see. Ah, look, the previews are about to start."

She swiped his licorice right before he was about to take a bite. "Come on. Just tell me."

"Fine. I'll tell you when you answer my earlier question." His hand captured her wrist, and the sudden seriousness in his gaze made her wonder if he hadn't been working her this whole time.

She tugged her hand free. "Why do you care what I did in high school?"

"I just do."

He wasn't asking for a lot. Not even a sliver of what his friendship had already given her.

She watched the preview flashing on the screen and tried not to show the sacrifice it took to answer his question. "When we weren't driving to the beach or trying to get into a nightclub somewhere, we'd go to this place we found. The Point. We'd get someone to buy us a six-pack, and we'd talk and drink and sometimes even dream."

His warm hand curled around hers. It was strong, rough with callouses but comforting. It was a hand she knew would never ball into a fist or threaten her.

"What did you dream about?"

"What do you think? Leaving Fairfield. That was all any of us dreamed about." They'd been so young, only teenagers, and yet they'd had it all figured out, down to their neighboring homes with white picket fences. Chad and Laila would get married, and Katie would live a blissful single life with oodles of men falling at her feet.

The air turned heavy. Asher's hometown had been her prison. His positive childhood memories, her nightmares. Of course he didn't understand her need to forget the past. He'd had a beautiful one.

"Popcorn and Hot Tamales." His hand slid away, and his voice shed the counselor's purr it'd contained minutes before.

"What?"

"My favorite food combination. You mix popcorn and Hot Tamales together."

"And you said mine was gross?" She faked a gag.

"See, this is why I couldn't tell you. Now I have to go get some and prove I'm right."

"But the movie's about to start."

He jumped out of the back of the car. "I'll be quick."

Katie let out a long breath as she watched him walk across the dimly lit parking area to the concession stand. He'd somehow guessed she needed a moment alone to push away the sadness.

She slid from the back of the SUV and walked around it. Leaning against the side, she tried to imagine what it would have been like to spend her weekends here instead of drowning in whatever substance she and her friends could get their hands on. Wondered what it would've been like to date Asher back in high school, before her sins had become too numerous to escape.

She would have been happy. That much she knew, without question.

A sleek black Jaguar crossed in front of her, bouncing as it navigated the potholed gravel. An elbow hung out of the open window, and Katie immediately recognized the snake tattoo an inch above it. Her eyes followed the line of the man's bicep past his shoulder and up to a profile she could still draw in her sleep.

Slim.

A man in jeans and an army-green T-shirt approached the driver's side, bent down to the window, and blocked Katie's view. Seconds later, he walked away.

An exchange. Quick. Stealthy. Dirty.

Katie knew the drill. She knew it so well, her mouth went dry and her stomach knotted until she felt the need to bend over and dry heave.

"Cash only," Slim said.

"It's worth way more than what you're giving me. Come on. I need this." She shoved the ring back in his face.

His gaze slithered down her front. "There are other trades that can be made."

"You know I don't play that game."

"And I take cash only."

"I'm one of your biggest customers. Do you want me to find someone else?"

His eyes became thin slits. "Okay, fine, I'll take it, but you gotta do something for me now too."

That night. That stupid, stupid night. And for what? A quick high. A fool's escape. A twist of reality that could never, ever be sustained.

She forced herself to stand and wiped sweat from her brow. The car had circled around and out of sight. Gone, but never far enough away to stop haunting her.

Katie's throat constricted, but she refused to cry. Asher had said she needed to feel, but he was wrong. Emotions were fleeting, uncontrolled, and dangerous. But at the same time, it was becoming impossible to tuck away the past. Everywhere she turned, there were reminders.

Maybe she'd been doing everything wrong. Maybe God hadn't just brought her back to Fairfield to help her parents. Maybe it was to give her a chance to fix her biggest regret. To go back to the beginning of the end and make restitution.

That one tiny piece of jewelry had set off an unstoppable chain reaction. If she could find it, if she could right that one wrong, then maybe the reaction would work in reverse.

Maybe then she could find a way to heal.

CHAPTER 15

Asher tapped on the glass counter as he waited for the popcorn to pop. The kid working concessions was new, and it took three tries before he could get the kernels spinning. The movie had started five minutes ago, but Asher was actually relieved to have a second to breathe. He'd broken through Katie's thick shield. Only a little, but enough to know he wanted more.

Chatter surrounded him, as did the steady *ping* of the arcade games in the corner. A little girl with pigtails begged her dad for chocolate, and Asher chuckled to himself as the man melted in her chubby little hands.

Finally, the popcorn and box of candy appeared in front of him. He handed the teenager a ten and waited for change. The scent of salt and butter swirled in the air and he inhaled, feeling comfort that for the first time in a very long while, that smell didn't bring regret.

He slipped his change into the pocket of his shorts and walked out, balancing his loot.

A familiar giggle raised the hair on his forearm. He shouldn't have looked, but it was instinctual. Platinum-blonde hair, blue eyes, a purse ten times bigger than she needed. All three blurred in front of him. He hadn't seen Jillian in six months. But there she stood, only ten feet away, purring while she kissed a man who must be the new boyfriend his mom had mentioned.

The two were oblivious to everything but each other, while Asher remained rooted to the concrete. He'd been on guard every other time he'd been at the drive-in, but not tonight. Being with Katie made him forget that demons lurked in the night.

The happy couple turned in his direction, their fingers interlaced, but Asher quickly walked the opposite way before he ended up face-to-face with the woman who made Jezebel look like a saint. The paper bag of popcorn shook in his hands, and heat engulfed his neck and cheeks. He wanted to curse. Or find something to hammer. Maybe he'd go ahead and tear out that tile in his bathroom tonight after the movie. Anything to make the hole in his chest close back up.

His quick steps brought him back to his car faster than he'd intended. Katie stood at the side of it, leaning with her head tilted toward the sky. She could be a model in a photo shoot, the way the residual movie lights reflected off her skin.

The sight of her was a balm to his ache. Jillian had dimmed something inside him, but Katie brought a hope that he could once again be whole.

She must have heard him approach, because her head dipped and she flashed a smile that continued to ease his pulsing anger.

"I didn't want to watch the movie without you." She eyed his tight posture and the death grip he had on the bag. "Everything okay?"

"Uh, yeah. Sorry I took so long." His voice sounded strangled.

She hesitated but didn't press. "No problem. I think all we missed were a few explosions anyway."

Asher attempted a weak smile, but he suddenly forgot how to pretend.

"And maybe a meteor attack, although it was hard to tell because the chick was in black spandex and her hair was way too perfect for an apocalypse."

Funny. Yet he couldn't laugh. Not yet. He climbed into the back of his SUV and helped Katie in over the bumper. She'd stopped talking and was watching him as if he, too, was about to explode. He wasn't, but his pulse still hadn't settled yet either.

A quick stretch over the seats to turn up the radio, and his speakers boomed with shrieks and feet pounding. They matched the turmoil in his head.

He wouldn't do this, let Jillian spoil another night. She'd already stolen so much; he refused to let his time with Katie be another casualty.

Asher poured some popcorn into a paper bowl and mixed in the Hot Tamales. "Okay, now *this* is how you should eat popcorn." He held up a finger when she appeared ready to protest. "Nope. No judgment until you try it."

The bridge of her nose wrinkled in the cutest way, and he felt himself relax.

She reached out and grabbed a handful of kernels and candy. With her nose still scrunched, she dropped the mess into her mouth and cautiously chewed. Quickly, her expression shifted from dread to surprise "Oh my gosh, that's so good."

Asher's tension uncoiled even more as he took his own handful. "Never doubt my knowledge when it comes to food."

"Noted."

She snuck more out of the bowl, and they watched the movie in silence until the acting got so bad that Asher couldn't stand it anymore.

"This movie is terrible," he said.

She burst out laughing. "The absolute worst." Her expression shifted to feigned panic. "Oh, Hansel, what will we do? New York is destroyed. I will never wear Jimmy Choo again!"

He lowered his voice to a deep bass. "Not to worry, my pet. I have fifty-inch biceps, so I can save the world when I flex."

"Oh, my hero." She drew her hands to her chest. "Let me kiss you with music in the background while two cars explode right next to us."

He shook his head and crawled to the front to turn off the stereo. "How in the world did this film get production dollars?"

"Hot girls in spandex. Equally hot guys in spandex." She leaned back on her elbows and stretched out her legs. "I remember now why I never go to the movies."

Asher laughed, and the act finally felt genuine. A breeze whistled through the back of the car as they both watched the screen in silence. A nice silence. One that wasn't awkward or forced.

She shifted her attention to him. "You don't have to talk about it if don't want to. But you seemed really upset when you came back from the concession stand."

He still hadn't adjusted to Katie's bold honesty. Jillian would have ignored the two-ton elephant and pretended they were having a wonderful time. That was the church way, right? Put on the smile, the mask; tell everyone you're fine when really you're dying inside.

He didn't want to be that person anymore.

"I ran into my ex." Even with effort, he couldn't keep the disgust from his voice. "Our breakup wasn't under the best of circumstances."

Katie sat up and faced him. "Who did the breaking up?"

"I did." He ran a hand through his hair. "But she certainly did the most damage."

"I really hate when people pry, but if you want to talk about it, I'm a good listener." She played with a dangling bracelet on her right wrist. "Although my past relationships don't exactly give me any authority on the subject."

"Why's that?" He welcomed the shift in conversation. Focusing on her was easier.

She pulled her dress farther down over her crossed legs. "I have a bad habit of picking men who aren't good to me. It's a character flaw. Really. It's like I know going in: this guy is cruel, selfish, and stubborn. Yet that's always who I end up with."

Asher scooted toward her until their knees almost touched. There was something about Katie when she let down her defenses that wrenched his insides. Made him want to hold her. Comfort her. "Maybe you were trying to punish yourself by being with them."

She shrugged. "Maybe. I think it's more habit. There's a draw to the familiar, even when it's no good."

Knots tightened in his stomach. Jillian had been familiar. Perfect on paper. Her father was a deacon, her parents close friends of his own. They had the same social circles, the same taste in movies and music, the same value system. Maybe that was why he'd felt so trapped. Heck, he used to get asked weekly when they were getting married.

"Do you regret the split?" Katie's blue eyes flickered over his face.

"No. I regret what happened before the split."

"What happened?"

"Things got complicated. Lines got crossed. Mistakes were made. The usual." He'd moved closer than he realized, and at some point his hand landed on her knee. The dress underneath his palm was stiff, but also soft.

She inhaled. "But you still care about her?"

"No. Trust me. The only thing I feel for Jillian is relief that she's out of my life."

Katie smiled then, and he liked that his words were the cause of that smile. She was so beautiful and real and unlike anyone he'd ever known.

She carefully laid her hand over his, and when she lifted her forehead, he was startlingly close to her face. Close enough to see a scattering of freckles by her nose, the small ball of silver in her earlobe, the quick way she swallowed when their eyes met.

Her fingers trailed a line down his forearm, exploring, inviting.

He shouldn't do this. It was too soon for both of them. But her breath touched his chin, and soon all rational thought disappeared.

Her hand traveled to his shoulder, and her thumb traced his collarbone through his shirt. His eyes closed, his pulse jumped, and soon his own hand sought out the hot skin of her neck. Fingers danced on both sides. His near the shorter strands of her hair. Hers tightening around his collar, pulling him closer and closer until his lips trailed centimeters above the sharp line of her jaw.

Just one taste, and he'd pull away.

But as his lips brushed the patch of skin he'd imagined kissing more times than he cared to admit, a rush of guilt consumed him. Katie was vulnerable. She'd told him she didn't like to feel. Told him she looked for ways to numb herself, and he'd almost given her permission to do the same with him. He abruptly let go, forcing space between them that was nonexistent just moments before.

"I'm sorry," he whispered. "I didn't mean . . ." But he had meant it. Just not like this. Not as an afterthought or an escape, and especially not before he had time to truly grasp what this step would mean for both of them.

"It's fine." She pulled her hair back at the nape of her neck and then released it. She wouldn't look at him. "I'm thirsty. Are you thirsty?" She grabbed her purse and slid out the open tailgate.

"Katie . . ." Her name lingered in the air, and the warning in the tight line of her mouth brought on a new surge of regret. He'd failed her. "I'll take a root beer," he said, even though his cooler was still full.

She glanced at the screen as the hero walked past a row of waiting soldiers. "I'll be right back. I'm gonna have a field day with this scene." With a forced smile, she ducked out of his line of sight.

As it turned out, when it was needed, Katie could act with the best of them.

CHAPTER 16

Katie almost turned around twice but in the end found the courage to pull into Fairfield Fellowship on Sunday morning.

She'd been avoiding Asher, mostly because she needed to figure out what the heck she was feeling. Figure out why, when she'd hopped out of the car, half of her was grateful they'd stopped and the other half was furious at the horror in his expression.

Her mother's words ticked inside her brain for the hundredth time.

I've seen his type. She was tall, blonde, innocent as a daisy, and practically wore a halo.

And Asher deserved all of that. He deserved someone good and honest. Not someone who would inevitably hurt him. So why did she feel so shaken?

Car doors slammed all around her, and the sanctuary stood boldly in her line of sight. She shouldn't be here, not at Asher's and Mary's church. But she needed to feel some kind of encouragement, especially when she planned to confront a fire-breathing dragon this afternoon.

She'd made a decision. She'd go to that neighborhood. To her old dealer. And find out what he did with the ring. She'd find a way to make it right again.

With a determined sigh, Katie walked down the sidewalk to the entrance. She'd come on time today so she could be sure to get to the far right side, away from Mary Blanchard's seat. Not that Mary would shun her. What Katie dreaded was worse: Mary would be kind and loving and completely oblivious to Katie's betrayal.

The glass door swung open before she could reach for it.

"Good morning." An old man greeted her with a smile. He had a full gray beard and wore black slacks and a polo shirt with the church's logo stitched on the front.

"Morning," she said, and stepped through the door with her head lowered.

She moved past a gaggle of people who stood in a circle talking and found the seat she wanted. Her row was empty, as was the one in front of her. Katie fumbled with her Bible, searching for anything to read while she worked to remain unnoticed.

The voices around her grew louder, and a few people slid by her to get to the inside seats. She kept her head down and held her breath until they were seated and engaged in conversation amongst themselves.

"Hi."

The new voice came from in front of her, but she didn't look up.

"Is this your first time at Fellowship?" the voice persisted.

Katie swallowed, no longer able to deny that the woman was talking to her. She raised her head and let out a breath of relief when she didn't recognize the lady.

The woman had twisted in her seat, draping her elbow over the chair. Her brown hair was curly and impeccably styled and hung just above her shoulders. But what pushed Katie past her unease were the kind eyes and genuinely warm smile that awaited her answer.

"Second time," Katie choked out. She did a quick check to her right and left. The sanctuary was even more full than it had been the last time she'd come. More people would see her. More people would talk. It seemed the buzz in town had been fairly quiet, but she doubted that would continue, especially after the little field trip she had planned for later that day.

"I'm Annie. We moved to Fairfield a couple of years ago, and half the time I forget who all I've met."

So Annie was a transplant. Good. "I'm Katie. I was born here, but I just recently moved back to town."

"Really? Well, I love it here. When my husband picked this small town, I thought he'd lost his mind, but who knew we'd be so happy?"

This woman liked Fairfield? Moved here on purpose?

"Why?" Katie muttered before realizing she'd spoken out loud. "I mean, why did you move here?"

"My husband works in Jacksonville, but the prices anywhere near the city were outrageous. We found this amazing plot of land with twenty acres for a third of the price we would have paid in Florida. And it's a good thing we grabbed it when we did. Word is getting out about this town, and land values have skyrocketed. An hour from Jacksonville, thirty minutes from the coast . . . it's really amazing Fairfield has stayed so small."

Katie's mouth surely hung open. Since when had Fairfield become desirable? They were only a few miles from swampland, and she'd always considered her small town to be the armpit of the Southeast.

The band started their set, and the congregation stood.

Annie turned around fully and rested one knee on her seat cushion. "So, we have a home group that meets on Wednesday nights. Since you're just getting settled, I'd love for you to come. There's only about eight of us, so it's real casual."

Home group? What the heck was a home group? "Um, yeah, okay, maybe." *Never. Not happening.* Why was this woman still talking to her?

Annie tore a piece of paper from her notebook and scribbled in handwriting as cheerful and bubbly as she was. "Here is the information with my phone number and address. So nice to meet you. I really hope you come." With one last grin, she turned back around and stood next to her husband.

The paper crinkled in Katie's hand and she rose slowly.

Judgment, she'd expected. Cold shoulders, quiet mutters, rude glances. All those things came with the territory of attending church in her hometown.

But friendliness? An invitation to someone's house?

Mind-blowing.

Katie didn't see Asher until the end of the service, when he stood and greeted a bunch of his parents' friends.

He was in a suit today with no tie. His sandy blond hair curled just slightly over his ears, and his mouth moved in short sentences. She'd spent enough time with him to know he wasn't relaxed. His neck and shoulders were strained, and his attention kept drifting to the left side of the sanctuary.

Curiosity got the better of her, and Katie let her gaze roam across the seats where several people still mingled in bunches and a few kids ran between the rows, laughing.

She stopped her search when her eyes landed on long, bleached-blonde hair, carefully arranged over one shoulder. The girl was store-bought pretty, with too much makeup and a dark tan that looked like it had been sprayed on. Katie knew the difference because Laila had the same coloring, only hers was natural.

The girl wore a long, strappy sundress with multiple thin bracelets on one wrist. Her other hand was latched on to the arm of an equally attractive guy with extra-broad shoulders and short brown hair. With their plastered-on smiles, the two could star in a toothpaste commercial.

Was that really Asher's ex? Was that the type of girl who appealed to him?

Katie stared down at the dress she'd last worn under her high-school graduation gown. It wasn't ugly or too out of style, but it certainly wouldn't land her on any "best dressed" lists. Neither would her flip-flops and cheap hoop earrings. She'd been called white trash her whole life but had never owned the title. But compared to Asher and his blonde Barbie, that was exactly how she felt now.

Her old minister's words pushed through her doubt. *God doesn't care what you wear on the outside. He only cares about the condition of the heart.* Reverend Snow had said a lot of things to Katie that no one had before. Things that pulled her out of her darkness and depression. He'd also found her a job, a rented room at a church member's house, and a prayer partner. She'd gone from homeless to cared for in less than a week.

She clutched those memories and ignored the pressure building in her chest. She'd find the ring, get her parents secured, and then return to the people who cared. People who didn't see her as the queen of darkness or the town misfit. She was in Fairfield for closure. Period.

Without another look in Asher's direction, Katie left the church.

Slim would still be home, if he hadn't moved. He never took calls before two in the afternoon. She knew because she'd tried so many times to get him to.

His neighborhood was just south of downtown and past the railroad tracks. Katie's beater of a car moaned as she rolled over the metal brackets. The wood between the rails was rotten and broken, creating huge dips for her small tires to traverse.

Familiarity tugged at her. She'd traveled this route a thousand times. Through high school, after graduation. Even after Laila got married and quit partying, Katie still craved the high. It was the thing that had kept Cooper and her together. The thing that kept her dependent on him long after he'd shown her his darker side.

Slim's house was down the hill and to the right, tucked behind three duplexes and the old fire station. It wasn't the worst area in town, but Katie had rarely gone there without a buddy. She passed an old Dodge Dynasty up on blocks, its rims either stolen or pawned. A string of empty beer cans littered the yard next to Slim's, and she had no doubt there were pipes and syringes among the debris.

Saying one last silent prayer, she pressed the doorbell. It'd been four years since that night. Four years since she stood right in this very spot and made the worst decision of her life.

No answer. She rang the bell again.

Finally, she heard several clicks and the door swung open. Slim was in boxers with no shirt. A long scar ran down his right side and into the dragon tattoo that started at his hip. In his hand was a pistol pointed toward the floor.

"Katie Stone. I heard a rumor you were back." He spoke like a well-bred southerner, not the drug-dealing street thug he was. "Only you would have the nerve to come here this early on a Sunday." He set down the gun on a nearby table and opened the door wider. "Come in."

Katie swallowed. She wasn't dressed for this. She needed her ripped jeans and black mascara. She needed the old attitude that had slipped away months ago. "No thanks. I'm not staying."

"Baby, you know I don't do business in public." That was a lie, but she knew he'd much rather corner her in his house. It would give him control and the upper hand.

Katie clamped her fingers tight to keep the shaking under control and didn't move from her spot outside his door. "I'm not here to buy. I want to know what happened to the ring. The one I traded before I left town."

His lips quirked up as his gaze drifted over her body. "I offered a different trade. One that didn't require you to give up your precious jewelry. You declined."

A shiver curled down her spine. Four years might have changed her, but he was the same slimeball he'd always been.

"I want the ring back. I'll pay you what you spotted me, with interest." Katie had just enough in savings to cover the debt, unless the amount of interest he charged would make the exchange impossible.

Slim's feigned amicability faded, and his face grew caustic. Katie knew she was navigating a minefield. He didn't like complications or loose strings. He expected payment in cash. He'd made an exception for her only because doing so benefited him at the time.

"I'm not a storage unit, Katie. I moved that ring the minute you left with your score."

Her chest caved. She'd known he'd probably sold it long ago, but there'd been that tiny sliver of hope that maybe . . . "Who did you sell it to?"

He stepped toward her, but she didn't budge. She couldn't show fear. "Now you're in my business. And you know what happens when people get nosy."

The possibilities sent a chill through her bloodstream. But she met his eyes and stared into their cold, dark depths. "The cut wasn't right. I don't know if you were trying to save money or if you laced it with something stronger, but, either way, you knew that supplier was shady, and you let me take it anyway. That's why you did the trade. It wasn't a favor to me, it was an experiment." She knew from the tic in his jaw that her calculated guess was spot on. "I could have ratted you out, could have blown up your reputation on my way out of town, but I didn't. That loyalty should matter now."

He was close enough that Katie could smell his nicotine-coated breath. She wanted to shove him back but knew better than to try. He'd taken much bigger men to their knees for less. He didn't say a word, and each second that passed curled her insides tighter and tighter.

"Who did you sell it to?" She stood motionless, nose to nose with a man who'd done jail time for assault and many more crimes he'd never been nailed for.

His expression darkened. "There are six pawnshops within fifty miles of Fairfield. I use them all." He roughly grabbed her chin. "That enough information for your *loyalty*?"

Katie slapped his hand away. She wasn't one to be manhandled without a fight.

He only smirked and stepped back over the threshold into his duplex. "Don't come to my house again unless you plan to make it worth my time."

Katie fought rising nausea as Slim slammed the door right in her face.

CHAPTER 17

A warm breeze blew through Katie's car as she drove home, cooling her flushed skin. Driving down country roads with her hair whipping around her face had always brought a sense of calm. And she needed something to tamp her growing anticipation. After leaving Slim's, she'd stopped by the library to research pawnshop locations. One was in town; the other five were each twenty to forty minutes away, in an array of directions.

Her fingers tingled. The printed list of addresses was the first tangible sign that her new mission might actually work, even if she lacked the courage to start searching. For today, having that piece of possibility in her hand was enough.

A new Ford F-250 was parked in the grass when Katie made the turn into her driveway. The gleaming blue paint sparkled in the sun, and Katie felt a twinge of envy when she cut the ignition of her rusty vehicle. She'd had a picture of that same truck on her vanity mirror for years. Super Duty. Lariat.

She strolled by the truck, trying to appear casual, and peeked in the window. Wood grain. Leather.

Footsteps crunched across the gravel. "It's nice, isn't it? Just got her last week."

The muscles in Katie's neck coiled tight.

Cooper's hand landed on the truck bed next to her. "I guess all those years of you staring at that picture finally had some influence on me."

Knowing Cooper, he likely bought the truck just to spite her. "So you came here to gloat?"

"You didn't really think you'd run me off that easy, did you?" The calm in his voice was more alarming than his rage. Both of which Katie knew well.

She met his eyes. "What do you want?"

He reached inside the truck bed and pulled out a Freon tank. "Right now I want to fix your parents' air conditioner. You seem to have forgotten it, but we take care of our own in this town."

He dropped the metal cylinder on the ground and raised himself to his full height. He wore jeans and a green John Deere T-shirt that was well past its prime. She remembered that shirt. Remembered way too much about their two-year relationship.

"The unit's around the back," her dad called from the porch. "Braves play in twenty minutes. Let's get this done."

Cooper grinned. "Mind if I stick around and watch the game?" His question was for her father, but he never took his eyes off her.

"You get my house cool and you can even stay for dinner. Katie's got something cooking in the Crock-Pot that smells so good my mouth's been watering for an hour."

Despite the compliment, Katie cringed, and of course, Cooper noticed. He winked and stalked toward her dad, Freon cylinder in hand. "I'd love to. I miss Katie's cooking." The two of them stomped around the side of the house until they disappeared.

She trudged toward the front steps, all her earlier victory sucked away.

Her mom waited at the top, balancing herself on a new, sturdier three-pronged cane. "Should I say I told you so now, or later?"

Katie shook her head, refusing to answer. "I'll be in my room if you need me."

It was a sad escape. The air upstairs was thick and suffocating. Katie stripped out of her dress, tugged on thin athletic shorts and a tank top, and pulled her hair into a ponytail. Even with the layers of clothing gone, sweat dripped past her temple.

The ceiling fan spun overhead, rattling as if it were ready to sail across the room, but she didn't dare turn it off. The breeze from its blades was the only bit of relief in the stuffy room, which still smelled of wet cardboard and dirty laundry.

One task at a time.

She pulled her comforter tight and fluffed the pillows. Another drop of sweat rolled down her arm. There was no way she'd be able to stay upstairs through the entire baseball game.

She'd have to go . . . somewhere. But where? She had no friends. Everything she used to do was off-limits to her now, and things with Asher were . . . well, she didn't know what they were, but she certainly wasn't going to find out while she was under Cooper's scrutiny. Katie sat on the freshly made bed, her shoulders sagging. She was trapped. Trapped in a house-sized sauna with a man who knew all her secrets.

Agatha jumped into her lap and purred, rubbing her side against the front of Katie's tank top. It was as if the cat knew Katie didn't like her and made a point to deposit as much fur on her clothing as possible.

She pushed the cat to the floor and brushed a hand down the front of her shirt.

"At least I'm not the only one you're too good for now." Cooper strolled into the room and lifted a hand to the vent above her bed, checking the airflow. "Nice and cool. You're welcome."

She continued to pick off cat hair. "Thank you. Now go."

He sat next to her, the mattress dipping under his weight as his thigh brushed against hers. She scooted over until there was space between them again.

"I found this in my dresser the other day and thought you might want it." With one quick motion, Cooper pulled a scratched old keychain from his pocket. It was the one her father had given her the day he brought her Toyota home, and for a fraction of a second she remembered that not every memory she shared with Cooper was a bad one.

He watched as she ran a finger along the bright pink word KATIEBUG that was etched next to the image of a grinning caterpillar.

"I'm sorry I was so harsh the other day," he said.

She tucked the keepsake into her fist. "Harsh? You threatened me." Typical Cooper. His apologizes never came with true remorse.

"Because you insulted me."

"Only after you cornered me and demanded we talk."

His voice rose. "I wouldn't have to demand if you'd stop avoiding me."

And there they were again. One second of peace followed by days of unrest. Better she just rip the Band-Aid off now, even though part of her didn't want to know. She'd enjoyed the cocooned bliss she'd been living in.

"Did you tell Laila what happened?"

"No. You were right. I was bluffing." An old affection sprang up in his voice but died out again as quickly as it had appeared. "Besides, I see no reason to hurt her more than you already have."

Katie laced and unlaced her fingers several times. Maybe this exchange was good. They'd get it all out. Have closure. She shifted to face him. "Well, you're here. And I know you well enough to know that's where you'll stay until I talk to you. So?" She lifted her hand, giving him permission to start the conversation he'd been demanding.

The room went silent, and Katie immediately wondered if she'd made a mistake. She'd given in. Cleared a path. With someone like Cooper, that was a slippery slope.

"Do I have a kid?"

She studied his face to make sure he was serious and not just toying with her in a new way. "You thought I was pregnant?"

"That was one of the rumors: I knocked you up, and you left town to take care of the problem."

For a few seconds she couldn't speak. "And you believed them?"

He rubbed a hand over his face. "I don't know. I knew you wanted to hurt me."

"Enough to hide a kid from you?" The only thing Cooper had ever truly wanted was to be a father. To have a real home. To create the kind of stability they never seemed to be able to achieve together.

His eyes narrowed, his mouth a tight line. "Don't act so holy, Firecracker. You know it was bad that night. It's not insane that I'd consider the possibility."

He was right. It had been horrible. The stuff they'd snorted—it was all wrong. Made them both crazy. Katie swallowed. "I was never pregnant."

He exhaled, not with relief but with what seemed to be disappointment. "Yeah, I guess I knew that. Besides, your dad pretty much told me those rumors were a load of crap."

At least someone didn't think the worst of her, although the truth wasn't a whole lot prettier.

She walked to the dresser and started sorting through the stacks of papers she'd already categorized. Finding the ring would make it right. It would end the shame. End the sickness lodged in her gut.

Katie felt him before she heard him. His body stood centimeters from her back in overbearing closeness; his breath lingered on her neck. He flattened one hand on the dresser and the other on the wall in front of her, caging her in. "We were a family. Me, you, Laila, Chad. Everything fell apart when you disappeared."

She squeezed her eyes shut, wishing the memories of that weekend away. "It fell apart long before I left."

"Fine. So we were a dysfunctional family. Who cares?" He dropped his hand from the wall and shifted so they were face-to-face. "You don't just walk. You don't just take off. And you especially don't get to come back afterward and act like none of us exist."

The tug-of-war between them was as real as ever. The simmering resentment, yet also a desperation that drove them back together time and time again. Only this time, she refused to play the game. "You asked your questions. I answered them. Now you can go do whatever it is you do these days."

His hand smacked the dresser with a bang loud enough to make her jump. "Enough! I'm done with this cat-and-mouse game you keep playing. You blew up my life when you walked out."

She didn't hesitate. She knew that tone. Knew the violence in his eyes. She'd been on the other side of a boyfriend's closed fist too many times not to know when to flee. Though Cooper had never actually hit her, he'd come close that night, and she knew all too well that years of bitterness could ruin a person.

She made it to the stairs before he caught up with her. He jerked her to him, and her arm ached under his tight grip. His fingers were pressing hard enough to not only stop her descent but also make a point.

"If you cared, I could forgive you for how selfish you've been. If you wanted to fix things, I could forgive you for the destruction you left behind. I could even forgive you for Chad if you showed an ounce of remorse. But I won't accept this lie that you've moved on. You don't get to start over while the rest of us are still bleeding."

"I don't need your forgiveness or want it." She tried to pull her arm away, but his fingers only tightened.

"Yeah, but you need my silence, don't you? 'Cause if I told, there'd be no one willing to forgive you. Not even in that fancy church you seem bent on attending."

Her cheeks burned and she lowered her head. She hated him. Hated him in that moment almost as much as she had that night.

CHAPTER 18

His body crammed under his deck, Asher wrestled with the final hose connection. He'd wanted the propane for the grill to stay out of sight, but he should have considered the enormous pain it'd be to change the tanks.

With a final twist of his wrench, he shimmied out of the crawl space. His hair was drenched. Sweat droplets rolled down his cheek and dripped from his chin. His T-shirt was all but ruined. But the grill was installed and functional, which meant frozen dinners were a thing of the past. It also meant that the task he'd used to distract himself all weekend was complete.

Katie hadn't even acknowledged him at church. Not a wave. No eye contact. Nothing. He grabbed a towel, wiped his face and neck, and threw it back on the lawn chair. He wanted to talk to her. To apologize once again for behaving so badly.

Suddenly the faint smell of pot roast permeated the air, and he lifted his gaze. Katie stood on the deck, a covered plate in hand.

He'd never been one to freeze up in uncomfortable situations or fumble over words, but he was already so twisted up inside, he could barely get his tongue to move.

"Hi." She said it as if she'd been standing there a while, just waiting for him to notice. She shifted her weight to her left foot and lifted the plastic in her hand. "I thought you might be hungry."

Her hair was pulled high on her head, and she wore a green tank top that exposed her bare arms. She wore no makeup, but Katie didn't need any. Her face was unique and exotic and far too interesting to cover up.

"You brought me food?" He fastened a thumb in the pocket of his jeans and tried his best not to look as guilty as he felt.

"Are you hungry?"

His stomach growled as if in response. It was almost six, and lunch was a distant memory. "I'm always hungry."

She smiled. "Good. I needed an excuse to come over, and this seemed to be the obvious choice."

They stood there, both of them tense and fidgety. Katie finally stepped forward and passed him the container. It was an expensive one with multiple food slots and a thin plastic cover to keep in the heat. Through the transparent lid, he saw a mound of meat, potatoes, and carrots.

"Fancy," Asher said, lifting the lid. He was used to paper plates and aluminum foil. After multiple trips back to retrieve her dinnerware, his mom had quickly switched to disposable containers.

"Keep it. We have, like, three hundred at the house. Don't ask me why, because I couldn't begin to tell you. But if there is ever an apocalypse, you can be sure that the Stones have enough food-storage containers to feed the town."

Her words came out quickly. She was babbling, which she seemed to do when she was nervous or anxious. He sat, hoping that would calm her down. Or maybe it was to calm himself down. Either would be good.

Katie handed him a package of plastic utensils, which even included a moist towelette for his hands, and then took the chair next to him. She played with the strings on her shorts and tapped her foot.

All their actions were familiar—normal, even—but a thin layer of awkwardness coated every movement. They'd crossed a line, and jumping back over it seemed impossible, especially since he still felt an urge to pick up right where they left off.

"This is tasty," he said after two agonizing bites. The food was good, but in such a stressful situation, the meat landed like a rock at the bottom of his stomach.

Katie sighed and bolted to her feet. "Okay, this is weird. And I can't have you being weird to me." She shook her hands out as if she were trying to bring feeling back into them. "We're friends. Good friends, I thought, and I don't have any others right now. All I have are people in my life who don't understand me or who resent me or are out to prove I'm a fraud." She paced back and forth. "We had a moment. So what? We're two adults. It was dark. Those things happen. I know you don't think of me . . ." She paused. "Like *that*. I mean, I'm totally not your type at all. So there's no need—"

"Katie."

She stopped her outburst.

"Sit down."

She did as she was told and Asher took two more bites of his dinner, enjoying it much more now that she'd blasted away all the pretense with one long, awkward explanation. He chuckled. "I'd forgotten how straightforward you are."

She stretched her hands high above her head, her relieved sigh audible. "I will add that to my long list of vices."

"It's not a vice." He tightened his grip on the plastic fork. "In fact, if I'd been less of a coward, I would have been the one to bring you dinner."

"Maybe, but it wouldn't have been edible, so I think we both win."

There was a smile in her voice. A small one, but it was there. Katie had a habit of ambushing him, and for some reason he respected her for it. So many people had been tiptoeing around him since the breakup. Letting him hide and brood all alone. He liked that she wasn't one of them. "I'm sorry about last night. I haven't been this close to someone in a long time, and I never should have put us in that situation."

She traced a circle on her kneecap with her fingertip. "I'm a big girl. Besides, I knew you were in an emotional funnel cloud and . . . well, it takes two." She looked right at him for a second and then back at her knee. "I think I saw Jillian today. In church. Blue dress? Had a beefy escort?"

His muscles tightened, and he willed them to relax. "Yep. That was her." He'd seen her too, but thankfully not until the end of service.

"She's pretty."

"I guess." He couldn't see her that way anymore. He still heard her cries and accusations. Still felt the sting of her viciousness.

Katie lounged back in the cloth chair and examined the trail of clouds in the sky. "You can talk about her, you know. It doesn't bother me."

It was an invitation he'd been given many times. His parents. His best friends. His old youth pastor. They had surrounded him in love as the lies floated around, but he'd been too ashamed to ever talk through what really happened between him and Jillian before the split.

"It's not my finest moment," he admitted.

"Well, don't let that stop you. I've had a million of those."

For some reason, her words snapped the zip-tie that had been holding his secret. She'd just given him permission to be flawed.

He returned the cover over his half-eaten plate and set it on the ground. "Jillian and I dated for almost a year. After about seven months . . . I don't know, I began to wonder if she was right for me. Being around her was becoming work, and I was starting to relish times when we'd be apart." It was so much deeper than just realizing they weren't compatible. It was also the recognition that life with Jillian would include everything he hated about life as a pastor's kid. She'd wanted the image more than the real person.

"But you stayed with her?"

"I did. And not for the right reasons." He wouldn't mention that Jillian had stripped naked in his living room right after his proclamation that they were drifting apart. Or how, after resisting temptation for twenty-five years, he'd finally given in, even knowing that doing so wouldn't fix things. "We'd become physical, and then it felt wrong to walk away."

She sighed like she completely understood. "Sex only complicates a broken relationship. How bad did it get?"

He quietly mulled over his response. Things had improved at first. He and Jillian had this new, wonderful thing to distract them from all the red flags in their relationship. But it hadn't lasted. After a few months, they were ten times worse off than they'd been before. "We fought a lot. She was pressing for a bigger commitment, but I couldn't seem to follow through any time I looked at rings. After I began to pull away, she upped her game. Manipulation, guilt, tears. Every tactic in her arsenal, but I felt this suffocating pressure against my windpipe every time I thought about marrying her, so it all just made me retreat further. I don't know. Maybe I am the scum her parents accused me of being."

"You're not scum. Relationships come and go. I've seen very few that last a lifetime."

Asher knew she was trying to make him feel better, but she hadn't been raised the way he had. She hadn't been taught from a very early age to respect the sanctity of marriage. To treat everyone she dated like someone's future spouse.

He ran a hand through his hair. "The breakup was monumental. I asked for some time to get my head in order. She gave me a week and then started attacking me. Privately at first, and then very publicly. She told her dad that we'd been intimate, and he went ballistic. Called the elders together, called my dad. I'd been serving as the media director for years. Even through college, when I did it all remotely. Jillian's father demanded I step down."

Katie lightly laid her fingers on his. "I'm sorry."

The words scraped against his open wound. He was the one who was sorry. And ashamed and humiliated. He'd made a mistake, and it'd been practically plastered on a billboard at the church.

"It still blows my mind. We were consenting adults, but it felt like I was a sixteen-year-old getting reprimanded by her daddy. It wasn't their place. It wasn't their business. Yet somehow my personal life had become a topic for discussion among the deacons. He even had the audacity to call me a predator." The words shot out of his mouth with a disdain he could taste. "If it had been anyone else, they would have handled things differently."

"You mean, if you weren't the pastor's kid."

"Exactly."

She drew her hand back to her lap. "Not that it justifies Jillian's behavior or her dad's, but women tend to put a lot of weight on that first sexual relationship. I imagine it's worse when you're actually taught to consider it special."

Asher rolled his eyes. That assumption was at the core of why he'd spent most of the past year angry and bitter. "Yeah, I'd buy that, except Jillian wasn't the virgin. *I* was. And I spent a month fighting her off before I finally caved. Ironically, she left out that little detail when she told her father." He risked a glance at her face when she didn't say anything. Her eyes were blank, unreadable, the guarded Katie back and in extra armor this time. "That was too much information, wasn't it?"

"No, not at all. It just surprised me." She seemed to choke on the words, and he realized the blank stare wasn't a shield after all. It was shock. "I just assumed it was the other way around."

"You and half the church." The old, familiar rage pressed against his rib cage. "The sad thing is, if I were anybody else, half this town would have congratulated me for finally becoming a man." His boiling emotion got the better of him, and he jolted from his chair.

"But you aren't like other men, Asher. You're better. And frankly, I don't know why that expectation bothers you."

He spun around, his arms waving, his heart pounding. "Because it's an impossible standard."

"At least you had one." Her voice held an unsettling intensity. Even seated, she owned the moment, her biting tone more powerful than his frustrated rant. "My first experience was at fourteen with a boy who never bothered to ask me out again."

Suddenly it turned quiet. There was not even a breeze to awaken the trees around them. Those imperial blue eyes had always demanded distance, and their sudden spark of frailty sucked the anger right out of him. He sat back down, felt the weight of her confession. "He took advantage. You were too young to make that call."

She shrugged as if to undermine the gravity of what she'd just admitted. "It's life. We all make our choices based on the convictions we're raised with. I never once felt guilty for my actions, but I did feel *less* after it happened. I think that's the hardest part about mistakes: Sometimes the consequences aren't physical. Sometimes they simply chip away at the essence of who you are."

Compassion overwhelmed him. "And sometimes they force you to change and become more than you ever thought possible."

She squeezed his hand, and he wrapped his fingers around hers before she could withdraw them. With his other hand, he pushed a stray hair back behind her ear. He wished he could show her how beautiful she looked, with her melancholy eyes and trembling lips. She said he was better than other men, but he doubted she realized how unbelievably special and unique she'd become. That rawness, that real, honest truth: he knew better than most that those qualities didn't exist in too many people.

Swallowing hard, she pulled her hand away and shook off her shattered expression.

"You wanna take a walk?" She tightened her ponytail. "I could really use a walk."

"Sure." And he knew exactly where he wanted to take her.

CHAPTER 19

A chill chased down Katie's arms even though it was muggy and hot. Asher had once again stripped down her defenses, exposed her in a way that terrified her. She was just supposed to bring him a meal, not dump her sad story on him.

They walked down from his deck. "There's this path I made that goes down to the reservoir," he said. "I take it sometimes when I need to think or pray."

"Sounds perfect."

He led the way, their steps pounding softly on the leaf-ridden trail, and pulled a small aerosol can from his pocket. "Let me spray you. Trust me, you'll thank me for it."

She stood quietly while Asher sprayed repellent over her bare arms and legs. The act of kindness was a natural one, and hardly meant to be arousing, yet her pulse spiked and her cheeks flushed with the same heat she'd felt in the back of his SUV.

He extended the bottle. "You mind?"

"No." Katie cleared her dry throat. "Not at all."

He spread out his long, tan arms, allowing her to spray his exposed skin. Every beautiful, muscled square inch of it. He dipped his head so she could get to the back of his neck, and the desire to kiss a trail to his ear slammed into her like a freight train. This was ridiculous. Her hormones were raging worse than a preteen's.

He tucked the bottle into his pocket and placed a hand on her back to guide her forward. She startled at the contact and speed walked until she took the lead by several feet.

Tall, thin trees with overgrown shrubs sandwiched in between lined each side of the path. The air was thick with humidity, bringing out the sharp aroma of dewdropped vegetation and moss-covered bark.

She peeked at him over her shoulder. "How did you ever clear this path?" The land was the same here as it was behind her parents' place, where thick thorny vines and large-limbed bushes blocked off any kind of entry into the abandoned woods.

"There's this fabulous tool called the chainsaw. It works wonders on the trees. The mosquitoes, not so much. The first day, I wore shorts and a T-shirt."

"Oh no."

Asher laughed. "Oh yes. Head-to-toe welts. Now I keep a can of bug spray with me any time I venture outside."

They fell into a companionable silence, the snapping of twigs under their feet in harmonic rhythm with the surrounding nature.

A few steps later, the trees cleared some, and the path grew wide enough for Asher to move into the space next to her. Their arms swung close together, their hands almost touching along their sides.

"I'm thinking I might build another deck down by the water. I can picture little boys running up the path with a bucket and fishing poles." She heard longing in his voice. Buried hurt. His feet slowed until he drifted to a stop in the middle of the trail.

"I really am sorry about Jillian. I know it's been hard for you."

He kicked a rock off the path, watched it bounce until it landed by an unsuspecting tree. "I'm realizing these days it's less about the breakup and more about the future that will never be."

She wanted to kick a rock too, just to show him that she, too, understood what it was like to lose a preplanned future. But unlike her, he deserved to have all his dreams. "You'll find someone better one day. And then you'll have your boys and your deck."

He peeked over at her. "You think so?"

A flutter shot through her abdomen. She blamed his complete lack of arrogance. He had no idea how desirable he'd become. "Um, yeah. Women are likely falling over themselves for a shot at Fairfield's most eligible bachelor."

"And what about you?"

She didn't know how to interpret the new gentleness in his tone, or why it vibrated against her insides. Maybe because if things had been different, she'd be doing everything in her power to knock out the competition.

Fire burned her cheeks. "I don't think women are going to be falling at my feet anytime soon."

"So there's no man in your life?" He didn't change his tone or even react to her cheesy joke. "No one's waiting for you down in Florida?"

"I've never dated a man who thought I was worth waiting for."

He hesitated, then kicked another rock. "You've dated some really stupid men."

"Yes, I definitely have." But even as she said it, Katie felt the weight of Cooper's threat. How different would this chat be if Asher really knew her secrets? He saw a wounded girl. A victim of circumstance and poor parenting. But she'd long ago buried the innocent version of herself.

She started moving forward again, faster this time. She and Cooper were both destructive, dark. Asher was all things good and bright. Mixing the two would only tarnish his shine.

The crescendo of insects drowned out her sad thoughts as she and Asher sank deeper into the forest. He'd gone silent again, and despite her heart warning against their growing attachment, she wanted to know the rest of his story.

"What about your parents? How did they respond to Jillian's dad?"

He grabbed a stray branch that blocked their way and snapped it off so they could pass. "They asked me outright what really happened. I told them, and they prayed with me." He shook his head. "My dad fought the elders' decision for a month. But in the end, I couldn't be there, knowing what was happening behind the scenes. I left the church and hadn't been back until that first Sunday I saw you."

The thought warmed Katie's chest. That was why he'd looked so relieved to see her. He understood. "I was there this morning."

"I know."

The squawk of a bird told Katie they were nearing the water. "A lady invited me to some group in her house."

Asher stumbled as he attempted to cut down another limb. "Are you going?"

"No. Definitely not." Although Katie wasn't sure she believed her own words. Annie had been kind. Too kind. The idea of brushing her off felt wrong, for some reason. "I don't know. What do you think?"

He ran a hand through his hair. "I think it's up to you. Home groups are a good way to meet people who share your faith. They may really be an encouragement to you."

"Or a room full of people judging every word out of my mouth."

"That's true. I guess you'll have to decide if it's worth the risk."

"Have you ever been to one?"

His pace slowed, and she could feel his burden return. "A long time ago. Before the Jillian thing."

She wished she could think of something perfect to say. Something to chase away his sorrow. "Is there anyone that you still talk to? Friends?"

"Right now?" His gaze was a caress as much as it was an apology. "It's just you."

Her heart tumbled to her stomach. She ached to touch him. To hold his hand or bury her fingers in his messy blond curls. He made her feel special, and she'd never been special. Different, crazy, a good time. But never special.

He glanced away, through the trees. "We're close to the water now."

The walkway began to slope down and curve. The trees parted, and immediately the sour smell of algae and decaying foliage hit her as the watering hole appeared before them. The simple pond had a diameter of maybe fifty feet, its shoreline a mix of swamp trees and thick mud. The still water glistened in the sun while invisible insects created tiny ripples. It wasn't a majestic sight, but being in the midst of Asher's dream spot made the experience unforgettable.

"It's beautiful," Katie whispered.

"You think? It kinda smells like dead fish." But the affection in his voice contradicted his words. He loved this place. She could see it in the way he held his chin, in the smile that touched his lips the minute they stopped.

"It also smells like adventure and nature and everything your future sons will love."

"I hope so." He stared off into the distance again, to a memory or maybe into the future he wanted so badly. "Jillian hated it. She only came once and complained the whole time."

It surprised Katie how much his statement bothered her. She wanted this spot to be theirs alone and not marred by the ghost of the fake blonde who'd cut him so deeply. "It sounds like you've also dated your share of stupid people."

He laughed, but there wasn't any depth behind it. Squatting down, he picked up a few stray rocks and tossed them into the serene water. "I'm tired of being bitter," he admitted.

"Then don't be."

His hand froze midthrow. "The whole 'no feeling' thing isn't as easy for me as it is for you."

"I don't think feeling is your problem." Her voice tightened defensively. She wasn't used to his sarcasm being directed at her. "Seems to me all you've done is feel. You've told me you've been sad, angry, and hurt. I think the greater question is: when is it going to be enough? When are you going to stop punishing yourself and everyone else for that one mistake?"

Lord knew if Asher couldn't find forgiveness, her plight was hopeless.

"I don't know." He stood, brushed his hands against his jeans. He'd been far away the entire walk, deep inside his own head, but when he looked at her this time, he was present, focused. Determined. "Maybe this is where it starts. Right here."

She didn't move when he came closer, his eyes lingering on hers long after the words had become an echo in the air. She'd been so careful to keep her distance, to minimize any accidental touching that could drop them back in that dark car where impulse trumped good sense. But he suddenly felt magnetic.

His mouth turned soft, and so did his voice. "I'm not the only who needs to stop punishing himself."

And reality came crashing down. He lifted his hand, but she moved away before he could consider making contact. The cruel twist of irony was that she hadn't been punished. Not really. Not for any of it.

Katie feigned interest in the sky. "Sun's gonna set soon. We'd better get back."

Confusion flashed across his face, but he gave her the space she desperately needed.

They weren't the same. Not even close.

In his story, Asher was the victim. In hers, she was one of the villains.

CHAPTER 20

Katie spent the next three days hiding. From herself, from Asher, from the million tasks she needed to accomplish. She had the name and address of the first pawnshop and had even driven halfway there at least three times before turning back around. As much as she wanted to find the ring, she also knew her search was likely to be futile. Pawnshops rarely kept inventory that long, and Katie wasn't ready to trade the idea of a yes for a probable no. Not yet.

She took a bite of a grease-soaked chicken leg. Her dad had brought home fried chicken, okra, and a gallon of sweet tea. A nice reprieve after she had cooked all week.

Her parents tore into their own pieces, neither one saying a whole lot to the other. There'd been the casual "How was your day?" and "How are you feeling?" Both questions were answered with "fine," and then they returned to their dinner. She wondered why she'd worked so hard to clear out the kitchen. Her dad seemed almost disappointed to lose his excuse for eating dinner in front of the TV.

Katie wiped her mouth with a napkin. "How were sales today?" She'd spent most of the day in her room, sorting through the dresser stuffed with papers. She had planned to finish the living room first, but she'd needed to get away from her mother's verbal jabs.

"Three closed out. I've got the boxes ready for you to take tomorrow."

"Good."

And silence won out again.

Katie tapped her fingers on her leg. It was rare for both parents to be in one place at the same time, and Annie's words about the town's rebirth had been stewing in her mind since Sunday.

"So, Dad, did you know that Fairfield is now considered a growing town? I even heard land prices have doubled in the past few years."

Her dad monotonously chewed, then swallowed. "That's the rumor."

"Have you priced out your place? I mean, you're sitting on ten acres of land." Land they had no way of maintaining.

"No reason to. We're not going anywhere," he said.

Her mother was fully engaged now, staring at Katie like she was sifting through every syllable to get to its hidden meaning. There wasn't any. Katie just wished she could see her parents in a place they could actually keep up. She wasn't going to be in Fairfield much longer, and the thought of all her hard work going to waste, and them falling right back into filth, was unacceptable.

Katie clutched her napkin. "I just think maybe you two should consider the future. Your back has gone out twice just since I've been home, Dad. And Mom, wouldn't you be happier in a wider space where you could move around freely?"

Her dad dropped his fork with a loud, frustrated clang. "We're not sellin' our home. Just get that thought out of your head." He shoved away from the table, rattling the dishes in his haste. Flinging open the refrigerator door, he threw her one last warning glare before grabbing his faithful after-dinner beer. "I'll be in the living room."

Katie sank lower in her chair. Her parents were unreasonable and stubborn.

"You haven't even been home a month, and you're already trying to stuff me into some nursing home." The ice in her mom's voice could have chilled a room full of hot coals.

"That's not what I'm doing. I found this place; it's a community of houses. They mow your yard, have group dinners. There's even a full-time nurse available for home visits."

"Like I said, I ain't going to some old folks' home." Her mom's hand jerked, missing her glass by mere centimeters. Her skin was blotchy, her frizzy brown hair a snarled mess. "The doc said this medicine could reverse the damage. I ain't giving up until it does."

The operative word there was *could*, and Katie hadn't yet seen any signs of reversal. If anything, her mother had become less stable, needing longer and longer breaks between activities. She needed a walker, not a cane.

"I just think y'all should consider it. Have a Realtor come—"

"Stop!" her mom shouted, her head twitching erratically with the adrenaline rush. "You worry about fixin' your own messes and stop prying into mine. I knew you were here to try and milk money out of this house. Well, it ain't gonna work. I ain't like old Ms. Blanchard, believing that you have a soul, when deep down we all knew you were waiting to shovel a hole for her burial."

Katie tried to set her fork down, but it hit the plate with a clatter and skittered across the table. That may have been who she was before, but not now. "Do you honestly think I'd slave over this house for some greedy payout? I had a life, Mom. A life that was good and stable and finally on track. I left it to come here and help you. But you refuse to see the difference."

"You call this a difference? What's changed, Katie? Other than you've replaced Cooper with Asher."

"That's not true."

"Isn't it? You bounce from people to people, leaving scars on everyone you touch. What about Laila and Chad? I clearly remember you telling me I wasn't your family, they were. You swore you'd take a bullet for them, yet here you stand, and they're the ones destroyed." She made a disgusted sound, and the lines deepened in her face. "And now you're on to your next casualty with that poor boy next door. What do you want from him? Another house? Another family? Is that it—you want the preacher's wife to be your new mommy?"

A rush of anger fired through Katie. She stood up abruptly, her hands shaking almost as much as her mother's. "If she had been my mom, I probably would have turned out a whole lot better. We both know that mothering me wasn't your top priority."

"Bull." Her mom didn't even flinch. "Some people are just rotten apples. No matter what tree they fall from."

The words shouldn't have hurt. They should've bounced right off her skin like they did all through high school and beyond. But this time something inside Katie broke. Not her heart, but something worse. Her belief that things could be different. That she could be different.

She grabbed her purse and slammed the front door so hard the windows rattled in protest. She didn't bother looking toward Asher's property. There were no answers there, just confusion and longing and a picture of what could have been if only she wasn't so screwed up.

She turned her key in the ignition, and the engine roared to life. She didn't know where she was going; she only knew that she had to leave. Slamming on the gas, she peeled out of the driveway, sending a spray of dust behind her old Camry. She needed to drive. To drive and escape and do something stupid and reckless and crazy.

She screamed at the windshield and squeezed the leather wheel until her knuckles turned white. She hadn't felt so out of control in a long, long time. Her body trembled, her foot pushed the gas hard enough to cause the rpm needle to shoot all the way to the right, and she wanted a drink so badly she could taste the burn.

Her purse lay in the passenger seat, and she drove with one hand while furiously searching for her wallet in the other. She'd drive out of town, hit a gas station, and go out to the beach. What did it matter anyway? No one believed in her. Why not prove them all right?

But her hunt found only two donation receipts and the crisp folded paper she'd been given on Sunday. *Annie.*

Katie pressed the gas harder, but with every mile marker she passed, her heart clenched tighter. Drinking at the beach wasn't the answer, yet the alternative was just as terrifying. She jerked the wheel to the right and slowed to a stop on the side of the road.

"Is this what you want?" she shouted at her roof, waving Annie's handwritten note. "Because I still can't figure out why you brought me back here." She'd asked for a miracle and instead felt swallowed up by the quicksand of her old wounds.

There was no audible answer, yet she still spun her car in the opposite direction—toward a group that would almost certainly judge her for being thirty minutes late and dressed in cutoffs and a faded blue Braves T-shirt. Maybe she was a masochist. Maybe she secretly enjoyed getting dirty looks and scornful stares.

Maybe her mom was right. Maybe she truly was beyond hope.

Ten more minutes had passed by the time she knocked on Annie's door.

"Katie?" Annie's expression was a mix of mild surprise and confusion.

"I'm sorry. I know I'm late, and I shouldn't have come. I was just driving and thought . . ." Katie's voice trailed off because she couldn't think of an excuse good enough to justify why she'd be driving by a farmhouse tucked five miles away from any other populated area. "I don't know what I thought."

Annie's cheerful smile appeared, and soon Katie was wrapped in her arms, Annie's light, flowery perfume surrounding them. Katie was too stunned to hug her back and just stood there like a frozen side of beef.

"You thought we might just be what you need. And you know what? You were right."

CHAPTER 21

Fairfield's only coffee shop was located two buildings down from Home Wares, where Asher had just dumped a few thousand dollars on new outdoor furniture.

Furniture he'd picked out alone.

It had taken him almost a year to delete the bookmarked page of his and Jillian's dream, but the burst of freedom that came with that simple click was confirmation that he was finally ready to move on.

Asher dumped another sugar packet into his coffee and stirred as the creamer turned the dark color a light brown. Katie had been right. He'd spent months rolling around in the agony of his mistake. Months feeding on hatred and grief. It was time to let go. Let go of the "what ifs" and the "if onlys." It was time to allow that painful chapter to close.

A bell jingled over the door, and he glanced up.

"Hey." Katie's expression held as much surprise as his.

Man, she was cute. Her hair bounced around her shoulders, and her shorts fell just high enough on her thigh that he had to actively stop himself from staring at the sheer perfection that was Katie's legs.

"Coffee after seven? I thought I was the only night owl," he said.

The door closed behind her, and she joined him at the counter. "I was in town anyway, so I figured why not?" She eyed his pressed khaki shorts and polo. "You?"

"Picking out furniture." He pulled the folded catalogue page from his pocket and handed it to her. "Should be here next week."

She backed up to an empty table and stared at the glossy sheet, turning the page to examine it from different angles. "It's exactly what I pictured."

Asher's chair scraped loudly on the floor as he pulled it out, causing the lone other patron to glance their way before returning to his book. "Yeah? You don't think the fire pit is a little much?"

"Not at all. I mean, it'll be a while before you use it, but come December you're going to be glad it's out there." She carefully folded the sheet in half and handed it back to him. "You have great taste."

"Thank you." He stood. "What do you want? My treat."

She pressed her lips into a mischievous smile. "Hmmmm. Well, if it's your treat, I want the large triple espresso java latte with extra caramel."

Asher furrowed his brow. There was no way he could recite back the description of that monumental mix of sugar and caffeine. "Say that again, slower."

She kicked his shoe with her sandal. "I'm just kidding. A small coffee is good. I have moral issues with spending six dollars on a drink."

"A small coffee, coming right up."

The young girl behind the counter swiped Asher's bank card and handed him the warm cup. He turned and watched for a moment as Katie scraped at something on the table. Her nails were unpolished, short, and chewed, but she didn't hide them like other girls would. In fact, when he came back to the table, she reached out her hand for the coffee like an impatient two-year-old.

Katie was real and raw and so beautiful it sometimes knocked the wind right out of him.

The decision that had seemed so muddy in his head at the drive-in felt wonderfully clear tonight. The ghost of Jillian was gone.

Katie took a small sip through the slotted lid. "You will never guess where I've been."

"Yeah? Where."

"That home group Annie invited me to."

He eased back in his chair. "You're kidding." He couldn't read her mood. She didn't appear to be upset but didn't seem especially happy either. "When did you decide to go?"

She studied the top of her lid. "I had an explosive dinner with my parents and went driving. A few minutes later I ended up at her house." He sensed there was more to the story, especially since her fingers were trembling as she lifted her cup for another sip.

But the why didn't matter as much as the result. He wanted to tell her how proud he was that she'd turned to people for help. That she'd chosen a healthy outlet. But it sounded condescending, even in his head.

"How was it?" he asked instead.

"Interesting." She paused, and a small V appeared between her eyebrows. "Okay, so explain to me why Christians have to use such gigantic words. I mean, seriously, these questions had at least three five-syllable words. Isn't there an easier way to say 'sanctification'?"

She went on spouting out terms he'd known his entire life.

"It's like you have to learn a foreign language just to have a conversation." She ended her rant with a deep sigh. "I'm sorry. It's just that for some of us, our history alone makes it hard to feel comfortable. Add in the fancy terms, and I don't know . . . it's like I have a banner on my head that says: *I don't fit in here.*"

"Don't worry about the vocabulary words. You fit in because you share a common belief." Asher paused. "Did they make you feel like you didn't?"

"No. Just the opposite. They were all really nice and friendly. Almost everyone was a transplant, so none of them knew my dirty little past."

"I think you're missing the point. Home groups are where you're supposed to share the ghosts from your dirty little past. It's meant to be a place for accountability."

She extended her hand like a game-show hostess. "And the six-syllable-word prize goes to . . . Asher Powell."

He laughed. "Sorry. They help you to not repeat your mistakes."

"I have no intention of repeating my mistakes." She went silent and was too pensive for his liking. Their normal banter was there, but something was different. He sensed an underlying sorrow that hadn't been present in weeks.

He lowered his head and scratched above his eyebrow, searching for the words that would somehow get her to open up to him. Unfortunately, the bell above the entry rang at that moment, and a group of loud, chatting women plowed in like clucking hens.

Katie smirked, and he could practically hear the running commentary in her head.

"Asher Powell?" A high squeal pulled his focus away from his tablemate.

A brunette with hair piled high on her head in a messy bun stood over him. He recognized her immediately. "Michelle?" In one swift motion, he stood and embraced his old friend. They'd been in band together for three years before her parents split up and she moved away the summer before their senior year. "How are you?"

"Good. Really good."

They released each other, and her smile faltered when she noticed Katie seated at the table. She tilted her head as if to make sense of who Katie was but gave up, turning her attention back to Asher. "So, how is your family?"

"Exactly the same. Are you living in Fairfield again?"

"I am. I've been taking classes at the community college. Only three more to go." She glanced at her entourage with humor and affection. "Our final is tomorrow, so we're loading up on caffeine."

The women at the counter laughed among themselves, more interested in the glass display of desserts than in Asher's conversation.

Michelle studied Katie again, her eyes widening.

"Well, it was good to see you," Asher said. "You should come by Fellowship. It's grown a ton in the last couple of years."

But she didn't hear him; she was too busy gawking at his neighbor. "Katie Stone? You went to high school with us." Then her gaze darted from Katie to him and back to Katie. "Wow, are you two . . ."

"Friends." Katie smiled graciously, even though Asher could tell she had no idea who Michelle was. It didn't surprise him. Katie's circle had been small and very exclusive.

Michelle pulled out a chair and sat, seemingly forgetting Asher was standing there. "You probably don't remember me. I was kind of a band geek with Asher here. So, wow, how have you been? How's, um, what's-her-name? The blonde girl you were so tight with . . . um . . . Laila. I heard she ended up being homecoming queen the year after I left."

"Runner-up," Katie said in a monotone.

"That's right." Michelle let out a string of snorting giggles, and the sound took him right back to band practice. She had a kind heart but had always been painfully awkward in social situations. Time hadn't cured her of this. "I remember that time in gym when you and Laila protested because the guys were able to go shirtless while we had to wear those horrible scratchy cotton uniforms." She glanced Asher's way as he sat back down. "Were you there? Katie came out in her bra and said she'd put a shirt on when the guys did too. Three more girls took off their shirts then. Not me, of course. I was way too shy, but gosh, the horror on Coach Foster's face! Priceless."

"I was suspended for three days." There was no inflection in Katie's voice. No humor. No victory.

"Yes, but the guys had to wear shirts, so you won." Michelle grabbed a sweetener packet and passed it between her fingers. "I just thought all of you were so cool. I even had the biggest crush on Chad Richardson.

All that leather and bad-boy vibe." She peeked at Katie through lowered lashes. "Wonder what he's up to now? Are you guys still super close?"

Asher took Katie's flinch as his cue that it was time to end this trip down memory lane.

"Michelle, I think your friends are waiting on you." He stood and offered her a hand that she accepted with a smile.

"Right. Yes. Anyway, it was so neat to run into you. Both of you." Her eyes flickered between the two of them again, as if she still couldn't believe they were having coffee together. "I'll see you around."

Moments later, Michelle and her friends left in a swirl of chatter and laughter, and he was sure he heard Katie's name dropped at least twice in muffled whispers.

Katie turned her head sideways, fixing her eyes on the now-vacated doorway. "I bet Michelle thinks she just saw pigs fly. Here I am, the queen of darkness, having a cup of coffee with Holy String Bean." There was a heavy, dead sound in her voice, as if someone had ripped all the fight out of her.

"I hate that nickname. Both of them."

Her gaze whipped back to him. "I was just teasing."

Was she? If anyone could hide truth behind a joke or useless small talk, it was Katie.

She spread her arms wide. "Well, I guess our secret is out." He didn't like her sarcastic tone or the way her jaw muscles jumped. Being seen together wasn't a bad thing. They weren't in high school anymore. There were no barriers or cliques to deal with.

"I never considered you a secret." And it bothered him that she had.

"I know. It's just weird to think people are going to be analyzing us now." She gulped down the rest of her coffee and traced her finger over the logo on the cup.

She was shutting down, closing him off. He reached across the table and took her hand in his. He needed the contact, and the way her shoulders relaxed told him that she did too.

"You shouldn't care what people think."

The switch in her expression was immediate. Proud Katie suddenly appeared. Fighter Katie. The only Katie he'd known before this year. She rolled her eyes and pulled her hand away. "Trust me, I have way more practice at tuning out rumors than you'll ever have." She rose, made three furious strides to the trash can, and dumped her empty cup. With her back still to him, she placed her palms on the counter and just stood there for five agonizing seconds.

He hated it, but stayed seated in the chair. There was still so much to learn about her. When to act. When to wait. When to force her out of the ridiculous shell she lived in.

She finally turned, calmer now, and returned to the table. The frown lines in her forehead had deepened, but her eyes had lost the earlier spark of anger. She was the one to reach out this time. To take his hand in hers.

"I'm sorry." She sighed. "It's just . . . I'm not worried about what they'll say about me. I'm worried what they're going to say about you."

CHAPTER 22

I t was nearly five p.m. on Friday when Katie pulled up to the first pawnshop on her list. The tiny town was located twenty miles north of Fairfield, but the drive had given her time to gather enough courage to actually step out of the car when she got there.

The run-down metal building was sandwiched between a title-loan office and a used-car dealership. All three had bars protecting the windows and shared a parking lot so beat up that most of the asphalt was marred by potholes and spiderweb cracking. A large red sign flashed **METRO PAWN** on a green metal overhang, inviting patrons to sell off their valuables for quick cash.

Taking one last stabilizing breath, Katie marched forward and pulled on the door handle. Inside, a long glass counter held the jewelry for sale, and seemingly endless shelves along the back wall held guns, computer equipment, and several guitars.

"Can I help you, miss?" An elderly gentleman with droopy eyes that appeared sleep-deprived stood behind the counter.

She approached the glass slowly, browsing past the necklaces, earrings, and watches. The far left corner housed the rings, in four different velvet cases. Katie's gaze slipped over each of them while her heart slammed in her chest. Engagement rings of every size, shape, and color sat in row after row. But not one resembled the vintage emerald ring she desperately wanted to find.

"I was looking for a ring. It's an older one. A rose-type gold, with a flower design. There is a round emerald in the middle." She hesitated. "It's kind of ugly. I know that sounds harsh. But looking at it, you wouldn't be especially impressed."

He rubbed his chin. "Hmmm. Sounds like an Edwardian ring. That style was real popular in the early nineteen hundreds. Rose gold was too."

She inhaled sharply. He knew vintage rings. Surely he'd know if one had come in here. "It would have been about four years ago. Do you remember anything like that being pawned?"

The man scratched his wiry white hair. "Nah. I'd remember a ring like that. Especially if it was in good condition. Those rings can pull a hefty price online."

"You're sure?"

"Yes, ma'am. But I can take down your name and call you if I come across something similar."

She jotted her name and number on the back of a business card he passed to her. "Thanks. I appreciate it."

The man carefully placed the card into a drawer. "Any time."

The grim reason for her scavenger hunt came rushing back as she dropped into the driver's seat. There was no way she'd find a ring that had been sold four years ago. She slammed the back of her head against the headrest and squeezed her eyes shut.

Lord, this would be a good time to give me that miracle I've been begging for.

But no ring magically appeared when she finished her plea, only the red glow from the storefront sign.

Katie's defeat made the trip back to her parents' house long and frustrating. Worse, her engine had started making a high-pitched squealing sound every time she idled the car. Her father had given her the old Toyota six years ago, and it'd been the only truly reliable thing in her life. Now, even it was falling apart.

She hadn't spoken to her mom since the fight they'd had at dinner two days earlier. Their silence was mutual, reminiscent of the way they'd spent most of her senior year of high school.

Katie made the last turn into her driveway and felt a desperate urge to curse. Four trucks were parked haphazardly, each pulled into the field of weeds that was their front yard. Yet only one triggered the fight-or-flight sensation.

Cooper.

Tired, and done with his badgering, she slammed the door of her sedan and strongly considered fleeing to Asher's house. But the last thing Katie wanted was to pull Asher into the tornado of her past. Nor did she want anyone else in town gossiping about the two of them. Perry at the Goodwill station hadn't even tried to be subtle that morning. *"Asher Powell is a hottie. Can't blame you for tryin', but go easy on the kid. He's had a rough patch this year."*

Her denial had been dismissed with a hand wave.

Katie walked toward the front door, dragging her feet. She could hear loud music and aggravated shouts through the cracked weather stripping around the door and prayed the guys would be too absorbed in the game to notice her. Her father loved poker. A hobby, he claimed, but a win or loss could dictate his mood for a week.

As quietly as possible, Katie opened and closed the front door and tiptoed toward the stairs.

"Katiebug? That you?" Her father's voice reverberated down the hallway, and the slurring sound told her one sure thing. He'd broken his two-beer limit tonight. How long had it been since Katie had seen her father drunk? Ninth grade?

Guilt gnawed at her insides. It was the conversation about selling the house. She'd only wanted to give them options. Make life easier. Instead, she'd hurt his pride. Questioned his ability to care for his family.

"Katiebug!"

"Yeah, Dad, I'm coming." She tugged on the ends of her hair and forced herself to put one foot in front of the other until she reached the opening to the living room.

Five men lounged around a six-sided portable poker table. Blue, white, and red chips were piled in the middle of the green felt. Two sets of cards had been turned over, while the others remained clenched in the players' fingers. Cooper's eyes were the first to meet hers, and the triumphant spark implied he held more secrets than what was in his poker hand.

"There she is: my Katiebug. Came all the way from Florida just to help her old man." Her father lifted his beer can in the air, and the other four men cheered and toasted her as well.

"And we mightily appreciate it," said her father's old friend Clarence. He seemed to have aged ten years since she left. Deep grooves made parentheses around his mouth, while his cheeks sank in with each breath. They'd worked at the factory together for twenty years, and he'd spent more than a few nights at that very poker table with her father. "We haven't been able to fit this table in here for years. Been forced to cram down in my basement."

Katie's lips tightened. She hadn't spent two days cleaning and organizing the living room just to see it get trashed by half-toasted party guests. "Where's Mom?"

A man with red hair and a missing tooth slapped the armrest of his chair. "The girls are having their own fun tonight."

"Where?" Did this party house have handicap bathrooms? Would the ladies be able to help her mother if she fell? A chill shot down Katie's spine. Would her mother get drunk?

Her dad was still sober enough to shoot Katie a warning glare, and she bit back any further questions. Once again he was denying the obvious truth—that their life could never again be what it once was.

Cooper obnoxiously patted his knee. "Come here, Firecracker. You can be my good luck charm tonight." He wasn't drunk—Katie could tell that in an instant—but his smirk was calculated.

She forced herself not to cringe. "Why don't I make you guys some snacks?" It was an excuse to flee to the kitchen, but also a chance to get some food in her father's stomach.

The other men lifted their drinks to her in loud agreement, and her father demanded they finish the hand.

Katie tried not to slam the cabinet doors as she pulled out chips, crackers, and nuts. She couldn't identify exactly what she was feeling. Concern? Disgust? Judgment? Who was she to dictate what they could do on a Friday night? Hadn't she been a far worse offender just a few months ago? At least their substances were legal.

She pulled a container of sour cream from the refrigerator and plopped its contents into a bowl, stirring with a pent-up aggression that wouldn't subside. She added a packet of onion soup mix and whipped the dip until it was a dull gray. Hoping to help curb the excessive drinking, she filled the kitchen table with a display of bottled water.

"Nice spread," Cooper said from the doorway. He leaned a broad shoulder casually against the frame, and his alert gaze followed Katie as she put a stack of paper plates next to the dip bowl.

"Since when do you play poker with my dad?"

He shrugged. "About three years now. You leaving gave us something in common."

Katie froze. She'd picked up hints that Cooper had weaseled his way into her family, but his inclusion in poker night was a sickening confirmation.

He scooped up a fistful of the peanuts she'd just poured into a serving dish. "There's been a lot of chatter about you lately," he said before popping a few into his mouth.

"All very glowing, I'm sure. Let me guess: you added your own observations to the bunch."

"Nope. Just listened. I'm trying to figure out your angle."

She clutched the top of the chair. "There is no angle." She knew her words didn't matter. Cooper wouldn't believe her. Every action he took had an ulterior motive behind it.

"Really? Fairfield's notorious atheist is all of a sudden a churchgoer?"

"I was never an atheist. I just didn't care one way or the other. Now I do."

"I see. So having coffee with the pastor's son is just an added perk?" His eyes trailed the length of her, as if checking every inch would help him figure out her evil scheme. "Or maybe . . . he's your new target." He clapped his hands twice, slowly. "Bravo. I knew you hated Pastor Powell, but this is genius. There's no better way to take down a legend than to destroy his kid."

"I never hated Pastor Powell. And I would never hurt Ash . . ." She stopped herself. Cooper didn't need an explanation. He'd just distort whatever she said anyway. Turn something pure and beautiful into something ugly. "Don't you have a hand to play in there?"

"I folded. Come on, Firecracker, we were always better as a team. Let me in on the plan."

"Give up the conspiracy theories. Asher and I are friends."

"You already have friends."

Katie fled to the sink, pumped the soap container twice, and let the cold water calm the raging heat only Cooper could unleash.

He moved in behind her when she turned off the faucet. "Laila and Chad got divorced. Did you know that? Happened about a year ago, after Chad left rehab for the third time."

She swiped a towel from the rack, ignoring him, and frantically dried her hands. He maneuvered around until she was forced to acknowledge him.

"You remember Joe? You know, the guy who used to bail you out of every sticky situation you'd manage to find yourself in?"

Her glare was lethal. Of course she remembered Joe. He was more than the town bartender. He'd been her confidant and mentor, sometimes the only person who truly understood her. She went back to meticulously wiping each finger.

Cooper jerked the towel from her hand. "Did you know he asks about you every time I go in there?"

"Stop it." She'd wanted to see Joe, but Laila worked at his bar, and avoiding her former friend had been her top priority. Plus, Joe would never understand why Katie needed her distance.

"Stop what? Giving you the truth? Making you see how much you're hurting everyone with this ridiculous charade you have going?"

She scrubbed her hands over her face and tried to lower the volume in her voice. "It's not a charade. It's not a con. I just don't want that volatile, broken life anymore."

"You can't possibly think I'm stupid enough to accept that explanation. You ran off without a word for four years and now you're back, pretending to be a saint? You forget: I know you. I know you well enough to know that you could never change this dramatically."

"I'm done with this conversation." Katie shot toward the back door. "Could you tell the guys the food is ready? I'm going to take a walk."

"I'll go with you. It's getting dark."

She spun around, her hand still on the knob. "Are you hearing-deficient? How many different ways do I have to tell you to leave me alone?"

Cooper was at her side with lightning speed and, before she could protest, had pulled her out the door and onto the porch.

"Let go of me," she hissed.

His fingers bit into her arm, and despite her struggles, he didn't soften his hold until they were a good ten feet from the house.

With a final jerk, she broke free and stood there, shaking violently. She hated this. Hated him. Every detestable instinct she'd been trying to quash was balled inside her chest, glowing hot and red.

Cooper threw his hands into the air. "Is this what you were hoping for?" he hollered. "You want to see me lose it? You want to push me until I turn into the monster you keep accusing me of being?"

"Your temper is not my fault," she spat back.

He stepped forward, his eyes burning into hers. "You know my buttons and yet you push and push and push. Just like that weekend you vanished."

"You locked me in a room!" Her anger was alive now, making her feel dizzy and sick. She used to welcome the rage, but now it caged her in, pulsed under her skin like a virus that couldn't be cured.

"Because you were crazy tripping. I grabbed the keys from your hands five times. And you kept swinging at me. Do you even remember that night, Katie? Do you? Because somehow I've become the villain in this scenario, when *you* were the one who bought the drugs."

For a second she couldn't get enough air. Spots danced in her vision. Yes, she remembered that night. Every single horrible moment of it. She was the addict. The criminal. The devil. Cooper was right.

She had no one to blame but herself.

Asher hadn't meant to eavesdrop. In fact, everything he'd just heard made him wish he hadn't gone outside to investigate the shouts filtering in through his ancient windows.

Katie stood across the yard. Her back was to him; the guy she'd been yelling at towered over her with a familiarity that didn't seem recent. Who was he? Why hadn't she mentioned him?

The burly man seized her shoulders and said something Asher couldn't hear. Whatever it was made Katie push him away and take a step back.

"Don't bring up that weekend." Katie's voice echoed in the distance.

"Then tell me something that makes sense."

She pressed her temples. "Please, Cooper. For once, just let it go. You win, okay? I'm the bad guy. You're exonerated. As far as I'm concerned, you were never there."

Cooper. Asher let the name float through his mind, searching for any glimmer of recognition but not finding any. The guy hadn't gone to their high school.

"I don't want to be exonerated. I want you to stop pretending to be something you're not. I want Chad to come home and Laila to stop walking around like her heart has been ripped out." Cooper's shouts had turned hoarse, as if his own heart were being ripped out with each word.

Katie's shoulders sagged and for a moment, the violence around them disappeared. Cooper reached out and touched her face, set his forehead to hers.

Asher suddenly felt sick. Sicker than when they'd been yelling, sicker than when he heard the play-by-play of Katie getting high. He couldn't define it, the twisting pressure in his gut, but it wouldn't subside, even when Katie shoved the guy away.

"We can't go back to how things were. I know it. Laila knows it. That's why she hasn't come here demanding to talk. It's time for you to accept it too." She left him standing there and walked toward the path in the woods, her head lowered, her arms wrapped around herself.

Cooper marched back to Katie's house and slammed his fist into the porch column. The wood cracked underneath his knuckles. He pulled on the door, but stopped. His motion seemed pained when he turned back, dipped his chin, and placed his hands on his hips. Katie had told Asher no one was waiting for her, but everything in Cooper's crestfallen posture indicated he wasn't going away without a fight.

Asher watched her disappear behind the tree line. Caramel hair and dark blue shirt, long legs and worn-out tennis shoes. She looked delicate and lost.

He'd wanted to rescue her, but he didn't know her. Didn't know anything about her.

Even worse? That was exactly what she wanted.

CHAPTER 23

Asher held the vibrating Weed Eater an inch from the sidewalk as he walked along the edge of his parents' front lawn. He focused on creating a perfect line, sweat rolling down his back despite the early dawn hour. It would be hot today. High nineties.

Good. He craved that sweat and the burn of his muscles.

A flash of brown slippers caught his eye, and he glanced up to see the raised eyebrows of his father. With a flick of his thumb, Asher silenced the equipment and pulled off his protective earmuffs.

"Hey, Dad. I thought I'd take care of the yard for you."

"I see that. Did you happen to notice that it's six-thirty in the morning?"

Yeah, he'd noticed. He'd noticed the time all morning. At two, when he was still trying to push Katie's argument out of his head. At four, when all his tossing and turning failed to ease the sickness in his stomach. At five, when he'd given up trying to sleep and worked on a website update for his client. But busywork hadn't been enough to keep his gaze from drifting out the bedroom window.

"Sorry. I wanted to stay ahead of the heat."

His dad crossed his arms. "Last time you manicured my lawn at the crack of dawn, you dropped a bomb on me afterward. Let's go inside. Get some coffee."

Asher's gut tightened. The last time had occurred the morning after his big breakup with Jillian. He'd been as lost then as he felt now. But he didn't want to talk with his dad about the previous night, much less admit that he'd fallen down another relationship rabbit hole. He'd thought Katie was different. He'd thought she'd been vulnerable and real with him, but all their conversations had been filtered by what she thought he wanted to hear. That wasn't friendship.

"I'm fine. Let me finish up and I'll come in when I'm done."

"Son, you turn that thing on again and your mom is going to have a conniption. You know how much she loves her lazy Saturday mornings."

Asher let his head drop. "Sorry." He'd forgotten Saturday was the one day his mom allowed herself to sleep in. He had no right to take his misery out on his parents.

He followed his dad into the garage, where he dropped the equipment and took off his grassy shoes. His father was wearing gym shorts and a baggy T-shirt. His hair was sticking up in two places, and his normally smooth face had a gray shadow of stubble.

Asher walked past his parents' closed bedroom door to the coffee-pot. His dad must have pressed Start before heading outside, because the dark liquid was almost to the top of the glass container.

"You look tired." His dad pulled out a kitchen chair and sat, opening the newspaper he'd grabbed from outside.

"Couldn't sleep."

"Jillian?"

"No. I think that dark story has finally come to an end," Asher said with, remarkably, no bitterness. Figures he'd heal just in time to get shot again. "I ordered the furniture for the deck. A set I love that she would have hated."

That had been the same day he'd seen Katie in the coffee shop. The day he'd felt sure their public "outing" was the beginning of something monumental.

When the coffeepot had puffed its final hiss of steam, Asher poured two mugs, adding sugar and cream to his. He thought of her again when he slid the black liquid to his dad, and immediately resented the memory.

She'd lied to him. Well, okay, maybe she'd just chosen to leave out some details, but he still felt a deep sense of betrayal. He'd trusted her with his greatest shame, while she conveniently sidestepped any real detail about her life.

"They finally unloaded that old building downtown. You know, the one that's been boarded up since the tornado," his dad noted, spreading the paper wide in front of him. "Two other buildings were bought up last month. I think Fairfield's about to boom."

Asher nodded, staring into his cup. He didn't want to be sitting there, talking about real estate. He needed to be moving. Working. Doing. That was his coping mechanism: Keep busy until the disappointment goes away.

His father laid the paper on the table. "You're obviously upset. So we can either sit here gabbing about nothing, or you can talk to me like I know you want to."

Asher tried to figure out where to start, but there weren't any words for what he felt. At least nothing that made sense. "Remember how I told you Katie Stone moved in next door?"

"Yeah."

"Well, we've become friends." He took a sip of coffee, trying not to choke on the word. Friends didn't lie to each other. Friends didn't pretend.

"Your tone implies that's a bad thing."

How had he ended up here? At his dad's table . . . again? He was a grown man. Past the point of needing his parents' advice. Yet his dad was also his pastor and his mentor.

"Of course it's a bad thing. She's Katie Stone." A nibble of guilt bit at him, but he pushed it away. He wasn't judging her for a past she couldn't change. He was angry because she'd acted one way with him while living a secret life with that Cooper guy.

"What happened? Your fists are clenched for a reason."

Asher relaxed his hands. "Nothing. She's just not who I thought she was. That's all."

His dad set down the coffee cup with enough force to catch Asher off guard. "Son, I'm going to tell you something you won't want to hear, but I think it's time you hear it."

Asher knew that tone. He'd heard it many times in his life—right when a lecture was coming.

"You put people on a pedestal."

Asher sat straight. "I do not."

"You do. Your mom and I are way up there. The church. Jillian. And the problem is, it's only a matter of time before whoever is up there falls off."

"I know that. I've been fighting against that pedestal my whole life." Now he was getting angry. He hadn't set unrealistic expectations. He'd been betrayed.

"Yes, you have. And I think that might be part of the problem. You're simply holding people to the same standard you hold yourself to."

"It's not—"

"Let me finish." His father's no-nonsense tone made Asher clamp his mouth shut. "You idealize people, and when they turn out to be just people, with flaws and weaknesses, you're devastated by the fall." His dad pushed his cup away. "Now, I'm glad you've had a life where people rarely failed you. And I'm glad you're the stellar man you've turned out to be. But let's be real here: Katie grew up in an environment you cannot possibly understand. She's seen and done things you cannot possibly fathom, but the girl is trying—and doing so without any real support."

His father leaned back in his chair and lifted a palm in Asher's direction, inviting him to speak. His dad's breathing grew steadier in the silence, his uncharacteristic burst of adrenaline appearing to wane.

Asher sorted through his feelings. Had he done that to Katie? Had he created this person in his mind—this idea of her—that wasn't real?

But as he tried to sort out what was real about Katie and what was idealized, a new truth hit him even harder than his dad's words. It wasn't a romanticized version of Katie he desired. It was just *Katie*. All of her, from her ratty, obnoxious T-shirts to her heart-wrenching questions, sarcastic wit, and self-deprecating tendencies. It was her bringing him dinner because she cared enough about their relationship to fight for it, and the way she worked—day after day, without fail—to help her ungrateful parents.

He wasn't disappointed in her. He was . . . jealous.

And even though the emotion was absurd, because Katie's body language had clearly indicated she didn't want Cooper near her, Asher felt sure they'd been intimate in the past. Cooper had a part of her, and he hated that.

"I'm not putting her on a pedestal," he admitted.

"Then what are you doing?"

Asher crossed his arms on the table and dropped his head on his hands. He was crazy. There was no way he'd come out of this without deep scars. "I think I might be falling for her."

His dad went silent. The kind of silent that heightened tension and made every surrounding noise, no matter how tiny, seem like machine-gun fire.

Asher raised his head and met his father's eyes. "I know what you're thinking, but you don't have to worry. She's a genuine believer. A new one, but her conviction is stronger than that of half the people in our church." He could tell his dad was trying to understand the appeal of someone so habitually self-destructive. And honestly, Asher didn't fully understand it himself. He and Katie, they made no sense. Yet somehow they completely did. "She challenges me, all the time. And she's fun and interesting and totally unpredictable."

"Sounds like you've already made up your mind."

If only it were that easy. "She has secrets. I thought I knew them, but I don't. What if it's more than I can handle?"

His dad cleared his throat. "You need to make a decision. Either be with her and accept the bad with the good, or get out of her life. Because like it or not, you represent Christ to her, and the last thing she needs is for you to walk away when things get hard."

"Like I did with Jillian."

"I didn't say that."

"Yeah, you did. You said I put her on a pedestal. How do I know this thing with Katie isn't going to be the Jillian situation all over again?"

"Don't let it be." His dad leaned in, his eyes reflecting the same passion Asher had seen from the pulpit. "Learn from your mistakes. Take things slow. Keep communication open and honest. And don't confuse your emotions with physical intimacy this time."

Shame wove its way through his already chaotic mix of emotions. He should have stayed strong. All this time, he'd been putting the blame on Jillian. But in truth, a great deal of his anger had been directed at himself.

"What about you? How would you feel if I dated her?"

His father chuckled. "Son, I've known Katie her entire life. If you do manage to tie that girl down, you're not going to have time to worry about what I feel—or about what anyone else thinks."

Asher smiled without warning. How had Katie put it? The queen of darkness and the Holy String Bean. He shook his head.

If this was God's plan, He seriously had a sense of humor.

CHAPTER 24

Katie quietly shut the front door, hoping the noise wouldn't disturb her mother, who'd been bedridden since her MS attack yesterday. No doubt the result of her Friday night blowout with clueless friends.

Everyone wanted to act as if things were normal. They weren't. And since when had Katie become the only adult in the house? Her father had been passed out on the couch until noon yesterday, and the whole house still reeked of stale beer. At least Cooper hadn't stayed, although he hadn't needed to. He'd already inflicted the damage he set out to do. She'd spent most the night thinking of Laila and Chad. Agonizing over the part she'd played in their failed marriage.

Katie closed her eyes and took a deep breath. She'd deal with those feelings later. Right now, she needed to get to church and somehow forget about Joe and Cooper and her parents' stupid choices.

"Morning," Asher said, approaching her from his yard.

She smiled, not just because his presence felt as comforting as homemade chocolate chip cookies but because his church-wear always took her off guard. The pressed slacks and crisp blue shirt were as foreign as his slick hairdo.

"You clean up nice."

"I considered putting my mowing clothes back on, but I knew my mom would banish me from their house if I did. And I rarely miss Sunday lunches."

Katie patted his stomach. "Better be careful. You know what they say about men as they approach thirty."

He pressed his hand over hers, holding it in place against his shirt. "No. What do they say?"

Butterflies swarmed her stomach, a sensation she hadn't felt since the fifth grade when Joshua Holt kissed her in the back of the school bus.

She swallowed. "I don't remember."

"Then I guess I'm safe." He gave her a lazy, way-too-sexy smile. It was the bug spray fiasco all over again. Ugh. She was blushing.

His fingers still wrapped around hers, he lowered her hand slowly and let it go. "I thought we could ride together. I heard your car squealing the other day. It sounded like the drive belt is loose."

Katie winced. "I was trying to ignore it."

"Never a good idea. Come on. Hang out with me this morning, and I'll replace it when we get home."

"I thought you never miss Sunday lunches."

"For you, I'll make an exception."

They had walked halfway to his house when she suddenly stopped. "You sure you want us to ride in the same car?"

"Of course. Why wouldn't I?"

"Because it isn't some hole-in-the-wall coffee joint. It's me and you—together—in your dad's church. Not really the best move for a man who wants people to stay out of his business."

"I thought we'd already established that being seen with you isn't an issue. At least, not for me." He paused. "Does it bother you?"

"No. I guess not." What did it matter anyway? Cooper had already used his knowledge of their friendship to lash out at her. How much worse could it get?

"Good." Asher wrapped an arm around her shoulder and pulled her toward his driveway. "Because I plan on us spending a lot more time together."

His touch made her uneasy, but he either didn't notice or didn't care. He'd never been so affectionate with her before. In fact, apart from the occasional hand squeeze, they usually kept at least six inches of space between them.

She matched his stride, forcing herself not to read too much into his strange behavior. "Really? Let me guess: you're all geared up to start a new project."

"Something like that." He tickled the nape of her neck and then quickly dropped his arm.

She felt her nervous tension ease a little. Their six inches were back.

He paused at the passenger door, his hand resting on the handle. "So, what'd you do this weekend? I haven't seen that many cars in your yard since New Year's."

"You don't want to know," she answered dryly, waiting for him to open her door. He didn't move.

"You don't have to hide things from me. You know that, right?"

Her insides ached. If only that were true. "Yeah. Sure."

His face fell as if her answer disappointed him. "Okay then." He opened her door and quickly shut her inside.

✕

Asher's frustration had eased by the time he parked outside Fairfield Fellowship. He'd made a decision. Her past didn't matter. He liked Katie, and he could sense she had feelings for him too. But he'd have to find a way past her wall.

"Are we waiting for something?" She had opened her door, but paused when he didn't turn off the car.

"Nope," he said, killing the engine.

Several couples walked by as Asher pressed Lock on his key fob. He noticed them doing a double take and even whispering a little when they saw Katie. She stood there, giving no sign that she'd noticed, but he knew it was just because she was used to the gossip.

His lingering disappointment transformed into a fierce sense of protectiveness. They didn't get to hurt her. Not with him standing right there.

This week's greeters opened the doors, and he ushered Katie through, his hand lightly touching the small of her back. It took monumental effort not to grab her hand. But Katie's unusually straight posture and tense shoulders were enough to hold him in check. This was more difficult for her than it was for him.

She leaned in close. "Are you going to make me sit up front?" There was a panic in her whisper, and Asher realized he'd never thought past the car ride over.

"No, but do you mind if we swing by and let my mom know I'm here? She tends to worry."

"You want me to meet your mom?"

"Katie, you've lived in this town your whole life. I'm pretty sure you've met my mom at least twenty times."

"Not in church," she hissed. "And I'd bet my car that I was rude nineteen out of those twenty."

"I doubt she even noticed."

Katie stopped dead, her mouth tight and her head tilted. "She noticed."

He tugged her arm, and she finally moved. "That was before. It's different now."

If she wanted to protest more, it was too late. His mother had seen them and was waving him over.

He hugged his mom when they reached the front row. "Sorry I woke you yesterday."

"You're forgiven. I saw the new gazanias you planted, and they're beautiful." Never one to hesitate or hang back, she let go of him and embraced Katie. "It's so good to see you. How's your mom feeling?"

Katie stood dumbfounded, her arms hanging at her sides, while his mom hugged her. When the uncomfortable moment ended, she straightened her dress. "She's fine. Getting better. Thanks for asking."

Her mother was neither fine nor getting better, but Asher didn't contradict her. "We're going to sit in the back today."

His mom glanced between the two of them, and he could see a million thoughts running through her head. "Sure. But I insist you bring Katie by after service for lunch."

Katie tensed next to him. "Oh, I can't, but—"

"We actually have plans today," he said, cutting her off midsentence. "Her car needs some maintenance work. But next week, we'll both be there."

Katie slammed her mouth shut, but her silence seemed loaded. He quickly guided her away from his mom and down the side aisle.

When they were out of earshot, Katie spun around on him. "I never said I would go to lunch with your family. You just committed me."

"I gave you a whole week to prepare."

"That's not the point."

Asher had to bite the inside of his cheek to keep himself from laughing. Katie was even cuter when she was angry. Her silvery eyes darkened, and her face and neck erupted with color. She'd never really let him see this side of her before.

"You've turned me down twice already. Give a guy a break." She started to open her mouth, but he stepped closer and whispered in her ear. "This is important to me. Please?"

She exhaled, and the act seemed to release all her aggression. "Fine. But I'm *so* not going to feel bad about you fixing my car. In fact, I'm going to sit out on the porch, drink my iced tea, and watch you sweat."

Her delicate chin jutted into the air, but her defiance only heightened his attraction. He wanted to kiss her. Right then, right there. Just to see how she would respond.

"Hello, Asher."

The familiar voice made the oxygen catch in Asher's lungs. He took his eyes off Katie and stared into the face of his ex-girlfriend. She was with her boyfriend again and hanging on his arm like a draping scarf.

"Jillian."

Katie turned around when he said the name, and soon the four of them were a spectacle in the aisle. People slipped around them on their way to their seats, but not without taking notice of the awkwardness.

Jillian's companion extended a hand. "I'm Coach Mack. Nice to meet you."

Mack? Really? With stiff shoulders, Asher shook his hand. "Asher Powell."

"I'm happy to see you here." Jillian's voice was soft and hesitant, and he even heard a hint of remorse in her words. The coach squeezed her close as if sharing some of his strength.

Watching them together, Asher felt nothing. Not hurt. Not anger. Not jealousy. For the first time in a year, he felt he might be able to forgive her. And himself.

"It's good to be back." This time his words weren't strangled. He meant them.

With a repentant smile, Jillian passed them and slid into her row. The gesture wasn't exactly an apology, but he figured it was as much as she was capable of giving.

A cool hand touched his, and Asher remembered he was still standing in the aisle. With a tug, Katie pulled him to the back row.

"Interesting morning," she said once they'd settled in. "How are you doing?"

He stretched his arm out over the back of her chair. "Surprisingly fine, considering that's the first time I've spoken to her in almost a year."

She patted his leg. "Good. You deserve better."

He thought of Cooper and how Katie had curled into a shell of herself when he shouted at her. "So do you, Katie."

Confusion played across her features, and she slipped her hand back into her lap. She wasn't ready to open up to him yet. He'd accepted that. But soon he'd show her that his feelings weren't conditional. He'd learned from his failures with Jillian, and this time, he was determined to do it right.

CHAPTER 25

"How's it going over there?" Katie called out from her cushy chair on Asher's front porch. He'd insisted that moving her car to his house would be easier than hauling his tools over to hers. She didn't mind. His porch wasn't rotting—and he actually had furniture a person could sit on.

"Just fine," he said with a strangled grunt as he pulled again on his wrench. The final bolt was practically cemented in place, and he'd been struggling for the last ten minutes to loosen it.

With a frustrated jolt, he detangled himself from the car and threw the wrench on the ground. Katie was impressed that she didn't hear a curse word fly out, although she was pretty certain a few had flashed through his mind.

He lifted one grease-covered arm and wiped the sweat from his forehead. He'd changed into a thin T-shirt with the sleeves cut off at the shoulders. She hoped it wasn't a sin to admire the cut of his arms on a Sunday, because she'd barely noticed anything else since he started his work. Well, that and his backside when he leaned over—but she was pretty sure that wasn't allowed either.

Katie lifted the glass of tea she'd poured for him and shook it. The few melting ice cubes that were left rattled against the glass. "I have iced tea, and it's still cold."

As if taking a drink was the same as giving up, he shook his head. "Not till I beat this bolt. I need more torque." He glanced down at his toolbox as if it held the answer.

She didn't think it did. Asher had already tried the staring-for-answers bit earlier, with no grand epiphany.

He gave up after only a few seconds this time. "Would your dad happen to have an old pipe? Something metal with a small diameter?"

"I have no idea, but we can check. The shed is packed with who knows what." She bounced down his steps and flashed him a smile that was all sass and attitude. "Betcha wish you hadn't committed me to a lunch date with your parents."

He leaned in close, as if he were going to say something to her, but instead wiped his sweaty, greasy forehead on her exposed shoulder.

"Oh my gosh! Gross!" She pushed him off and used the strap of her tank top to try and wipe off the sweat. Asher bent over, laughing. "You're disgusting," she said once she'd finally removed the last of the slimy mess from her arm. But she didn't really mean it.

In fact, as she watched his face beam and his eyes dance with mocking pleasure, she felt a twinge of something she couldn't identify. It felt like drinking hot chocolate while snuggled in front of the fire, yet also like swooping down a roller coaster. She wanted to laugh, but also to cry, because neither reaction alone felt exactly right. She wanted to hug him for making her feel such peace, yet hit him for bringing on a whirl of confusing emotions.

"What?" he asked when she continued to gape at him. He wiped at his face like he'd missed something that needed to be cleaned and in the process left a grease smudge that hadn't been there before.

She shook off her whole train of thought. "Nothing. Just wanted to see if you'd blink first." She shrugged. "You did, so I win." She took off toward the shed, hoping the escape could also shrug off her unexpected reaction to him. Well, *unexpected* wasn't exactly the right word.

Her reactions to him were getting more predictable and less platonic every day.

Footsteps pounded behind her. "Hey, you don't win. I didn't even know we were playing a game."

Oh, they were playing a game all right, and it was called *See How Fast Katie Can Get Her Heart Crushed by a Man Who, Even on a Bad Day, Is Ten Times the Person She Could Ever Hope to Be*. Sure, Asher liked to flirt. He might even enjoy her company now and then, but that was only because he didn't know the truth. He didn't know she'd ruined four people's lives in one twenty-four-hour period.

He caught up quickly and fell into step next to her. She jammed her hands in her pockets and wished for the millionth time that she could go back to that night and change the course of her future.

"Is your dad gonna throw a fit that I'm digging through his stuff?" Asher asked when they reached the metal building.

"He shouldn't. I've been doing it every day since coming home." She rolled the numbers on the combination and then tugged on the lock. "Got it."

Asher pulled open the door, and heat billowed out like a wave of steam. "Yikes. When's the last time he was in here?"

"Your guess is as good as mine."

He cleared away a few cobwebs and stepped into the shed. Katie waited outside, not just because she hated all things creepy-crawly. She also had no intention of getting shoved into a small space with her handsome neighbor. Her self-control had limits, and she was already approaching the top of the scale.

When she heard banging and what sounded like several items hitting the floor, she called out: "Find anything?"

"Yeah. A little too much of everything."

"Welcome to my world," she mumbled to herself.

He emerged a few minutes later, beaming as if he'd just conquered the jungle, a foot-long metal pipe in his hand. "Yep. This should do the trick."

"I know I'm mechanically inept, but how is a pipe going to solve your problem?"

His lips curled in a way that caused Katie's cheeks to overheat. "Leverage. Sometimes it just takes a little distance and an extra dose of force to make a stubborn object move."

Maybe it was the way his eyes never left hers or the way his stare turned from humorous to deadly serious. But she felt sure he was talking about more than just her car's alternator bolt.

※

He'd done it. He'd conquered the blasted drive belt, with only minor cuts to his hands and a few hits to his pride. The job had taken twice as long as he'd anticipated, but getting to spend the day with Katie had made every agonizing minute worth it.

She'd fallen asleep about ten minutes earlier and was now curled up in the outdoor love seat, still clutching her empty glass.

Asher washed his hands under the water spigot at the side of the house, not wanting to wake her. It felt right having her there, just hanging out, talking. She was interesting and funny and way smarter than he'd ever realized in high school. He knew her choice to drop out of college had nothing to do with capability. Maybe one day he could convince her to give it another shot.

He splashed water on his face and over his head and neck. It helped, but he was still hot, sweaty, and in serious need of a shower. With a quick whip of a towel, his face and hands were dry and only a little bit stained from the oil.

And still she slept, her breath coming in steady streams through slightly parted lips.

He approached quietly, wanting to watch her just a minute more, and crouched in front of the love seat. For all her references to being the queen of darkness, to him she embodied only peace and light.

With a gentle brush of his fingers, Asher traced a trail along her cheek, pushing aside the piece of hair that had fallen over her face. Smooth, silky soft. Just as he'd imagined.

She awoke slowly, her eyes fluttering open. If he leaned just the slightest bit closer, his mouth would be on hers. And the thought of it shot a jolt straight to his abdomen. But despite his desperate need to touch her, he wouldn't do that. He'd give her the choice.

"Hey," he whispered when she began to sit up. "You fell asleep."

She rubbed her eyes and blinked twice as if to focus. "How long was I out?"

"Only about fifteen minutes. But you missed my grand celebration."

"You did it?" A smile crept through her sleepy disorientation. "Well, congrats. You officially can do it all: build fences, create gorgeous outdoor kitchens, plant weird-named flowers for your mom, and now fix cars."

She stood and he followed suit, determined to take his moment now, while he had the courage. "If I'm so impressive, go out with me."

Katie froze in midstretch, her hands high in the air. Her arms dropped back to her side. "What?"

He stepped closer, grabbed one of her hands in his. "On a real date. Go out with me." His thumb pressed into her palm, caressing it.

She wiped her eyes again. "I must be still half asleep. Either that, or I'm totally hallucinating."

His pinched brow made it clear she wasn't, but that knowledge didn't bring the smile he'd longed for. Instead, her eyes were cast in shadow, troubled and intense.

"Don't do this," she said, pulling her hand from his.

"Do what? Take action on what we're both feeling? I know I'm rusty with the whole wooing-a-woman thing, but I think I've been pretty clear about my feelings for you."

Her shoulders remained stiff as she stomped down the steps. "Just the fact that you used the word 'wooing' should tell you exactly how crazy this is. I'm not the wooing type, Asher. I'm the bad girl."

He jumped off the porch and moved in front of her to keep her from bolting. "Don't be a cliché, Katie. This isn't about who you used to be. It's about who you are now. Who we are together."

"You don't know me." Her lips trembled, which surprised Asher enough that Katie managed to slip past him. He'd seen tears in her eyes. Real, live tears on a girl who never cried. A good sign. She wanted more than friendship too. He just had to convince her that he was worth the risk.

He took off after her again. "I want to know you. The good and the bad. It's never been about pretense with us." The faintest brush of his hand on her arm stopped her. "I overheard you the other day. With Cooper. I heard about drugs, and I know there's still history there. I don't care. I just want you to trust me. I'm asking for you to give us a real chance."

She shifted. It was only the slightest movement, but it put distance between them, and she made her point. His admission to eavesdropping hadn't helped his cause any.

But this was Katie's default. Building walls, pushing him away. He was tired of climbing them, just to find another one. He wanted a bulldozer, anything to finally break through.

Frustrated, Asher ran a hand through his wet hair. "Just think about it, okay? Later, when you're not so mad at me for listening. When it's quiet and you don't have a million reasons not to date me going through your head, stop for one second and think about what it could be like. A real relationship. One based on honesty and trust and friendship. One based on a shared faith."

"I don't have to think about it. What we have now works, and you're ruining it." She flung out her hands in exasperation, but Asher didn't need the dramatics to tell she was angry. Her tone said it all.

He let his shoulders drop, realizing for the first time that she really might refuse him. "I'm done pretending. It's the one lesson I learned this year: I am who I am. And I like you. I want us to be more than we are now. I think about it every time we're together."

He stared at the V in her neckline, the way it flexed every time she took an angry, shallow breath; the edge of her jaw, straight and determined; the planes of her face, all downcast and mournful.

Her mouth. Her eyes. Her mouth again.

He waited for that mouth to make the words she was too afraid to say.

I care about you.

I'm willing to try.

She stared at her feet, and he fought every urge to take her in his arms and show her how amazing they would be together. But it had to be her choice.

"Take some time and then come talk to me. I'm right next door." He forced himself to walk away. He wouldn't play games, and he wouldn't lie to himself.

If that meant losing her, then it wasn't meant to be in the first place.

CHAPTER 26

Katie stared out the upstairs window. It'd been four days, and Asher had never called. Or texted. He'd hardly even stepped outside. She knew because she'd been watching for him like a lovesick puppy. The space he'd promised didn't feel like breathing room. It felt stifling, like a rope closing around her windpipe. She'd broken her own rule. She'd come to depend on him. Cared about him. Too much.

She tried to focus on the house. The upstairs was half finished now. Only her parents' room remained, and half the drawers in her dresser, but Katie knew the last stretch of work would be significant. She couldn't think about it now. At this point, the house was decent enough that she could talk to a real estate agent. Get an idea of its value. The kitchen was clean, the living room functional, and the yard . . . ? Well, the yard might be a problem.

With a sigh, Katie forced herself to stand and stretch. *One task at a time.* She'd focus on what was in front of her. What she could control. Not the looming unknown.

"Katie," her mom called from downstairs.

She was glad to have a reason to move. Maybe her mother would even come up with an errand or two for her to run.

"I need the boxes from the top shelf," her mother said when she entered the dining room-turned-office. Though her voice was dismissive and cool, Katie could feel the frustration behind it. Her mom could no longer stand with just the cane alone, yet she still refused to use the walker Katie had picked up from the medical supply store.

"I've got them." She pulled down five flattened cardboard Priority Mail boxes and quickly assembled them so her mother wouldn't have to.

"I'm going to be closing out all my listings today," her mom said absently. "Your father and I will be in and out of town for the next couple of weeks. Do you think you can handle the house?"

"Of course, but what's going on?"

Her mom took the boxes from her and stacked them on her desk. "None of your business. Here's our schedule. Some trips will be more than a day."

Overnighters? Her parents? Katie studied her mother's sour expression. Wherever they were going, it didn't sound like her father was taking time off work so they could rekindle their romance. She took the paper her mother offered. They were leaving tonight for two days, then traveling again next week and the week after.

"Mom, I want to be—"

Her mom put up a hand. "Katie, when you're ready to spill all your secrets, then you can come sniffing around mine. Until then, keep your questions to yourself."

Katie's fingers tightened on the paper. "Fine. Have fun on your little trip, then. I'll try not to screw up everything while you're gone."

"Well, that'll be a first."

Katie grabbed her keys and slammed out the front door. She had promised herself she wouldn't fire back anymore. Was determined to be the one to stay calm and not tumble into their constant hateful exchanges. But her patience was dangerously close to running out.

Asher's SUV was in the driveway. She'd normally go over there, knock on his door, come up with some excuse to lure him outside. If he wanted her to miss him, then he'd succeeded, but it didn't change anything. Just as six weeks with her parents hadn't fixed the resentment between her and them.

She gripped the porch rail, ready to fling herself down the front steps and away from a situation that seemed to only get worse with time, but as she tightened her fingers around the wood, it splintered under them. A *crack*, and then she was tumbling. It happened so fast, she could only register the sharp pain in her back when she slammed to the ground and the mangled hole where the stairs used to be. The house blurred in front of her, then came back into focus.

She tested her arms and legs. They all worked. But the damage in front of her was irreparable.

"Aaarrrgh!" she screamed into the air as she scrambled to her feet. Couldn't anything go right? The stairs were hanging at an angle, their weathered strips of wood torn right in two, their jagged edges sticking straight in the air.

The front door swung open and her mom stood in the entry, using her walker for the first time. "What the he—" She stopped when she saw the splintered gaping hole in front of her. "Crap, Katie. How am I supposed to get out of here now? You know those back steps are too steep."

Katie scowled at the neglected, blackened destruction in front of her. This was her life. Filthy, rotting, disgusting debris that only pretended to be functional. When it mattered, when it needed to be strong, what did it do? It broke into tiny, mangled pieces.

Her mom slammed the wheels of the walker against the wood. "Well? How are you going to fix this?"

"I don't know. Okay?" Katie hadn't meant to shout, but the words simply wouldn't stop flowing from her mouth. "I don't have any answers for you. I'm trying my hardest. Every day, I'm trying to make things right, but you don't see it!"

She had to go. Had to get away from that horrible house. From every vicious memory that wouldn't disappear. And from Asher and his dangling carrot of a new beginning she knew wasn't possible for someone like her.

Another dead end. That was Katie's life: one dead end after another. The second pawnshop was a complete waste of time. They didn't even buy jewelry, only firearms and electronics.

She'd been gone for hours, driving aimlessly down deserted roads until her gas gauge was almost at empty. But she couldn't bring herself to go back to that place where there was so much work to do and no answers. She tried praying, even listening to some local Christian radio, but she kept struggling with the same questions: How was she supposed to move forward when her past felt like a weight dragging her under? How could God give her the same future as people who'd loved Him their entire life? The checks and balances just didn't add up. She hadn't been given the consequences she deserved.

A familiar ballad crackled through her Camry's old speakers, and Katie let the words fall over her like a warm blanket in the cold. With them came the memory of that moment when her life had completely changed.

She'd been unceremoniously kicked out of her boyfriend's apartment. He'd left her duffel on the top step along with a note that said he'd grown tired of her. It was January and freezing, and after spending two nights in her car, she swallowed her pride and sought refuge at the Tallahassee women's shelter.

Katie had thought the night she'd left Fairfield was her darkest moment, but this one beat them all. She was homeless, friendless, jobless, and so full of regret it was making her life rot.

It was at the shelter that Katie met Reverend Snow and he told her God's love was for the broken and lost. She had been both. And through trembling lips, she'd turned her heart over to the God of the universe.

She believed in new beginnings. She did. But Asher didn't know her. Didn't understand how deep her scars ran. He'd known her in high school where, sure, she was a punk kid with a quick lip and a pattern of continuous detention. But as an adult, she'd become something far worse.

He only thought he wanted to know the truth. But Katie knew that once he did, the sweet words and heated stares would all dissolve. In their place would be left disappointment and grief. She couldn't bear either.

Katie made the familiar right turn into her driveway. The sun was setting, which meant her parents were likely gone. It was a relief and, in some ways, the very reason she'd stayed absent for so long. Her dad would have come home a couple of hours ago. Maybe he'd figured out a solution to a problem for once?

Her question was answered when she parked the car. There, in front of the sagging porch and chipping front door, were three new steps and a handrail. The wood was raw and unstained, but Katie knew from the quality and precision that it hadn't been her father who'd fixed her mess.

She slammed her car door and walked closer to the new wood. Sawdust lay near the structure, evidence that Asher had used his favorite handsaw. Her fingers slid over the surface. The wood needed to be sanded, but it was sturdy and reliable, just like the man who'd spent his afternoon building it.

Katie wanted to curse but couldn't speak. Her sinuses were full, her eyes stung, and her throat ached as if she'd swallowed burning coal.

She would not cry. Katie Stone did not cry.

But even she couldn't deny the moisture spilling down her cheeks as she touched another thing he'd unselfishly done for her.

Ignoring him wasn't working. As much as she wanted to push Asher away, as she'd been able to do with every other person in her life, she couldn't. He'd infiltrated and claimed some part of her soul.

She hadn't wanted this. Hadn't asked him to come to her rescue time and time again. Yet he'd known her need, and he'd met it even after she told him clearly that she wasn't ready or willing to trust him. Why? It didn't make sense.

She wiped at the tears and stormed next door, more angry than sad. He wanted to know her? Wanted the bad along with the good? Well, fine. He was about to get a heaping dose of the old Katie.

Her fist pounded his door. She had no idea what she'd say to him, but this swirling, confusing, tear-causing sensation had to end. She jammed her hands into her pockets and paced back and forth in front of this door like a caged tiger.

Slowly, it opened.

"Hey," he said, surprise coloring his features.

He'd recently showered. It wasn't just the wet hair and freshly shaven face that gave it away, but also the smell of minty soap and spicy aftershave. His scent. The scent she'd come to rely on.

He was right. They weren't just friends. There was respect and admiration between them, that was true. But there was also chemistry and attraction. Their touches had become more intimate, more meaningful. Their conversations, more important.

"Why?" she demanded, feeling that ache in her throat again. She'd come to yell at him, yet her voice sounded strangled and weak.

He stepped forward with an expression she'd seen a hundred times. The one that made her believe she could actually be worthy one day. "You're crying. What happened?"

"*You* happened!" Her stomach hurt, her hands were shaking, and her instincts urged her to walk away fast. "Why couldn't you just leave it be?"

His mouth tightened. "Well, for one, your mother was cursing like a sailor when you drove off. Plus, I heard you scream. Sue me, Katie, but I actually care about your well-being."

"Not the steps, you idiot. *Me!*" She went back to pacing. "I wanted to come home, get my parents in a safe place, and then go on with my life. I can't do that in Fairfield. Don't you see that? No matter what I do, my mistakes will always be ten feet from me."

"Your past exists, whether you live in town or not."

"Maybe, but it's not right in my face. It's not luring me back every time I let my guard down."

"Yes, it is. Your past is your crutch, Katie. Your excuse to not even try." He stepped closer, putting two hands on her shoulders to calm her erratic movement. "I spent almost a year hiding away in this house, hoping to avoid the church and Jillian, thinking that would somehow make the pain stop. But it didn't. Not until you started showing up, asking me questions, challenging me to see past my bitterness, and encouraging me to trust someone again."

His words sank past her defenses, and just as quick as it had come, all the aggression left her body. Wiping her eyes, she gave him a wobbly smile through her tears. "I didn't know I was doing that."

"Well, you were. You did." His voice was soft, persuasive. His hand began stroking up and down her back, until it landed on the nape of her neck. "Not everything can be planned. Not everything is going to fit into precise, separate piles. You and I: we work. I don't know why, but we do."

"I'm not staying in Fairfield." But her resolve sounded weak, even to her. It was his proximity, the way his thumb caressed her skin, the way his gaze felt intensely focused yet gently intimate.

"I'm just asking for a chance." His lips grazed her forehead, and the feathery touch made her skin tingle as if little fireflies were dancing over the surface.

She closed her eyes when his lips traveled down to her temple. Her hands moved on their own, first to his hips, then to grip the T-shirt he wore.

"May I kiss you, Katie?" His lips were at her cheeks now, barely making contact. "I've wanted to for so long now."

She didn't want him to ask. Didn't want to have to be the one to make that decision. But she knew he needed her to agree. She also knew doing so with a man like Asher meant that she was committing to more than a moment of contact. It meant she would trust him. It meant she would allow him access to her heart and her soul. It meant a plunge into something different and unknown.

"Yes," she whispered, unable to answer any other way. It felt wrong to feel so much. To want his touch so fiercely.

He moved with a gentleness she didn't expect, not when the tightness in her chest felt like a raging mesh of heat and passion and need. She pulled at his back, pressed closer, demanded more. But his control didn't falter.

Then ever so softly, his lips met hers.

CHAPTER 27

Katie practically bucked beneath his hands, her body demanding he move faster, but Asher wasn't about to rush this moment. He wanted to savor her touch. Savor the way her cheeks were damp with the tears he had never seen her shed before. He wanted her to know what it felt like to be valued, to be cherished, to be adored.

Energy magnetized the small distance between them, and he finally gave in, brushing her mouth with his.

Soft. Warm. Glorious. His lips moved slowly, exerting just enough pressure to relieve the ache in his chest. He pulled her closer, wanting to feel her collapse in his arms, to feel her let go of distance and walls.

The need for more grew deeper. His hands were on her face, cupping her jaw, framing her ear; his fingers slipped into her hair. Shock waves poured down his spine. He needed to stop but felt his treacherous hands move down, under the loose hem of her shirt, until he could touch the remarkably soft skin on the small of her back.

She didn't shy away but encircled his neck and pulled him tighter.

Stop. His mind warned him to get control. He could feel the edge of her bra strap, knew that only a slight flick of his fingers could turn this moment into one of regret. That thought was enough to cool the heat surging inside. His hands found safety on her hips, as he slowed the frenzy that had overtaken them both.

He pulled away just enough to peer in her eyes, and when he did the ache returned with a fist. He'd seen them angry, excited, joyous, and lost. But now longing reflected in the silvery depths. It was more than desire. More than a touch that had been forbidden for so long. She trusted him. And this time, he would be a man worthy of that trust.

She swallowed. "That certainly opened Pandora's box."

His laughter caught him by surprise. He dropped his forehead to hers. "Leave it to you to fire-hose a moment with one sentence." He kissed her cheek and then let her go.

She patted down her hair and straightened her shirt, scanning the area as if someone had been watching them from afar. "I didn't come over here to kiss you."

He crossed his arms and leaned against the frame of his front door. "But you did want to see me. Admit it. You missed me."

She rolled her eyes. "No. Mostly, I just wanted to yell at someone."

He reached out and took her hand. "That's because you missed me." He gave a little tug, and she was back in his arms. "Admit it."

A grin fought its way through the scowl she was faking. "Okay, fine. I missed you. Happy?"

"Very."

He kissed her again, without losing his senses this time. It felt so strange to feel hope again. To see a silver lining where there'd only been bleakness. Sure, they had some challenges to face, but Asher wouldn't accept that any of them were large enough to knock down what they'd built.

Katie laid her head against his chest. "Are you sure you really want to do this?"

"I'm sure," he said firmly.

"It's going to be a hot mess." Her answer was equally sure.

He wrapped his arms around her. "I like messes. Keeps me on my toes."

She laughed. "You're insane."

He kissed a line down her throat. "Here's a thought. Let's throw in a pizza, watch a movie, and make up for the four days we lost with your stubbornness."

✕

He didn't let her protest. A second later they were inside his kitchen, hand in hand. Stainless steel and granite covered every surface except for the rich mahogany cabinets.

He opened a freezer drawer. "I have three-meat, supreme, and some kind of chicken spinach thing."

"Whatever is fine. I'm not picky." She couldn't think about pizza, not when her heart was racing. *Clean.* Everything in the kitchen was perfectly, beautifully pure and clean. Like him.

He shut the drawer and pulled a string to open the cardboard pizza box. "Three-meat it is. We'll stick with something I know will be good."

A few photographs were fastened to the fridge door with round magnets. She stepped in for a closer look while he rushed around, turning on the oven, pulling out a flat pan. She'd never seen him nervous or flustered before, but her being inside his kitchen seemed to be making him both.

She fixed her attention on a four-by-six photo of Asher with two other men. They were all sporting several-day-old beards, messy hair, and proud smiles.

"Would you like something to drink?"

"No thanks." She took the picture off the fridge, leaving the magnet in place. She didn't recognize them. She barely even recognized Asher. He'd had an entire life outside of Fairfield that she knew nothing about.

She heard the oven door shut and the *ting* of a timer being set, and then felt warm arms wrap around her middle. "That's our annual camping extravaganza. Three men, one week, no electricity or running water."

185

"Sounds fabulous," she said with sarcasm injected into the last word.

"It is. Being in nature, away from the stress of life. I don't know. I've had some of my greatest epiphanies on those trips." He pointed to the guy on the left with longer dark hair and bright blue eyes. "That's Dylan. We roomed together in college for three years." His finger slid over to the opposite side of the photo, pointing to the guy, as tall as Asher, with tight-cropped hair and big brown eyes. "And Will. He and Dylan are like brothers, but they can't live together. So he hung out in our place during the day and went back to his freakishly neat apartment at night."

"You're pretty freakishly neat too."

"Not like Will. The man has a checklist for his checklists." Asher chuckled. It was clear that he loved his friends, flaws and all.

She snapped the picture back on the fridge. "Was this taken last year?"

His arms slipped away. "No. I didn't go last year."

She watched him bustle around the kitchen again. He pulled out two glasses, even though she'd said she wasn't thirsty. "I won't ask if you don't want me to."

He set the cups down, held on to the counter for second, and then stood straight again. "I was in a bad place. It was about two months after the breakup. They'd just forced me to step down at the church. The last thing I needed was a week to think about the black hole my life had become. So I stayed home and renovated the kitchen instead. A week spent hammering cabinets can be quite therapeutic."

She gave him a faint smile, feeling a quick sting of jealousy. "You really loved her."

He moved in slowly, pulled her to him by her belt loops. "I'm over it."

"Good."

She raised a hand to investigate the rigid structure of his biceps, her fingers slipping just beneath the sleeve of his T-shirt. His muscles flexed with the contact, and she explored further: to the rounded edge of his shoulder, the thick muscle by his neck, the slight curl of hair beyond his ears. His eyes closed, and she knew he felt what she did. That heat, that ache deep in her belly that made her want to do a million things she knew they weren't ready for.

He lowered his head and laid it against her neck. His strong arms gathered her closer, both possessive and comforting. "I won't make the same mistake again. I won't confuse things by moving too fast." He let out a painful sigh and gently pushed her away from him. "And I want you a little too badly right now."

With his back against the island and his body now a good several feet from hers, reality settled on her shoulders. "What are we doing?" she said—only partly to him, mostly to herself. She'd ruin him. This beautiful, gentle, respectful man.

He smiled a lopsided grin that was meant to tease but only made him sexier. "Some people would call it dating."

"What would you call it?"

"I'd call a new beginning. For both of us. But . . ." His smile faded, and so did the mood. "I want you to tell me about Cooper."

She met his eyes, and the expectation in them hurt. He didn't just want her honesty. He needed it.

She twisted the edge of her T-shirt around two fingers. "Cooper and I met at Joe's not long after he moved into town. He had this dark, mysterious past, and I had this need to be with angry, complicated men. After a few rounds we each decided the other was interesting enough to do it again the next night. And then the next. We dated for two years, and most of those months were volatile." She dropped the wrinkled fabric and tried to find the right words to explain their relationship. "It's not a romantic story. We were two people immersed in self-destructive behavior who found kinship together." She shuffled away until her backside hit his enormous refrigerator.

"Two years is a long time. When did you break up?

"The night before I left town." She eyed the timer on the stove, wishing it would count down faster. She hated this conversation. Hated how Asher had gone all stiff and solemn, and how far away he seemed all of a sudden.

"Not much closure there." Asher didn't have any kind of nervous tic. His hands didn't shake like hers. He didn't grip his neck like her dad. He was just still. Which made the statement more important, because all of that focus was on *her*.

"Not everyone needs closure. Sometimes they just need a way out," she said.

"So why haven't you mentioned him before?"

Silence. A heavy silence that rattled the windows, shook the doors, and pushed all the air from the room. She couldn't tell him. Not yet. Not when she'd had a glimpse of what being cherished felt like.

Unwilling to let Cooper's memory tarnish the little happiness she'd found, Katie sauntered across the hardwood floor separating them until her palms were on his chest, over the slamming of his heart. "Can this be enough for tonight? There are some things I'm not ready to talk about."

His hands landed on her hips. Sturdy hands. Warm fingers. They gently pressed against her waistband and into the flesh above. He tugged her closer, and his nose brushed along her cheekbone.

"And it's definitely over?" His voice was deep and gruff, and every syllable caressed her soul.

"Yes. Absolutely."

CHAPTER 28

Katie Stone was dating Asher Powell. In Fairfield, of all places. Insane. Stupid. The town would protest in the street. They'd string up her sins along the light posts, spend their weekends convincing him of what she already knew to be true: she wasn't good enough.

Yet she couldn't walk away, because somewhere in the depths of her soul, she wanted to believe in second chances. She wanted to believe every sweet word he'd whispered to her.

A light rain peppered her windshield as she drove the ten miles south. Standard Pawn was the largest shop on her list and had the best rating on Google. It also advertised the most comprehensive jewelry selection in the county. Katie knew it was a long shot, but making the trip sounded like a far better idea than sitting at home trying not to think about her next-door neighbor or the fact that they'd spent two hours kissing in his living room last night.

Just kissing.

Katie hadn't done that since junior high. And even then, she'd let the boys explore under her shirt. But with Asher, it felt right to take it slow. He made her feel untarnished, special, worth waiting for.

She wanted so much to be all he thought she was, but in the dark recesses of her mind, Katie knew this dream world had an expiration date. But if she found the ring—if she could just set one thing right—then maybe they'd have a chance.

She parked the car and entered the large brick building. Unlike the other two pawnshops she'd checked out, this one felt like a retail outlet. Several teenagers wearing matching shirts walked around helping patrons find items. A stout lady with short hair and a manager's badge stood behind the counter. JACKIE was etched in the blue plastic.

Katie stood in line, waiting until the customer in front of her had paid.

"May I help you?" Jackie asked with a practiced smile. "We're running a ten-percent sale on all our old stock. It's noted by a green tag."

Katie glanced along the glass counter, eyeing the rows of jewelry underneath. "Actually, I'm looking for a specific piece. It's a vintage emerald ring with a flower design. It was pawned about four years ago."

The woman sighed. "I'm sorry, hon. We never keep inventory that long. One year, and the company policy is to mark it down or sell it online."

"Could I just check anyway?"

Jackie's face softened. "Sure. We keep our rings over here."

Katie followed her down the counter until they'd reached the far end. Two more customers were walking up to the register.

"Take your time. I'll come back in a second and see if you want a closer look at any of these."

But Katie didn't need extra time. There were only two rings with an emerald stone, and neither was the one she sought.

As promised, Jackie returned a few minutes later to check in.

"Would you have a record of the ring?" Katie swallowed the lump in her throat. "I mean, if you'd sold it online?"

"We would." The woman pulled out a blank sheet of paper and wrote the description Katie gave her and the general time frame of the sale. "I'll check when things slow down and call if it was here. We can't disclose buyers, but you can at least know if it was sold."

"Thank you. Thank you so much."

Jackie patted her hand in an unexpected show of compassion. It fueled Katie, gave her much-needed comfort and encouragement that she was doing the right thing.

That feeling only grew and emboldened her as she drove back into Fairfield. She parked in front of Bradley Properties on Main Street. Her parents were stubborn, but they weren't stupid. Maybe if she could just show them actual numbers, they'd consider putting the house up for sale.

A bell chimed as Katie entered the office. Cinnamon and vanilla welcomed her from a candle on the table. A receptionist's desk and three plush chairs filled the small waiting room, but no one was around. Katie checked her phone. Two fifteen on a Friday. Surely, someone should still be working.

She approached the desk and peeked around to the offices in the back. "Hello?"

"Coming. Sorry," a voice called from behind a closed door. A woman emerged a second later, wiping her hands on a paper towel. "Figures the one time I take a break . . ." Her voice trailed off.

Piper Wilson had fire-engine-red hair as loud and crass as her personality. She was three years older than Katie, but they'd crossed paths more than once, and not often on good terms. Piper had been as determined to steal Cooper as Katie had been to keep him. It made for a lot of drama on Friday nights.

Piper tossed her towel in the trash can with more force than was necessary, and her expression contorted into that of feigned professionalism. "Katie Stone. What can I help you with?"

Katie could feel the hostility all the way to her stomach. The judging eyes, the vicious smirk, the satisfaction in Piper's voice that said Katie was beneath her. "I'm here to speak to a Realtor. Is one available?"

"Cooper mentioned you were back." Piper glanced at her fingernails. "We're dating now, you know. Going on six months."

"That's nice." Cooper's standards must have dropped dramatically in the last four years.

"It's interesting, all the talk going on about you. The laughter too. Who knew that Katie Stone, infamous bad girl, would turn into the town joke?" She took her seat and fumbled with her desk calendar as if her words were insignificant. But her sword had been unsheathed. "Wade should be available. I'll check."

Katie knew people talked, but hearing about it from Piper and seeing the girl's amusement over the ridicule unleashed a part of her old self that she'd suddenly lost all ability to restrain. "Thank you, and when you're done, be sure to ask your boyfriend why he's been by my house twice since I've been back, trying to convince me we belong together." She shouldn't have felt satisfaction when insecurity flashed across the girl's face, but she did. In fact, she wanted to say more. To hurt Piper the way she knew she could with only a few choice sentences.

With a trembling sigh, Piper picked up the receiver. "Wade, Katie Stone is here to see you." A pause. "Okay. I'll send her back."

She hung up the phone but wouldn't look Katie in the eye. "He's the office on the right, after the bathroom."

With her back straight, Katie walked past Piper and down the hall, even though her conscience demanded that she apologize. She wasn't supposed to let herself get baited anymore. She was supposed to be different. To take the high road.

Wade's door was open, and he waved her in. "Katie. What can I do for you?"

She didn't know him personally, just by his reputation as a sharp-minded businessman. He greeted her with a smile and a handshake that eased the tension left over from her confrontation with Piper. "I'd like to discuss my parents' house. I'm sure you've heard about my mom's health, and I'm just trying to help them plan ahead. I've heard talk that the market is booming and that now is the time to sell." She took the seat he offered. "We live out off Forest Road on ten acres. The only other house out there belongs to Asher Powell." The mention of his name brought on a wave of sadness. He'd be disappointed in the way she'd treated Piper, using Cooper to hurt her when Katie didn't even care about their relationship.

Wade tapped some keys on his computer. "Yes. I know the area. Used to belong to the Winters family. They built your mom and dad's house as the second home for their parents and then broke up the land after Winters senior died."

Katie nodded. She hadn't known all the history, but she knew her parents had been the third owners of the property. "Could you give me a market value?"

"Absolutely. In fact, I have two buyers right now who would jump on that property."

"It needs work," she admitted.

"What old house doesn't? That won't be a problem." With excessive energy, Wade clicked at the keyboard some more and then stood to retrieve a piece of paper from the printer. "Here's some sales comps within ten miles of your house. Now, it will be hard to estimate without seeing the property, but I think we can stay in this range." He leaned over and wrote down a number that had Katie almost sliding off the chair.

"You're kidding."

"Nope. Supply and demand. Fairfield has a lot of undeveloped land but very few established homes with acreage. The last two I sold went above asking price."

Katie folded the paper in half. "Thank you. Um, they aren't quite ready to sell yet. But as soon as they are, I'll call you." She stood and shook his hand.

"You seem all grown up," he said with a hint of surprise.

She thought about her confrontation with Piper. "I'm getting there."

Wade walked her out, and Piper pretended to be too busy at her desk to notice. "My cell number is on the attached card. Call anytime."

"I will. Thank you."

As the door shut behind her, Katie took a huge breath of wet air and considered the number Wade had given her. Her parents could not only buy a safer home without a loan, they could also hire someone to help her mother. She had to make them see reason. She had to.

Katie glanced down the street, still amazed at the changes in Fairfield's downtown district. It was cleaner and brighter and showed all the signs of growth and potential. Her gaze fell on the black-and-white sign over Joe's Bar, and longing pulled at her heart. A drizzle of rain soaked the fine hair around her face, but she didn't move. Laila was probably in there, wiping down tables and glasses, preparing for the happy-hour crowd.

Katie clutched the paper tighter to her chest, protecting it from ruin. Even if she found the ring, it'd never change what she'd done to her best friend.

No matter how hard she tried, some mistakes just couldn't be fixed.

CHAPTER 29

Attending Fairfield Fellowship had been terrifying that first Sunday, but nothing compared to the dread churning in Katie's stomach when Asher parked outside his childhood home. The small one-story brick house with hedges, bright flowers, and two large trees was located in the center of the Whispering Pines neighborhood and only four miles from the church.

Katie had passed the sign to this neighborhood plenty of times but had never actually turned in. It was filled with middle-class family homes, families with two point four kids and smiles and happiness. These were the families she used to detest, mostly because she envied that kind of stability. And Asher's had been one of them.

"You ready?" he asked when she didn't move.

"How many people will actually be here?"

"Probably twelve to fifteen. Mom always invites the deacon of the week and his family, any new couples that come to church, and whoever else she thinks needs a home-cooked meal."

"Your mother is a saint."

"Yes she is. Although she'd correct you pretty quick if you ever said that to her."

He opened his door, but Katie stayed as if glued to the leather. "I can't go in there."

"Try it for ten minutes. If you feel uncomfortable, we'll leave."

"You promise?"

"I promise."

"Okay." Katie found a way to make her body move. Found the strength to open and shut the car door and even enough courage to walk around the vehicle and go stand by Asher.

He offered a hand, but she only stared at it. "I don't want them to get the wrong impression."

"What impression would that be?"

"That we're more than friends."

"We *are* more than friends."

"I'm not ready for everyone to know that yet. I'm barely used to the idea myself."

Asher tucked his hand into his pocket. "Right." She sensed frustration in his tone but wouldn't let herself feel bad. She had way too many complications in her life already.

They started down the sidewalk, having to duck under a low-hanging branch to get to the front door.

"I need to trim that tree one day. I keep forgetting," he muttered, cutting the now weighted silence.

The door opened before he could grab the knob, and suddenly his five-foot-nothing mother stood in front of them. Her graying blonde hair was sprayed firmly in place, while splotches of red sauce marred her *Best Cook in the South* apron.

"Hi! Come in, come in." She moved out of the way and let Asher and Katie through the door.

Asher kissed his mother on the cheek, then peeked into the kitchen. "Where is everyone?"

"I decided to just keep it small today." She smiled at Katie. "Crowds can be overwhelming."

There was a flash of emotion in Asher's eyes. "Thanks, Mom."

She reached out and squeezed his hand, her eyes glassy. "I heard about your phone call."

Katie's interest piqued. Asher hadn't said a word to her about any call.

He shrugged. "It was past time."

"I'm still very proud." Mrs. Powell released him and waved a hand in front of her face as if the motion would make her tears retreat. "Well, show Katie around. I'm just going to get the food set out so we'll be ready when your father gets here." She disappeared through the door.

"That must have been some phone call, to make your mom almost burst into tears," Katie said.

"Actually, it doesn't take much. A good TV commercial, a hug from a little kid, or a kind word, and my mom is Niagara Falls."

"Is that your way of telling me it's none of my business?"

He took her hand. "No. Although it is something I'd rather share with my girlfriend and not just some cute neighbor."

"Point taken." She focused on her feet. As much as she wished she could rush unashamedly forward with their relationship, she couldn't shake the feeling that a guillotine hung just above her head.

Asher led her down a hallway lined with photos of him from birth to college graduation. It was a timeline of smiles sandwiched between family photos at various vacation spots. Katie recognized Disney's Cinderella Castle, Mount Rushmore, the White House, and other landmarks.

She stopped to admire the last photo. In it, Brian and Laura Powell flanked their son and a very smiley Jillian. Beside them was a sign indicating they'd climbed Pikes Peak.

"That was taken almost two years ago."

"You look happy."

"I was." There was no hidden meaning in his tone. Just matter-of-fact truth.

"I'm surprised you didn't take her picture down."

"Forgetting the good memories would only deepen the tragedy. At least when I looked at this photo, I could convince myself the pain was worth the journey."

Asher stared at the snapshot in silence, and Katie wanted to reach out and touch him, to pretend she could understand his loss. But she couldn't. There'd never been a time when she'd felt that kind of joy, not for an extended period, anyway, and never with her family. "Your life was very different than mine," she said instead. "Same town, same school, but very, very different lives."

He shifted, not just his attention but also the lilt of his voice. "So tell me about yours. What was it like growing up in the Stone family?"

"Cold. Unstable." She picked at a loose thread. "When I was a kid, my mom and dad worked a lot. And when they weren't working, they were off doing whatever it was they spent their time doing. I really don't know. By thirteen, I pretty much took care of myself—and them, too, when they'd overdone it." Katie remembered the shouts and the alcoholism. The threats and the multiple suitcases packed and unpacked. "When I turned fifteen, my dad quit drinking. Just cold turkey. Not sure what happened, but he stopped for a year. Then it was two beers a day and never an ounce more."

"Did things get better at home after that?"

"Probably. But by then I was too angry and independent to care. Mom and I have never really clicked, but it got worse when I was in high school. I never officially moved out, but I can say that since graduation this summer is the longest stretch of time I've ever consistently stayed at my parents' house." Katie pointed to the picture. "Family vacations: they didn't happen."

"I'm sorry."

"It's fine. You don't miss what you never knew existed." She took in the dated decor. The carpet was worn, and the walls needed a fresh coat of paint, but still the house exuded warmth and family.

"I took it for granted," he admitted, leaning a shoulder against the one spot on the wall without pictures. "That vacation—the Disney one. It was a gift. I was seven and I guess I told someone my dream was to go to Disney World. We had been saving up for it at the time, but it was a slow road. Two weeks later, there was a card on my father's desk that included our tickets and itinerary. I still don't know who paid for it."

"Wow."

"I know. This past year all I've thought about is the negative. The downside of being in ministry. But the truth is, up until the fallout with Jillian, this church had only loved me." A hint of regret echoed in his tone, a feeling Katie understood all too well.

She thought of Laila. "Sometimes one bad moment can destroy a lifetime of memories."

"Yeah. But it shouldn't." He said the words firmly. "That's what the phone call was about. I called Jillian's dad."

Katie rubbed at the goose bumps on her arm, fighting a slow creep of jealousy. "How was it?"

He barked a short laugh. "Awkward. Very, very awkward. But good. We both apologized."

"What could you possibly have to apologize for? They're the ones who lied and turned against you."

"I hurt his little girl. And though Jillian isn't absolved from blame, I can't say that I was completely honorable in that relationship. I wasn't." Asher brushed his thumb across her cheek. "And with that last ghost put to rest, I can focus entirely on you."

Her skin burned beneath his touch. Once again, he'd made her feel wholly precious. But fear soon followed. They'd been together less than a week, and the relationship had already become more serious than all her previous ones combined. "Asher . . ."

"Come on. Let's go test your coffee-table theory." His hands landed on her shoulders and he pushed her toward the kitchen as if he could sense her hesitancy. She welcomed the distraction.

The Powells' kitchen was the biggest room in the house, with a large stainless-steel oven being the predominant feature. Its wide gas burners were covered with a basin of pasta, a loaf of bread, and a bubbling pot of sauce. A brown salad bowl filled with spinach leaves and vegetables sat on the island next to bottles of various salad dressings and all the paper goods and silverware.

At the other end of the room, Laura fussed with a centerpiece, lighting two votive candles. "Your father just texted. He's on his way," she said without stopping her task. "Katie, what would you like to drink?"

"Oh, water is fine. Thanks."

Asher continued to push her forward, past his busy mom and into the living room. Her gaze landed on the wooden table in front of the couch.

"See? Normal."

Katie smiled, surprised he remembered their conversation in the park. She picked up a two-inch-thick book with a picture of the Parthenon on its hardback cover.

"My dad loves architecture. Especially ancient structures that have survived for centuries."

She ran a hand over the sleek exterior. "He designed your deck, right?"

"Yep. Every detail."

Laura walked up behind them, wiping her hands on a towel. "Oh, good. Asher told me to set that out weeks ago. I finally remembered. Are you into design too?"

Katie raised an eyebrow while Asher found something else in the room to focus on. "Organizing, more than design. So, what was out here before?" She kept her eyes on her sneaky neighbor, holding in the laugh that pressed against her chest.

"Oh, just his father's old Greek Bible. Nothing anyone could translate anyway."

They heard the front door open and shut. Laura patted Katie's shoulder. "That's Brian. I'll be right back."

She waited until Asher's mom was out of sight, then smacked him in the arm. "You are so busted! It doesn't count if you manipulate the scene."

Asher rubbed at the spot she'd hit, his face beaming with a smile that mirrored the one in the photograph. It sent a flush of joy through Katie to know that she, too, could make him so happy. "He already had that coffee-table book. I simply reminded them to put it out."

"It still doesn't count."

"Yes, it does." He stepped closer, his eyes challenging hers with a humor that felt both electric and sensual.

She narrowed her eyes and stepped in too. "No, it doesn't."

His breath fanned her face, his smirk a promise that he could do this all day. "It does." Mint mixed with the underlying spice of his cologne seasoned the inches that separated them. The room grew hotter. She'd become too used to kissing him, because she could almost feel his lips touch hers.

A throat cleared behind her and she turned abruptly, scrambling not to drop the book in her hand.

Pastor Powell stood next to his wife, his eyes flicking between her and Asher. Katie set the book down in haste. She felt sixteen again, trapped between his cart and the exit of Marty's drugstore, a stolen tube of lipstick in her pocket. He hadn't said a word back then, just motioned toward the aisle she'd exited. It had worked. She'd put the stolen lipstick back. Katie may have been a troubled, cocky teen, but even she knew when to back down.

"Hi, Katie. It's nice to see you again."

Her trembling hand shook his. "You too, sir. Thanks for having me." She let go as soon as she could and tried to breathe normally.

"Of course. You're welcome here anytime."

Silence engulfed the room.

After a beat, the pastor clapped his hands. "Well, I'm starved. Let's eat." He followed his wife back to the kitchen, chatting with her about the service and the music that morning. They filled the last of the glasses, working in the kind of unison that came from years of living together.

Hot breath tickled her ear. "You haven't moved," Asher whispered.

"I know." She couldn't seem to get past the intimidation. Pastor Powell wasn't like Reverend Snow. The old minister had only known the changed Katie. The one who'd come to him broken, seeking answers.

But Katie felt sure Asher's dad knew more about her sins than almost anyone.

What had she been thinking, coming here? She was that egg no one found during the annual Easter hunt. The one that made the park smell for a week. She didn't belong inside this beautiful, pristine family with their matching Disney shirts and homemade spaghetti sauce.

And she certainly shouldn't be dating their son.

✕

Asher knew the minute Katie began to doubt herself. She had a "tell" he'd noticed the first night they spoke. It wasn't her voice. She could control its sound better than anyone he knew, her words remaining silky smooth despite whatever anxiety she felt. Even her shoulders would relax as if she hadn't a care in the world.

But her hands told a different story. They were the one part of her body she constantly fought, the Achilles' heel of a girl who could stare down a dragon without blinking. And those hands were now clenched behind her back, trembling.

She'd remained frozen in place since his father's handshake. Asher lightly clasped her elbow and helped her take that first step toward the dining table.

He pulled out a chair and she sat, but there was a pallor to her face. He took the seat next to hers and brushed his finger along her forearm under the table. She met his eyes and he could see the unease.

It hurt that she still didn't trust him not to put her in a situation where she'd have to defend herself. One day she'd realize he wasn't like the other guys. He wanted to be her hero.

His mom placed the final bowl on the table and sat. "It's so quiet, I hardly know what to do with myself."

"Relax. It's nice for you to get a Sunday off now and then." His dad turned warm eyes to their guest. "Thank you, Katie, for giving my wife a reason to take it easy."

"Um, sure, although the credit goes to Asher. He's the one who forced me to come."

His dad burst out laughing, and Asher had to bite his cheek not to join in.

It took a second before Katie realized what she'd said, but as soon as she did, her face was awash in horror. "No, I don't mean it in a bad way." She dropped her head into her hands. "Forget it."

"Coercion is one of Asher's specialties," his mom said, attempting to ease Katie's embarrassment. "When the church was really small, they would bring all the kids up front for a children's time. Asher was so proud he knew all the answers, we told him to stop speaking out and let the other kids have a turn. Well, one morning our children's minister asked him a question, and he just shook his head and said—in front of the whole church, mind you—he said, 'Oh no, my dad is gonna take a switch to my hide if I talk. He said so last week.' Well, you can imagine the roar of laughter. And our complete mortification."

Katie's shoulders shook slightly, and she finally dropped her hands from her face. "I'm guessing you didn't *actually* take a switch to his hide."

Asher folded his hands behind his head. "Not only that, but Dad never again told me to be quiet in church."

"Yep. I was worried for a week that CPS was going to knock on my door. I guess it serves me right for using a figure of speech with a five-year-old."

When their laughter died down, his dad bowed his head and blessed the food. Even better, when Katie scooped spaghetti onto her plate, her hands no longer trembled.

She glanced Asher's way, and the sparkle in her eye made his neck flush. Somehow, he and his parents had managed to do the impossible.

They'd made Katie Stone feel comfortable in a pastor's home.

CHAPTER 30

Katie entered the large cafeteria-style break room madly clutching the handles of her father's lunch pail. He'd forgotten it this morning and asked her to bring it by. She hadn't wanted to, but since her father rarely talked to her anymore and even more rarely asked a favor of her, she'd agreed.

Rows of tables stood empty, as the morning shift didn't end for another ten minutes. She sat at the far right of one, pushing the edge of the plastic tablecloth away so it didn't shift. Salt and pepper shakers stood at three-foot intervals, as did stacks of napkins, bottles of hot sauce, and containers of sweetener packets.

She set the lunch box opposite her and folded her hands in her lap, trying not to wring them while she waited.

A few workers trickled in after several minutes. Two of them recognized her and waved. She watched the door and four more entered, but none of them was her dad. Tired of the curious glances, she shifted her focus to her phone. He would see her when he came in; she didn't need to keep watching for him.

There was one text waiting for her.

Asher: *Didn't see you outside. You working today?*

She couldn't help but smile. They'd been officially dating for two weeks, and every new day was better than the last. Maybe it was because they'd been friends first, but somehow with Asher she didn't need all the fillers she used to. They talked and watched movies and went for long walks together—all activities she would have found miserably stale and boring only a year ago, back when she fed off angst and emotional highs.

"That smile for me, Firecracker?"

Her phone slipped into her lap.

Cooper lowered himself into the chair across from her. He wore the same blue uniform she'd seen on him a million other times, only his name tag indicated he'd received a promotion. He was crew leader now.

"That seat's for my dad."

"I know. He asked me to tell you he had some paperwork to finish and he'll be out in a minute."

"Great," she said, not bothering to hide her exasperation.

"I heard you and Piper had a little showdown." His eyes twinkled with satisfaction. "Jealousy has never suited you, Katie, but I am flattered."

"I'm not jealous. You can do whatever you want."

"Is that so?" They both knew he wasn't talking about Piper anymore.

She said nothing because her words wouldn't matter anyway. Cooper wanted to twist the situation. He wanted to continue his game of "Will I tell or won't I?" and she was getting really tired of playing along. She'd been home almost two months. If he was going to tell, he would have done it by now.

"Your daddy know you're trying to sell the house from underneath him?"

She rolled her eyes and checked the door for her father. "As usual, your girlfriend is misquoting facts, but she did mention the fun you've been having at my expense. I suppose you two had many laughs about my so-called pregnancy." She picked up a sugar packet and rolled it around in her hand. The rumor bothered her more than it should.

My Hope Next Door

"Hey." Cooper's voice dipped, and his hand stilled her fidgeting ones. "I would never joke about a child of ours. If you had been pregnant, it would have been the greatest news of my life."

Katie studied their joined fingers. Angry, abusive Cooper she could handle, but this version—the sad, tormented, exposed one—got to her, every time. She slid her hand away. This was one more area in her life where God's mercy had intervened. An unplanned pregnancy with Cooper would have tied her to him forever. "Well, thankfully, that wasn't our story."

A muscle under his eye twitched, a familiar tell that he didn't like her response. He rubbed the anger off his face with the heels of his hands and tried again. "Chad called yesterday."

Her eyes flashed to Cooper's. This time his words had hit their target, and he knew it.

"I told him you were back in town."

"What did he say?" She tightened her fist, trying to squeeze away the sharp surge of grief and regret.

He relaxed his shoulders, remained controlled and deliberate. "Let's just say he's not your biggest fan anymore."

"Was he sober?"

Cooper faltered for the first time, his eyes accusing. "Chad hasn't been sober longer than a week since that night. But I suppose you don't care about that either. I mean, with your new life and all."

"I still care," she whispered, the weight of her transgressions pressing down on her more heavily than ever. He knew her weaknesses. Every one of them.

"Do you? 'Cause it seems to me that you and Chad are doing the exact same thing: he's hiding behind the bottle, and you're hiding behind religion." He reached out and grazed her hand with his fingertips. "You can still fix what you broke. I know Chad. He'll see you clean and get his life in order. Laila will get her husband back, and we'll finally be whole again."

A chill sliced through her, a coldness that no heater could dispel. It reached past her skin, past her muscles, and into her bones.

"He wouldn't come home for me." Her voice shook with the denial.

"Bull. Who handed him his first joint? Who convinced him not to join the army? He wouldn't even buy an engagement ring for Laila until you approved."

Once again Cooper knew the exact words that would make her want to curl into the fetal position and never move again. "Chad has always been his own person. He makes his own decisions."

"Really? So you think it's a coincidence that he went completely off the rails after you left? Lie to yourself all you want, babe, but I watched him unravel. And don't think for one minute you weren't part of why."

Tears threatened her eyes, which only elevated her anger. Cooper had crossed many lines, but she would not let him use Chad as a weapon. A calm descended, one that only came when she knew she had the power to shatter someone. "You're the one lying to yourself. You think we were a family? Not even close. I let you visit our world, but you were *never* part of us." She leaned in, fueled by the hurt burning in his eyes. "And if I had the power to erase those two miserable years, I would, right down to your name etched in that tree."

Cooper went still—like a rock—and the microwave dinged in the distance. The whole room seemed to hush when he stood, openmouthed and with ticked-off, wide eyes. Controlled outrage. She should have felt satisfied that she'd had the last word, but her gut twisted with guilt. She'd let her dark side win—again.

Cooper practically bumped into her dad's shoulder in his rush to leave the break room, mumbling a quick apology before disappearing.

"When you gonna cut that boy some slack?" her dad asked, taking the seat Cooper had just vacated.

When he quit tearing out her insides every time they spoke. "I hope that's not why you asked me to bring your lunch."

"Please. I'm too old for all your drama and breakups. I wanted to talk about your mother." He opened his lunch box and pulled out two sandwiches, chips, and an apple. "She didn't want me discuss it, but I think you need to know. You two have been going at it again and, I don't know, I thought maybe if you understood why she's so upset, you'd be a little more patient."

More patient? She'd hardly said a word to her mother since the porch explosion. "Okay. So what's going on?"

"The medicine ain't working. They've upped her dose, switched brands, but her body is still attacking itself. We've been seeing this specialist in Jacksonville, but they've just referred her case to some fancy doc in Atlanta."

Knots hardened in her stomach, and she laced and unlaced her fingers several times. She hadn't spent nearly enough time researching the disease. Maybe on purpose. Maybe to avoid knowing. "How bad will it get?"

"It'll kill her. Slowly and painfully." Her father's somber tone made her feel empty. He sounded like a man who'd quit fighting and accepted his bleak reality. "I need you to play nice with her. Mental stress only makes things worse."

"I'm trying."

"Try harder." He unscrewed the water bottle he always kept on hand and took a big gulp.

She nodded, because there was nothing to say when he told it like it was.

He took a bite of his sandwich, and she decided it would be better to mention the property now than in front of her mom.

"I talked to a real estate agent."

"This is not you helping her mental stress." He tossed down the sandwich. "Or mine."

"Just listen, Dad. Market value is double what you originally paid for the house and the land." She pulled an information packet from her purse. "These two-bedroom homes in Fairfield Community are only a third of that amount, with a small monthly fee for services. You just said she's getting worse. Can you honestly tell me that house can sustain her in a wheelchair?"

He ran a frustrated hand over his face. "No."

"Okay then. Just look it over. Think about it. If you honestly feel I'm wrong, I'll back off." She offered the packet and he took it reluctantly.

He spent the rest of his lunchtime eating while flipping through pages and asking her questions. By the time he'd finished, she felt a bit of hope that, for once, her dad might actually take her advice.

CHAPTER 31

Her parents were gone again. Their second trip to Atlanta. Katie had questioned her father in passing about his decision regarding whether or not to sell, but he'd just squeezed his temples and said they'd deal with the house another day. At least she knew where she'd gotten her ability to compartmentalize. Her father was a pro.

And tonight she'd do the same. Asher had asked her to dinner. A date. In public. Ready or not, she would once again be the talk of the town.

At least this time the facts would be correct.

Katie shut her front door and tried to stuff down the nerves. She felt good about herself, and that always helped when she was about to face a firing squad. She'd found another box of clothes her mother had tucked away, and half of them were her size. This outfit was her favorite. The slick navy capris had a mild sheen to them and were soft as satin. The champagne top was cut like a halter but sat high on her neck with a beaded collar, exposing only a hint of her tan shoulders.

Her hair fell in straight layers just past her neckline. She'd cut it again and loved the sophisticated and sleek style. She wanted Asher to feel good about having her on his arm. Like he'd felt with Jillian.

She practically jogged next door, her heels occasionally sinking into the grass. She was early. Ten minutes, but watching the clock and chewing her nails was getting old.

Asher pulled open the door after two hard knocks. "When are you ever going to let me pick you up?"

"I was restless. Besides, you take longer than a girl to get ready." Her eyes trailed down his body. The shirt he wore was thick and tight across his chest. It hung just below the waist of his jeans, where her eyes lingered. Katie forced herself to look up. This wasn't church Asher. Or sweaty outside Asher. This was hot, sexy, out-on-a-date Asher, and she felt herself swoon just slightly.

He noticed her noticing him and smiled that crooked, confident smile that made her wonder how she'd ever thought he was anything but gorgeous. "Seems to be working for me."

She shrugged. "Maybe."

He wrapped two arms around her waist, pulled her close, and nuzzled her neck. "You're stunning."

It was a crime how quickly he could light her on fire with just a faint touch to her skin, or with the trail of his lips as they made the slow trek to her mouth. "So stunning I'm having to remind myself why I decided we should go out in public."

"Let's not, then." She stood on her tiptoes, met his mouth with an eagerness that had his hand in her hair the minute they made contact. He didn't let her push him back inside, although she attempted to.

"Nice try," he said, putting some distance between them. "There's no way I trust myself alone with you looking like this."

She playfully slapped his chest but jerked back when she heard gravel crunching in the distance. That truck. That stupid blue truck was pulling into her driveway.

Cooper had called her three times since their argument at lunch. Each message of his grew angrier. First he'd played it casual, acting as if they'd chatted on the phone a million times in the last four years instead of never. The next call came at two in the morning. He was drunk and rambling about the wallpaper she'd put up in his room. Told her it was peeling in the corners and raged at her for marking up his life when she had no intention of sticking it out.

The final call had come two days ago, and she hadn't made it through even half the voicemail. He was past the threats, past the words. He was done, he'd said. Done holding on to a lie.

She should have known he wasn't bluffing this time. Should have known that her fantasy life with Asher was moments away from crashing to the ground.

⋈

Asher eyed the truck he'd seen parked at her house before. Behind it was another one, equally as big but black, with a keg mounted in the bed.

Katie detangled herself from his embrace. "Just stay here." She marched down the steps so fast she almost tripped.

He caught up in three easy strides. "I'm coming too."

She froze and spun around in a fury. "No. I'll handle them and then we can go out. Just like we planned."

The driver of the blue truck had hopped out and was now leaning against the hood, watching them. Asher couldn't see the man's face clearly, but he'd seen that silhouette before. Cooper.

The last time, Asher hadn't intervened. He hadn't known his place or what Katie wanted. But it was different now. They were different, and he wasn't going to let anyone hurt her again.

"I'm going with you."

A short redhead jumped out of the passenger side and wrapped her arms around Katie's ex-boyfriend, keeping her back to them. Cooper didn't move. He didn't hug her or shift closer. He simply kept watching, his eyes locked so tightly on Katie that Asher considered the multiple places he could hide Cooper's body.

Katie refused to budge. "Please. Just let me deal with this alone."

"No." They were eye to eye. Hers pleading, his getting more and more irritated. "That isn't how things work now. We're together. I've seen what he does to you, and it's not happening again."

Her expression turned cold, her face the same mask of indifference he'd seen countless times in high school. "I'm not a damsel in distress. I don't need your help, nor do I want you interfering in my life."

His jaw jumped. "I'm going over there." Sure, he could be soft and gentle, but that didn't make him weak.

"Why? Why can't you just trust me that everything over there is poison?"

"Because it's insulting that you think I'm going to hide in my house while my girlfriend fights off an army. Don't ask me to be less than I am."

"Fine," she hissed. "But don't you dare give Cooper any more ammunition than he already has. You and I are friends. That's it."

"I'm pretty sure our kiss debunks that theory."

"You don't know if he saw us."

"He saw us."

Three more people had climbed out of the second vehicle, and a girl with stilts on her feet hollered at Katie to get her "white trash booty" over there. Katie spun back around and scanned the crowd. Her face went sheet white.

"That son of a—" Her fist tightened as she swallowed the word. "He brought Laila."

CHAPTER 32

She was in hell and this was her penance for trying to have something she knew she didn't deserve. Her footsteps dragged across the dry grass, dread clasping her throat as the distance between her and her old friend lessened.

Asher wouldn't go away. He walked step by step beside her, inching closer to her as they moved in tandem.

Those boxes she had so precisely separated—her past, her future, her mistakes—all had been dumped together in her front yard, with Laila as the centerpiece.

Laila Parker had been her best friend from the time she could walk. They'd spent every summer, every weekend, and every pre-date shopping trip together. And yet they hadn't spoken a word since Katie took off in the middle of the night.

Her old friend stood next to a man Katie didn't recognize, looking exactly like she did so many years ago. Black shorts and a side-tied Joe's Bar T-shirt. Long blonde hair braided over her shoulder. Only a hint of makeup. The man had his hand around Danielle, one of Laila's coworkers, and each time the girl moved, the hand inched closer to her backside.

She should have known Cooper would attack with his entire arsenal. That was what he did. What both of them did. Rip each other to shreds.

Piper draped over him like a sloth on a tree, but he only responded to his clingy girlfriend when Katie met his eyes. Sickening. Piper was one more casualty. One more person destroyed by the dysfunction of their relationship. Cooper didn't want Piper any more than Katie wanted them standing in her front yard.

Once she'd finally made it past the end of Asher's property, squeals filled the air as Danielle rushed forward and tackled her with a hug that smelled like cheap perfume and Jäger shots.

Danielle jumped on her four-inch heels while her too-short skirt rode up her legs. She didn't acknowledge Asher, except for a dismissive glance.

"I can't believe you're back! Cooper said you were. He said if you wouldn't come to the party willingly, we'd drag you there. Where have you been?"

"I've been helping my parents."

"All work and no play makes for no fun at all," Danielle crooned. "So, girl, we are kidnapping you tonight. Don't even try and say no. Joe's is ready to go with at least fifty people. We just need our honored guest!" Danielle giggled until she tripped, and Katie had to practically hold her up. "And dang, girl, you look like some rich hoity-toity. I'm almost afraid to touch you." She fingered Katie's top. "Is this silk?"

Embarrassment flushed Katie's cheeks. Asher was seeing her life firsthand. Seeing the crowd she'd hung in. Seeing what she used to think was fun and exciting.

They stopped in front of Cooper, whose smile was as confrontational as it was victorious. "Hey, Firecracker. I heard your daddy was out of town tonight." His eyes flickered from her outraged ones to something behind her. "We both know what you like to do when given a little freedom." He pushed Piper away while Katie tried to detangle from Danielle's obnoxious embrace.

Katie's heart drummed a rapid beat, and a cold sweat broke out over her body, leaving her trembling palms clammy. Asher and Cooper slowly approached each other, and although Asher stood a good three inches taller than Cooper, Katie knew he could never compete physically with him. Cooper was a street kid, raised to take a licking and keep on fighting, the dirtier the better.

"Cooper." Her tone was a warning.

"Chill out, babe, I'm just introducing myself to your *friend*." He said it like a curse at the same time he offered a hand to her neighbor. "Cooper Myles. I'm the ex."

Asher didn't miss a beat, nor did he seem intimidated or thrown. He wore the same casual smile she seen him display in church or with her parents. "Asher Powell." He glanced at her only a second before adding, "The neighbor."

"That's right, you're the preacher's kid." Cooper's feigned surprise made Katie want to punch his arm. He'd known exactly who Asher was before he ever pulled into the driveway.

Movement to her right pulled her attention away from the guys and onto Laila.

She should say something. This was her friend, her only real support for years. But she had no idea how to reconcile who she used to be with the person she was now. Or how to begin to apologize for what she'd done.

Cooper's voice boomed throughout the yard, and judging by his focus on her, the excessive volume was intentional. "If they let ole Katie through the doors, I ought to get my own ticket to heaven. Compared with this one, I should get mine lined with gold and maybe an emerald or two."

She flinched, his gut punch quick and effective.

"It doesn't work that way," Asher said, hands in his pockets, shoulders relaxed as if they were talking about the weather.

"Really?" Cooper laughed into the air and reached for an eager Piper. "Dollface, we're about to get evangelized. Come on, preacher boy, give it your best shot. I guarantee better men have tried and failed."

"Just like old times, isn't it?" Laila's raspy, feminine voice was one of a kind, and it made Katie's heart pound against her chest. "Two guys sizing each other up. Cooper marking his territory like a dog on the loose."

"There's nothing to mark. I'm not the same person I used to be." This shouldn't be how they talked after all these years. Not with Cooper dropping hints about the ring and Danielle lining shots up on the hood of the truck.

"Oh, girl. We both know that isn't true." Laila's sarcasm came with an icy stare. This wasn't the girl Katie had known most of her life. This one was lethal, bitter, angry.

Katie suddenly felt dizzy. Too many important conversations were happening around her, and she couldn't follow any of them. Danielle was squealing, declaring the shots were almost ready. Cooper was harassing Asher, who brushed off every insult with a quick response. And Katie could feel Laila's hatred. It poured from her voice like lava.

"Cooper finally told me what happened that night."

Her stomach cramped. "What do you mean?"

"Don't play stupid with me. The ring. The drugs. Chad. Every stupid, idiotic choice you made. He told me."

A continual pressure built in Katie's chest with each horrible word. Cooper had actually done it. He'd said he would. He'd threatened and threatened her. She'd been stupid to think he wouldn't. That he felt as responsible as she did.

"I didn't know he'd take them." Katie could hardly breathe, let alone speak.

Tears pooled in Laila's eyes. She opened her mouth to speak but no words came. Then, as one tear after another slid down her cheek, she barely choked out, "I hate you."

"I know."

Laila stared at the ground, her right hand toying with her very bare ring finger. "No, you don't. You don't know anything about what these last four years have done to me."

Katie didn't respond. What could she say? It was true. She'd left and never looked back. She'd wanted to forget. Wanted to erase everything about that night.

"I used to admire your ability to detach from anyone at any time. No one ever hurt you. No one ever penetrated that cold heart of yours." Laila's tension came into her, charging the atoms in the air between them. "But only because I thought I was different. I thought I mattered more."

Katie swallowed the fire in her throat. "You did."

"Do you have any idea how much I needed you? We swore we'd never abandon each other, and you just left me here."

Because Katie couldn't have faced her. She couldn't face anyone. It was a month before she called a soul. And even then, it was only a message left on her dad's voicemail so he knew she wasn't dead.

Cooper was like a shark that could sense blood in the water. "You girls okay there? It's looking pretty intense." He cuddled Piper to him. "It's supposed to be a party, remember?"

Laila followed Cooper over to the shot glasses. She wasn't cruel by nature, but the devil would've shown more mercy than Laila did as she picked up the shot glass and unceremoniously toasted her. A threat? A promise? Katie had no idea.

A hand on her back made her jump.

"You okay?"

"I'm fine. Please, just go home." *Before they tell you too. Before everything is ruined.*

"Don't." There was an unfamiliar edge to his voice. Irritated and tight, just like his features.

With her free hand, Laila offered Katie her own glass. "Come on. You love this, remember? My first shot was at your house. What were we, fourteen?" She pointed to Katie's window. "Right up there with Chad and . . . what was his name? Oh yeah, Eric. A night of many firsts."

Everyone else grabbed their shots, leaving only two. Katie's and Asher's.

Danielle's boy toy gestured to the lonely glasses. "Come on, Katie. I've heard you can outdrink men twice your size."

"No thanks." She couldn't swallow that shot if she tried. They'd all come to humiliate her. And she could have taken it—she probably deserved it—if Asher hadn't been standing right there hearing every word.

Cooper smirked. "What about you, preacher boy? Or will Daddy get all hot and bothered?"

"It's Asher," he answered. "And I'm good."

Laila offered him a coy farm-girl smile, the one that sent most men to their knees. "He's a cutie, Katie. Well done for only having a couple of months on the prowl. And to convince him you're clean and a good girl now? That's impressive, even for you." She leaned forward, training her eyes on Asher's. "Here's a little secret, though: *she's a liar.*"

Cooper laid a hand on Laila's shoulder, pulling her back and silencing her at the same time. He lifted his glass, and his gaze drilled into Katie's. "A toast to Mary Blanchard."

Katie shook her head, her hands trembling so uncontrollably that she could feel their quiver in her knees. "Don't do this." She was pure rage. Pulsing, aching. Her chest vibrated with energy. Her hands clenched and unclenched.

"Mary Blanchard," he continued with his glass raised. "Sweet, God-fearing old woman who only made one mistake. She trusted the wrong person. Trusted Katie with her home, her health, even the key to her most valuable possessions." He stepped forward, stopped only a foot from Katie.

Blood pounded in her ears, her head, her eyes. "Shut up," she warned.

His lips curved. "And here's to Katie." His words came slowly, each one intended to encourage her restraint to crumble. "The ring-stealing junkie who ruined everyone's life."

※

With a guttural curse, Katie attacked like a rabid animal, giving Asher only a split second to step aside before Cooper's shot glass shattered at his feet. Laila jumped out of the way. The red-headed girl cried Cooper's name.

Katie punched, kicked, clawed, and hollered obscenities, the high-pitched stream of hate echoing across the air.

Asher grabbed her waist and pulled her off her ex-boyfriend, whose arms were busy protecting his face. She thrashed like a wild two-year-old, making it nearly impossible for him to contain her and still prepare for a counterattack.

But Cooper only stood straight, wiping a trail of blood coming from his bottom lip.

Katie surged for another round, and Asher wrapped his free arm around her chest, locking her arms down to her sides. "Stop," he hissed in her ear.

It was enough to break through her madness. She stilled, her chest heaving in and out against his grip while she glared at the man in front of her. The man who was now smiling like he'd won a war.

He came closer, and Asher pulled her back.

"There's my Firecracker." Cooper's voice was low and intimate, and it challenged Asher the way no fist ever could. Cooper placed his hands on his knees, came nose to nose with the woman in Asher's arms. "I knew you were still in there."

Katie deflated, and Asher needed the same strength it took to keep her from attacking to keep her on her feet. Asher backed toward the house while the group quietly loaded into their trucks. The air was hollow. Silent. As if the earth had stopped spinning for a finite moment in time.

The rear truck backed out of the drive and Cooper's soon followed, honking twice as he departed.

Katie wiggled out of Asher's hold, walked over to her new front steps, and dropped straight down. She sat, her arms limp between her knees, as if she'd witnessed carnage. She didn't speak, and her gaze fixated on the place where she'd just completely lost her mind.

Asher ran a hand down his face, his arms rubbery from the strength it had taken to hold her back. Words bombarded his mind. Mary Blanchard. He knew her. She had been his mother's widow for February and had come to lunch twice.

Katie's face was a blank mask. What had been raw emotion only minutes ago was now a chasm of nothing. He laced his hands on top of his head and paced, waiting for her to do something. Say something, anything, to explain how ten minutes could annihilate their world so completely.

The silence grew, as did his temper. "What just happened?" he demanded.

Nothing. Not a blink. Not a sigh. Not even a breath.

She had told him it wouldn't work between them. His dad had warned him that he had no idea of the depth of Katie's wounds. Heck, he'd heard Cooper and her fighting before. So why was he so stunned? Why was he ready to pound his fist into the nearest tree and dig out his shotgun?

His stomach clenched. *My Firecracker.* It wasn't just the words, but the ownership. The satisfaction with which Cooper delivered them. Like a right hook before a knockout. Cooper wanted to destroy all that Katie had become. And judging by the way she sat there, his plan had worked.

Asher crouched in front of her. "Listen to me. You're not the same. One moment doesn't define you."

Her cold stare didn't warm; it simply redirected from the ground to him. "You're right. But a lifetime does." She stood, brushed invisible dirt off her pants. He followed her upright, attempted to take her hand. She pulled away but offered a smile that bruised him with its pain. "I'm gonna have to take a rain check on our date."

Her words were simple, but her eyes said a thousand more things. *I told you so. This won't work. I'm not good enough.*

They were all lies and yet he had no way to counteract them. He watched her disappear, torn about whether or not to push. He'd just finally managed a grip, yet she was already slipping away.

CHAPTER 33

Katie was packed in an hour but waited four more before tugging her duffel down the stairs and out to her car. She kept her head down and her eyes focused on lifting the bag into her empty trunk, willing her stiff fingers to shut it.

She'd failed. Again. The ring was still missing. Her parents were still barely above drowning. The feeling shouldn't have been so debilitating. She was used to failing. Used to running when things got out of control. At least this time she'd left a note.

The engine started without the squeal thanks to Asher. She'd been home only a few months, yet it felt like a different life. But that's what it was, really. An illusion. A dream. A wish. The past can stay buried for only so long before it comes up and chases a person like the walking dead.

There was only one place left to go before she hopped on I-95, back the same direction she had come from. She'd been avoiding the land since she came home, but even though her chest felt barren and empty, she couldn't leave without offering a final good-bye.

Fairfield was desolate when she drove through at midnight. The sign for Joe's was the only one lit on Main Street, and even that would shut off soon. Katie didn't scan the lot for the blue truck. She already knew it'd be there. He'd won. He'd proven her a fraud.

She turned south into her old neighborhood, The Point. She'd lived next door to Laila and Chad until she was seven, but even after the move, she'd spent hours there. The trees were taller, the street worn with a few extra potholes. But other than that, it hadn't changed, not a bit.

She parked against the cul-de-sac's curb, down by the storm drain, and slid through the PVC fencing the city had put up to keep kids out of the greenbelt. A worn path through the line of trees said the attempt didn't work any better with this generation than it had with hers. Acorns crunched beneath her feet as she counted off the towering oaks, shining her phone's flashlight a few feet in front of her. When she was younger, she could find the tree house in her sleep, but years had changed the topography of the underbrush and nothing looked the same.

After circling back twice, Katie spotted the boards still nailed to the wide trunk. Two had been replaced, their bare, unfinished surface reminding her of the new steps Asher had built. Pain ricocheted against her heart. She embraced it. It was her own fault for creating false hope. The pain would remind her not to do it again.

Wedging her fingers into the edges of the boards, Katie put a foot on the lowest slat and pulled her body up. One by one, she climbed them, fearing only a little that the makeshift ladder was designed to hold a small child and not an adult. When the familiar platform appeared, Katie sucked in a breath and pushed down with her palms while pulling her legs onto the small strip of wood.

The tree house entry was as tight as she remembered, and it scraped and cut her side as she shimmied into the space only large enough to fit four grown adults. She knew because all four of them had come six years ago to carve Cooper's name into the wood. To make him part of their family.

Katie lit up her phone again, moved it in a full circle until she could find the corner that started it all. Walking on her knees, she crept toward the carving. *Chad. Laila. Katie.* A heart encircled them. The names were so worn, it was hard to make out the letters. Tucked next to hers was a smaller, newer one. *Coop.*

"I knew you'd come here."

Katie didn't bother turning around to face her former best friend. "I guess some things never change."

"And some things change too much."

The wood squeaked and cracked as Laila finished sliding through the small square.

"I saw you drive by Joe's." She came over to rest next to Katie, by the carving.

"I bet Cooper's celebrating big tonight."

"Cooper's hurt. And he's too proud to say it. He's only loved two people in his life. You and Chad. In one night, he lost both of you."

Katie moved away and sat with her legs crossed, her back against the far end of the tree house, as far from Laila as she could get. "I don't know what you want me to say."

"How 'bout you tell me what happened that night."

"I thought Cooper already did."

"He told me his version. I want yours."

Sweat broke out on Katie's forehead, and she wished she'd just driven to the highway like she'd planned. "Why? It won't change anything."

Laila tucked her knees to her chin. "I know that. But I have a right to hear what happened from my best friend, even if it's four years too late."

Katie slammed the back of her head against the wall. She didn't want to do this. She didn't want to relive that night. "Slim didn't want to make the sale. He knew the ring wasn't mine, even though I pretended it was. But after a while, he conceded on one condition. That I try out the stuff from his new supplier." She remembered her desperation. Remembered how little she cared that she was selling off someone else's possession.

"Of course I agreed, because I wanted the high too bad to turn it down. Cooper and I drove out to that dance club at the beach, and then we both did a line in the car. I kept the vial with me for when we wanted another hit. It was nothing out of the norm. We'd done it a million times before."

Laila played with the end of her braid. "I hated when y'all would go there. It always meant you were using." She didn't understand. Never could. It'd been Katie and Chad who had the cravings. Even Cooper kept his use recreational. Laila had only tried it once because they'd pressured her to, and then never again. She was their conscience. Their guardian in so many ways.

"Whatever Slim had given us, it was different. Stronger, I guess, or laced with something else. Because the second hit was titanic. It felt like my skin was crawling, like I couldn't move fast enough or dance hard enough. Cooper got real paranoid and jealous. He forced us to leave. Drove, even, which was just stupid. The whole way home was a nightmare. I needed to move and go and he kept demanding that I settle down, saying that we were going to get caught and something about cars following us."

Katie's stomach rolled. "We made it home, but things went toxic as soon as we did." She couldn't verbalize it. The screams. The accusations. The way they mutilated each other with their words. The way his fist raised and then slammed into the wall behind her. "I wanted to leave, but Cooper was too messed up. He thought I was going to the police, or that I was trying to kill myself. I don't know. He kept saying crazy stuff. So he locked me in our bedroom. I banged and threw things at the door. I ripped down the curtains, tore apart the bed. And finally, I crawled out the window. An extra set of keys were on his dresser, so he didn't realize I was gone until it was too late."

Laila turned away. She knew what was coming next.

"I went there to see you." Katie needed Laila to know that she hadn't meant to mess with Chad's head. "You always knew how to calm me down."

"I was working," she whispered. "Chad had to study, so he stayed home."

The sting returned to Katie's throat. The ache that meant tears were coming. She wouldn't cry. It would influence Laila. It always had, and

Katie had used those tears to her advantage too many times. She swallowed and the sting slowly eased.

"As soon as I saw you weren't there, I tried to leave again. Chad took my keys. He tried to get me to calm down. Even threatened to take me to the ER if I didn't stop spazzing out. Whatever he did, it worked. But the fall was as bad as the high. I started sobbing. My life was a mess. I was a mess. I had no future. No hope. Cooper and I were done. It was horrible. He said you were coming home soon and he didn't want you to have to deal with me. He said you were already overtired and stressed out. He said it was time we both grew up and stopped relying on you for so much."

A tear slipped down Laila's cheek. "Those were my words. We fought before I left for Joe's. I'd found an empty bottle of vodka in his closet. He'd been hiding it from me again." She straightened. Wiped her face. "Tell me what happened next."

"Laila, I didn't know he was struggling." The plea was weak.

"You gave an addict cocaine. What did you expect to happen?"

"I didn't just give it to him. Although I'm sure that's what Cooper thinks. I was planning to get rid of it."

"So why didn't you?"

Because Katie was weak and high and far too strung out to make rational decisions. "Chad asked me if I still had any left. I told him I did, but that it was bad and I was throwing it out when I got home. He said he would do it for me. He said I wasn't strong enough." Katie's eyes brimmed with moisture, only this time she had no ability to stop the tears. "Laila, I'm so sorry. When I left your house, he seemed so in control."

"How would you know that? You didn't even stick around to make sure he was okay." Laila's hitched, broken voice was more than a slap. It was a knife through the gut. A twisting, sharp ache of the reality that Katie was responsible for Chad's overdose.

Silence filled the tree house. There was no need for more words. Laila knew what happened next. She'd seen it with her own two eyes when she came home to find Chad unconscious on the bed.

"I called you from the hospital, like, fifteen times."

"I know." The call had woken Katie up. She was parked in front of Ms. Blanchard's house, although she had no memory of how she'd gotten there.

"That's why you didn't come."

"I couldn't face you." Her voice sounded as if someone else were operating it. Someone toneless and half dead.

Laila's gentle features morphed into disgust. "You know, for all your bluster and tough-girl act, you're nothing but a coward." She pointed out the small circle window. "I bet tomorrow night's tips that your car is packed up and the minute I leave, you'll be gone all over again."

Katie didn't deny it. "It's better this way."

Laila slammed her hand on the floor. "It's not better this way. It's easier for you. That's it."

The words struck Katie like a towel snap—hard enough to sting, but with the promise of deeper pain to follow. "I can't turn back time. I can't change what happened. What else can I do?"

"I'm not your fixer anymore. Figure it out." Laila stood, remaining hunched over so she wouldn't hit her head, and walked to the exit. She lowered to the floor, slid her feet out, and turned on her belly to leave. But something stopped her. "You know, all I've heard about since you've been in town is how different you are. Your hair. The people you hang with. The fact you've been in church on Sundays. But here's the thing. You can't just say you've changed. You actually have to do it. And hiding in your parents' house, running away, well, that's got old Katie written all over it. If you want me to believe some holy power has turned your life around? Well then, Katie, show me the difference."

CHAPTER 34

Headlights flashed onto Asher's street, and his pulse jumped. It felt like an eternity, not two hours, since he'd noticed her car was gone. He'd grabbed his keys to go after her but with a sharp pain realized he had no idea where to even start searching. He knew nothing about her old life, what friends she had, her old hangouts. He'd been blissfully ignorant of the gigantic storm brewing until it smacked into him with no warning.

So despite his galloping heart and desperate need to do something, he waited. At first in his house. Then on his porch. Thirty minutes ago he'd moved to her new steps, as if getting closer would somehow make time move faster or take away the voice in his head that said she was never coming back—and the even louder voice that said he should have never let her walk away in the first place.

A crunch of gravel, and then the blinding light turned off. Asher stood and was at her car door the minute she shut it.

Her pale eyes were Katie's eyes, her face was Katie's face, but she wasn't the same girl who'd sat, lethargic, only hours before. He didn't wait for permission this time. He wove their fingers together, pulled her close, and kissed her closed eyelids. "For a moment I thought you weren't coming back."

She sank into him. "For a moment, I wasn't."

She wore an old sweatshirt and loose-fitting jeans that had to be sweltering in the humidity. Even with the sun down, the air was thick with heat.

Traveling clothes.

He held her tighter, realizing just how close he'd come to another heartbreak.

"I need to tell you what I did. Why I left four years ago."

"All that can wait." He inhaled the scent of her, kissed a line down the side of her temple. He was entranced, his hands moving to her face, cupping her neck, pulling her in. His mouth seized hers, but not like before. Before he'd been in control.

This wasn't control. This was fear and need and recklessness. Everything she'd told him she didn't want anymore. But it was there, in both of them. There was no pretending the past didn't exist. It did. It'd shaped them. Brought them together. He never would have appreciated the rawness of Katie if he hadn't experienced Jillian's composed beauty.

She broke away, laid her forehead on his chest. "It will change things for you. I know you say it won't, but you don't know how dark the secrets are."

When she lifted her head, the tears made her eyes shine. Her lips were red, her skin flushed at her cheeks. "And it's okay if it does. The girl you fell for goes to church, and sorts through her parents' junk. She eats weird concoctions at the drive-in and makes fun of cheesy movies. I really love that person too, but it's not all I am. I wish it were."

She was so wrong, he didn't know where to begin. "The girl I fell for once spent four days in detention for pouring a line of fake blood from the girls' bathroom to the counselor's office. She bolted from church the first day she ever stepped inside. Her eyes light up like a furnace when she gets angry, and even if she doesn't say a word, you feel stripped down and beaten by just a stare." He brushed a piece of hair from her face. "The girl I fell for is strong. She's dynamic. And through her transformation, I've seen God more clearly than I have in years. It isn't just who you've become that appeals to me. It's the journey you took to get here."

Katie didn't say anything. She simply took his hand and pulled him to her front door. He hadn't meant to pour his heart out, but she needed to know he wasn't leaving. He was trustworthy and faithful, two qualities he doubted she'd seen much of in her life.

They continued in silence as she unlocked the door, shut it behind them, and flipped on the light. He'd been inside once, but it was only deep enough to pick up the ugly couch in the dining room.

"Just so you know, it's typically polite to respond after a guy lays out his soul."

She passed him in the hallway. "I'm not typical or polite. That's what I've been trying to tell you."

"Katie."

"Stop. I'm not going to let you say things like that without knowing the truth. You make it too easy for me to want to forget what I did and pretend those choices didn't affect anyone."

He followed her to her living room, where she plopped on the couch and hugged a pillow to her chest. "I'm selfish. And I'm a thief. I almost killed one of my best friends, and I might as well have, since his life has been a spiraled mess ever since."

Asher took a seat next to her, settled against the cushioned armrest, and listened. He knew whatever she said didn't change anything for him, but maybe telling him would change something for her. "Okay. I'm listening."

She took a deep breath. "I met Cooper a year before I started working for Ms. Blanchard. We both fell fast and hard, despite the fact that we were like dynamite and lighter fluid. When the job opened for a caretaker for Ms. Blanchard, he encouraged me to take the position. Said it was the perfect setup. She had no family. And if I could just get her to love me, then we'd be set. I figured, why not? She didn't need the money after she died anyway, and I enjoyed her company. The problem was, Cooper's plan worked too well. She did love me. She did trust me. And I betrayed her."

Ж

Asher awoke to light streaming through the windows. His back ached, and his head was wedged between the armrest and the edge of the couch. Sweat clung to his neck and forehead. Katie was cuddled up against his chest, her body a furnace in this heat-box of a house. He shifted, trying to work out a cramp in his leg, which had fallen off the couch cushion at some point during the night.

They'd talked for hours. Well, she'd talked. She told him more than he ever wanted to know. Enough to make any man want to stand up and walk right out the door. But his father's warning kept playing in his head. *You represent Christ to her, and the last thing she needs is for you to walk away when things get hard.*

Katie's eyes fluttered open. She paused, then bolted upright, her hair flat on one side, a line from his shirt etched in her cheek. "We fell asleep," she said, slightly disoriented. "Sheesh, it's, like, a hundred degrees in here." She pushed off the pillows and stood on shaky legs.

He stretched out his sore muscles and noticed his shirt was drenched where she'd been sleeping. "Is it always this hot?"

"Not since Cooper added Freon, but that was weeks ago, and the condenser has a leak."

His heart thrashed as he stood, trying to rein in the anger that name provoked. He'd thought he'd understood hate, but his feelings for Bob and Jillian paled in comparison to what he felt for that con artist.

"I'll take a look at it," he said through clenched teeth. "I don't want that guy anywhere near you."

She snorted. "Well, good luck with that. I've wanted him to disappear since I drove into town. Cooper doesn't take orders well."

"I think you should turn him in."

"For what? I stole the ring."

"He manipulated you."

"Yeah, he did. But it wasn't like I resisted all that much." She walked over to him, took both his hands in hers. "Go home. Shower. Heck, we both need one. We'll talk later, once you've had time to process everything."

Asher pulled her close, even though he figured he smelled like sweat and old laundry. "I want to go to the next pawnshop with you."

"You don't have—"

"Katie." His tone was intentionally firm. "I'm not going anywhere. Get used to having me around."

"Okay. We'll go today. There's three more options, but only one has a big jewelry selection. It's ten minutes east of here, just outside of Burchwood."

He kissed her forehead. "I'll be back in an hour, then."

CHAPTER 35

Katie fidgeted the whole way there. Not just because Asher drove in relative silence, but because he was with her. He knew everything now. Her secrets. Her fears. Yet he didn't walk away.

She tried to reconcile why. He didn't need her baggage. He was an attractive, successful, kind man who wanted a family. There had to be a hundred women in Fairfield who were better suited for him.

As if he could sense her thoughts, he reached over and slid his hand into hers. "Just a few more minutes. You nervous?"

Her stomach flipped. "A little. I think this is my last real shot."

His eyebrows drew in as if he was having a conversation in his head, but wouldn't say the words out loud.

"What?" She didn't like not being able to read him.

"Nothing."

She let go of his hand, feeling a heat in her chest that always came before she said or did something stupid. "Hey, you told me I had to be honest. It's a two-way street. If you have something to say, say it."

"I think you should tell her."

"Who?"

"Ms. Blanchard."

Katie bit her lip, wishing she'd just kept her mouth shut.

"Even if you find the ring, I think you should tell her what you did. And definitely if you don't find it. She has a right to know that she didn't lose a family heirloom."

Guilt swept through her like tumbling river. She'd known all along that confessing was the right thing to do but had refused to consider the option. Like facing Laila, it meant watching the hurt. Seeing the betrayal in Ms. Blanchard's eyes as she realized the cause of her pain.

"Let's just see what happens here." Katie stared out the passenger window, not sure if she regretted telling Asher or not. He'd said the word before: accountability. She didn't like him pushing her. It took things out of her control, forced her to say things out loud that should be reserved for the mind. His knowing made the impact of the secret so much greater.

Asher punched the dial for the radio, let music drown out their burdened silence. Her head fell against the warm glass.

Cat City Pawn was just off the highway in a freestanding building with **GOLD, CASH, JEWELRY, GUNS, LOANS** painted in bright yellow on every available window. Its red roof glimmered in the sun while displaying an even bigger sign that read: **FAST CASH**. This place obviously believed in billboard-size advertisement.

Asher parked the car and stared at the brick structure. He looked completely out of place in his khakis and soft linen shirt. But then again, Katie doubted he'd ever seen the inside of a pawnshop before, let alone sought one out to find stolen goods.

She gripped the door handle, wanting to run from the responsibility that weighed on her for bringing him here. "We gonna stare at it or go in?"

He cut the engine and scowled like her old English teacher. "You get cranky when you're being defensive."

"I'm not defensive. You wanted to come. We're here. Let's get this over with."

She shifted to escape, but Asher's hand slid to the nape of her neck and gently pulled her across the car. His brown eyes met hers. "I'm not your enemy. And I'm not judging you." He closed in, kissed the tip of her nose and then her cheek. "I don't understand your old world or the choices you made. I probably never will, but that doesn't mean you have to hide them from me."

She closed her eyes. How did he do this to her, make her want to share every thought racing through her mind? "I'm just ashamed. And you being here makes it worse."

"Shame is a choice, Katie. It's not how I want you to feel or how God wants you to feel. You're here because you've changed. You're here to right a wrong. And I'm proud of you."

His words fell against her skin like summer breeze, and it hit her. She felt safe. Despite everything. Safe and warm and cared for. And it was the first time she'd felt that way since . . . since that night she'd prayed with Reverend Snow. She nodded, afraid if she tried to speak, that horrible sting in her throat would return. She had already cried a lifetime's worth of tears yesterday.

"Okay then. Let's do this thing." He let go after another quick kiss and opened his door.

Katie exited her side, trying to shake the jolt of emotion. "'Let's do this thing'? I swear, Asher, you could dialogue your own cheesy apocalypse movie. It's a store, not a gunfight."

He wrapped his arm around her shoulder and clicked the lock. "And your inner sunshine obviously needs more than two hours of sleep."

The bell chimed when they entered, Asher guiding her in before him. A gentleman always, even in the drabbest of circumstances.

A stout man with bushy hair above his ears and nowhere else came up from the back room. "Can I help you folks?"

"We're looking for a ring that was pawned about four years ago."

He scratched his bare chin. "Okay. We have some old inventory in that far right case if you want to take a look."

"Thank you."

They walked to the glass display case, and Katie scrutinized each ring available. Nothing. Not even one that could be close.

Her shoulders sagged, and Asher's strong hand squeezed the muscle by her neck in support. "You don't see it?"

She shook her head. On to the next unlikely option. "Sir? Do you happen to sell inventory online? I mean, if I could describe the ring to you, would you be able to track if it was sold?"

He tapped fingers on the glass. "Not me, but my wife probably could. Let me get her."

A lifetime seemed to pass while they waited, but finally an equally plump woman with long white hair came to the front of the store. "I apologize for the wait. I had a customer on the phone. Everyone wants distance sales these days." She was all business as she dropped a binder on the counter. "Do you have the dates we bought it?"

"Yes. Sometime around April twentieth, four years ago. It was a vintage emerald ring. Um, I believe it was an Edwardian ring?" Katie said, reciting the terminology she learned from the ring collector at the first pawnshop.

The owner flipped several pages, then ran a finger down two of them before stopping. "Bingo. Vintage emerald rose, April twenty-second." She slid her finger to the right. "Sold it two years later with four other pieces. Online sale via eBay."

Katie gripped the counter.

"Could we get an email or any information on the buyer?" Asher asked, not knowing what she already did. That they weren't allowed to disclose buyer information.

"I'm sorry, sir. In this business, that's a quick way to go under, if you know what I mean. Can you imagine what a jilted fiancé might do to get his ring back? Not pretty." She smashed the book shut. "I'm afraid once things leave our store, that's it. They're gone for good."

X

They sat in the parking lot, staring at the shop that had so quickly dashed their hopes. Asher wanted to fix it somehow. Find a loophole or a second chance.

"I could contact eBay. Tell them what happened, see if they could give us any information."

His offer was met with a fierce head shake.

"No. It's done. I always knew it was a long shot. I guess I just expected God to do a miracle, though I don't know why. I don't deserve one."

Asher felt helpless. He was a problem solver, a doer. Just sitting there while she suffered drove him crazy. "We can go back to my place, talk more if you need to."

Katie let out a hollow laugh. "I'm done talking. And I'm tired. I just want to go home, curl up in bed, and deal with this later." She turned in his direction. "Can you take me home, please?"

He wanted to hit the steering wheel. "You don't have to deal with this alone anymore."

"I know." She squeezed his hand. "Let's go out tomorrow, have our date that was interrupted. I just need a recovery day."

What she meant was that she needed time to sort all her emotions into tidy boxes so she wouldn't have to deal with them. Like before, when she'd managed to talk to him every day for months without once sharing this monumental burden. He started the car, trying his best to swallow his frustration. He didn't want that kind of relationship again. He didn't want pretense. He wanted to share in her hurts.

But pushing Katie didn't feel like the right answer either. He'd wait, give her the space she needed, and push later.

Brushing a finger against her cheek, Asher conceded. "Okay, tomorrow it is. But I get to choose the restaurant."

"Fine by me."

She shrugged like it was no big deal, but he knew better. Tomorrow they'd make their big debut as a couple, and this time, Asher wasn't letting anyone ruin it.

CHAPTER 36

Asher hopped up the steps of Katie's house, feeling more nervous than he had since prom. She'd finally let him pick her up, which made tonight feel more significant than all the other times combined. Funny that their first date would come after he'd already lost his heart, but he should've expected no less with her.

He knocked on the door and waited with hands deep in his jean pockets. Her parents were home, and part of him was optimistic, the other part, anxious. Her dad had begun returning Asher's waves, but they still came with a scowl. Katie was an adult. He didn't need their permission or blessing, but he wanted it. Maybe because he'd been raised to respect his elders, or maybe just because he knew they needed at least a few people on their side.

The door opened in front of him. Mr. Stone blocked the entry and then walked out, closing the door behind him. The man wasn't tall and had packed on extra pounds around the middle, but there was still an air of intimidation. It was one all fathers held when dealing with their daughters' suitors.

"I don't like this," he said, his voice gruff as he ran a hand through thinning hair.

At least the man didn't pretend. Asher could respect that.

"Katie's been, well, she's finally been somewhat stable. And it's been nice to have her home without all the drama and headache. But she doesn't deal well with chaos, and when things get out of control, she usually follows it up with something stupid and self-destructive."

"And you think I'm her next self-destructive thing?"

"I just can't figure out what a guy like you, from your upbringing, is doing with my daughter."

Asher's mouth tightened into a line.

"Now don't get me wrong, I'm not saying Katie isn't good enough for you. I'm just noting you're from two different worlds. And usually it's your world that has the biggest problem with someone like her."

"With all due respect, sir, my world has welcomed Katie with open arms. It's yours that's been so quick to judge."

Mr. Stone tugged on his neck and stared out into the front yard. "She's more fragile than you think. She just hides it better than others."

"I won't hurt her." There were few things in life Asher felt sure of, but this was one of them.

Her father chuckled. "I'm not worried about you hurting her. Katie will take you out at the knees long before you ever get that close. It's just, when Katie loses interest in the whole religion thing, I don't want to see you and your family run her out of town. Her being here has been . . . nice." He nodded a few times, as if deciding whether he had more to say, and then walked back into the house without so much as a glance at his guest.

Asher had planned to reassure her dad of his intentions, but was left feeling emasculated and unsure. Mr. Stone had actually laughed at the very idea that Katie would care enough to be hurt.

He pushed down the gnawing tumble in his gut. The same one he felt when she'd driven off without so much as a good-bye.

After a moment, the door clicked open and Katie stepped out, shutting it behind her.

Then they were looking at each other. He and Katie. Her face was cheerful, but only until he read her eyes. His gaze dipped to her soft, witty smile that could lie about every raging emotion she felt inside.

He took her apart, one piece at a time. Forehead, nose, cheekbones, chin. Those eyes, silvery blue like shards of glass under moonlight.

She touched his arm. "You okay?"

No, he wasn't okay. He was lost. Hooked. Completely at her mercy. And he had no idea if she'd even be around long enough for his feelings to matter.

He swallowed. "I'm good. Just had a little chat with your dad."

Her smile deepened. "No blood. It must have gone pretty well." She slipped her hand in his and pulled him toward his waiting car. She'd worn a dress tonight. Blue, with a slight ruffle on the bottom edge. It made her seem feminine and soft. Nothing like the lethal siren who had completely rocked his world. The one he'd barely just begun to rebuild.

He couldn't shake the insecurity. Couldn't shake the unease, even when they'd piled in the car and she'd rattled on about clearing half her mom's closet and the treasures she'd found there.

Because it was a lie. She'd just had her world blown apart, and she was acting as if the last few days hadn't happened. Trust wasn't just sharing secrets. It was sharing hurt, fears, and failures. And even though she'd given him her history, she'd yet to let him anywhere near her heart.

"You're quiet tonight," she said, when another five miles had passed without a word from him.

He considered what he wanted to do, which was demand more honesty from her. But he didn't want to be that guy who put her on edge, who backed her into a corner and forced her to lash out. He would simply show her. Show her what vulnerability looked like.

His fingers wrapped around hers and pulled her hand close enough for him to kiss the inside of her wrist. It trembled while her pulse raced against his lips. These moments reminded him why they worked. There was only so much she could hide when he was truly looking.

"Maybe I'm stunned silent by your beauty."

A rose color filled her cheeks and made him smile. He stopped and just stared at her for a split second as her eyes danced with genuine joy. This was Katie with her guard down. Katie without fear.

And those rare moments she gave him were enough to make him take the risk.

She fluttered her eyelashes, the pretense back with a fake southern drawl. "Am I pretty enough that you'll let me choose where we eat?"

"Not a chance. I've been craving Fiesta Grill all day."

She bristled at the name, her hand going slack in his. "That's right downtown."

"So?"

"It's Saturday night. The place is packed on Saturdays."

He knew that. It was part of why he'd chosen to eat there. He wasn't hiding the two of them. Not from anyone. "So it's a good thing I called ahead and got us on the wait list. We should be seated right away."

She turned away to stare out the window. They were close. Only two more stop signs and they'd be pulling up to the restaurant she feared so much.

"Did you go there a lot?" he asked, wanting her to turn back around so he could see how much truth came with her answer.

"Every weekend, practically." Her voice was quiet, reflective, and even a little sad.

"Since you've been back?"

"No."

"Why?"

He could see the flashing sign over Joe's and the crowd mingling outside the restaurant, and he pulled into the lot in front of the dollar store. She watched people through the windshield, her eyes round, her jaw tight.

"Are you worried he'll be here?" Asher didn't want to say Cooper's name. It was dirty and created an acid taste in his mouth.

"It's not about him," she said, more defensively than he liked. "It's about me. This side of me that I don't want to revisit. Why not go to a restaurant by the highway or take a drive out to the beach? I told you I wanted a break from the drama."

She was too far away for them to have this conversation. With a flick of his wrist, he turned the car off and jumped out. She didn't move, even when he opened her door and unlocked her seat belt.

She spun around in the seat, poised for a battle, but he pressed a finger to her lips. "A gentleman gets the door for his date." Hands tight on her waist, he pulled her closer until he was locked between her knees.

Her eyes could burn holes through him, they were so fierce. The little flecks seemed to flash. The tiny creases around the edges deepened. "What are you doing?"

He wouldn't give her a fight. Not when she used angry words to push people away. "I want the people in town to see us together," he said softly. "I want you to be you, no matter where we are."

She frowned, a deep slash forming between her eyebrows. "I don't even know who I am. Not totally. With you, it's different. It's safe and clean. Here it's messy and uncomfortable."

He tugged her hand, and even though she resisted, a step later she was out of the car and next to him.

"I like messy and uncomfortable." He shut her door and locked it, then wrapped an arm around her waist and kissed her temple. "Trust me to be a better man than you think I am."

She nuzzled her face against his chest, let him pull her into a deep embrace. "That's the problem. You're the best man I know."

Her lemon shampoo filled his nose as he ran his lips over the silky strands. "Only if you let me be."

CHAPTER 37

Every footfall made Katie cringe as they crossed the street to Fiesta Grill. Asher's arm was around her shoulders; hers was around his back. It should feel natural and exciting to walk that way with someone she cared about, but she had to force the contact. Had to force herself to go forward and not run back to his SUV.

It was evening, but summers in Georgia meant nightfall didn't come until after eight. They were exposed, completely visible to anyone in a quarter-mile radius.

The stares came quickly. Mostly from groups waiting outside or eating on the terrace. She scanned the parking lot again, just to be sure. No blue truck. No Cooper. Her relief was shallow. Dating Asher in public would be the last layer of salt she could apply to that wound, and Cooper was notoriously unpredictable.

Katie stopped outside the door, ran a hand over her arm. She recognized the group of three women taking a selfie with a phone. They'd see her in a minute, and she didn't want Asher standing right there. "I'll wait here while you check on the table."

"You sure? It should be ready."

She pushed him slightly toward the door. "I'm sure. I'll be right here."

He, thankfully, complied, squeezing her arm as he passed by. Katie turned away from the group, still hoping they hadn't spotted her. But turning brought a new wave of nausea. She was looking directly at Joe's Bar, looming only ten feet away. Through the open blinds, she could see faces from her past. Some had aged poorly; others were just barely old enough to be in there. A shadow passed the window, holding drinks on a tray. The blonde braid was unmistakable, and Katie's throat did that horrible stinging again.

She wondered how Laila was doing now that she knew the truth. Wondered why Cooper hadn't told her about the drugs years ago. Wondered where Chad was living and if she'd talked to him.

A hand touched her shoulder, and Katie practically jumped out of her skin.

"Sorry," Asher said, pulling her back to him. "I didn't mean to startle you. I said your name, but you didn't hear me."

She found a smile from the depths of her soul and tried to push back the moisture in her eyes. "They ready for us?"

"Twenty more minutes. You were right, this place is insane tonight." He glanced over to Joe's, having noticed, of course, that she'd been entranced. She didn't know whether she loved or hated that about him, how deeply he looked. It was unnerving.

The door to Joe's opened, and her heart stuttered. Joe hadn't aged a day. Faded jeans, old black T-shirt, white beard that just barely covered his chin, and knowing eyes that bore into hers. He had no purpose, just stood there watching, waiting for her to do something or say something. Finally, he shook his head and disappeared back where he came from.

Guilt festered within her. She should have waved, should have acknowledged him in some way. He'd been a loyal friend, a shoulder to cry on more times than she could count, and she had just stood there wishing she could erase the last twenty-six years.

Asher was talking to her again, but she heard only the last word. She should say something back, but it was too hard to speak. The stinging clawed at her. Ringing pierced her ears. "I need to go in there." The words came out a whisper, but they were the antidote she needed to get back under control.

He tensed. His eyes jumped to hers, then past her to the closed door of the bar. "Joe's?"

"Just for a little while. If you're uncomfortable, you can stay out here." She eased away, ready to do this on her own. But just as he had with the ring, Asher fell in step next to her.

"I'm fine. Let's go. They'll text when the table is ready anyway."

They only made it five feet before her palms began to sweat. She wiped them on her dress, but her anxiety only worsened. In the past, she never would have shown up there dressed this way. Guys would have hit on her, which would either tick her off or get Cooper into a fistfight. Both scenarios led to fiery showdowns between them later. But that had been their life: one argument after another. One battle either lost or won.

Asher laced his hand in hers. "You're trembling."

"I know. I'm terrified."

"Then why are we going in here?"

"Because I'm more terrified of what happens if I don't." She knew it didn't make any sense. Just like searching for the ring didn't make sense. There was a reason she worked so hard to compartmentalize. Because when faced with her demons, she always ran, and she didn't want to be that person anymore.

A blast of cold air hit her face when she pushed open the door. Smells that took her back in time bombarded her senses, as did the black laminate bar, dark-leathered barstools, and mismatched tables shoved everywhere to accommodate patrons.

Music drifted from corner speakers, and Katie couldn't stop the grin. It must have been Laila's night to choose. Acoustic, depressing alternative rock filled the room.

Joe walked in from the back and stopped short when he saw her and Asher standing right inside the doorway. His gaze slid to their joined hands, and while Katie tried to pull away, Asher tightened his grip. She hadn't planned to make a statement, but they'd done so all the same.

"Well, call me a chicken and fry me up. Our Katie has finally come home."

She'd expected sarcasm, disappointment, scowling. She didn't expect the warm bear hug he gave her or the kind way he shook Asher's hand. She didn't expect him to offer a round of drinks on the house or to compliment her.

But he did all those things, in perfect Joe fashion.

"Sit down. Sit down," he said, patting the bar. "Tell me all that you've been up to."

"I just came in to say hi really quick. We're waiting on a table."

"Well, you can wait here just as good as out there." He strolled behind the bar, grabbed two glasses. "Asher, what can I get you?"

"A Coke is good."

"Me too," Katie added after seeing Joe pull out the liquor bottles to make her favorite drink.

He raised an eyebrow but poured their soda without a word.

Asher acknowledged a group in the corner, and two of them shoved their glasses behind menus. He smirked, probably used to people reacting that way.

"Wanna go say hi? They're some guys from the gym I used to play basketball with," he said.

Joe wiped down the counter, watching her.

"No, you go ahead. I want to talk to Joe anyway."

She couldn't tell if it bothered him, but he didn't argue. He walked over to the table, long legs carrying him confidently across the bar as if tomorrow his name wouldn't be on the lips of everyone in town. She was good at making everyone believe she didn't care what they thought, but Asher truly didn't. It was inspiring.

Joe came back around the bar and sat, patting a stool next to him. "Come talk to me."

She did with trepidation, keeping an eye on Laila, who hadn't once acknowledged their presence.

"Interesting company," he said before Katie even settled. "I'd heard the rumors, but man, seeing it myself was just as shocking."

"Does it bother you, Asher being in here?"

"Me? No. Christians. Non-Christians. They all pretty much look the same around last call." A smile tugged at his bearded lip. "Now his church members, on the other hand, are all a little squirmy."

Katie laughed, remembering how she used to think the same, that all Christians did was notice and judge everyone's actions. But the truth was, she didn't have time to judge everyone else. She was too busy judging herself.

Laila slammed her tray on the bar a few feet from them and filled two glasses of draft. Mouth tight, eyes locked on her goal, she looked ready to implode at any moment.

They watched her until she disappeared back out on the floor.

"She'll come around," he said. "Laila can't stay mad at the people she cares about. We all know Chad exploited that virtue as much as he could when they were together."

"How is he?" Katie nursed an inch of her soft drink and avoided eye contact. If she looked at him, he would see how responsible she felt. He would see that Laila had every reason to hate her and probably would for the rest of their lives.

"Bad. He's been gone a while but still calls when he needs money."

Katie nodded, expecting no less. When Chad was sober, he was the kindest, funniest, most amazing man in the universe. Off the wagon, he was a manipulative train wreck.

"What about you? Seems a lot's happened since I saw you last. And don't bother lying to me. I can see right through you, and Cooper's already told me everything."

She wanted to slam her hand on the bar. "When?"

"Not long after you left. He got a tip that a friend had seen you up in Atlanta. He took off, even got put on probation at the factory. Two days later, he came in here, told me what went down, and never said a word about you again." Joe rubbed his chin, a motion he did only when he wasn't sure whether to spill or keep his mouth shut. The man had more dirt on people in Fairfield than anyone, but he rarely talked. "You messed him up pretty bad, kid."

"The damage was mutual."

His voice softened. "That's probably true. So Jacksonville, huh?"

"Yeah. Then Tallahassee."

"Who'd you stay with?"

"Friends. Strangers. Whoever would take me in. Sometimes I stayed in my car."

"You could have come to me. I would have helped you."

She met his eyes. "How?"

He didn't have an answer to give her, because there was none. Just like now. Her only chance for restitution had been smashed in the pages of that plastic blue binder. "I found the ring, but it was sold two years ago on eBay. I thought maybe, just maybe, if I could make one thing right, then all this pain I've caused would go away, or at least be lessened."

She'd spoken without thinking. She shouldn't be saying these things out loud. Not here. Not to Joe.

He exhaled. "It's just a ring, Katie. An object. Finding it, not finding it. Who cares? It doesn't change anything. But walking in here tonight, coming to see me after years in hiding. Now that's how you start to heal hurts."

Katie saw Asher approach and slid off the stool to meet him.

"Text says they're ready. Are you?"

She eyed Joe, who was still watching her with that thoughtful stare. The one that said she should stay and try to reconcile with the people she'd so callously left behind.

"I'm ready. Good to see you, Joe."

He stood, disappointed. "You too, Katie. Don't be a stranger anymore."

Asher said his good-byes, and they left the bar. Only fifteen minutes had passed, yet the sky was now darker, the mood between them altered. Once again her past had ruined what she wanted to build with him.

"Was that horrible for you?" she asked when he didn't say anything.

"It was interesting." He stopped, carefully watched her. "I won't lie. That place isn't somewhere I want to go on a regular basis. It's not me."

"I know that. It's not me anymore, either." She threw herself into him, wrapping her arms around his waist, burying her face in his chest. "Why am I so confused?"

His chin rested on her head and he squeezed her close. "Because you can't have a future until you accept the past. That doesn't mean you have to live the way you used to, but it does mean you can't deny what made you who you are. You made mistakes. Own them and move on."

"Okay." Her voice came out hoarse. "I'll tell Ms. Blanchard what happened. I'll tell her after church tomorrow."

Asher's hand cradled her face, his mouth touching hers with a softness reserved for only the most precious of moments. "And I'll be right there with you."

CHAPTER 38

Katie couldn't move. She could only sit and stare at the small white house she hadn't seen in years. A sad déjà vu flickered in the air. That night had been an avalanche of one bad choice after another. The regrets. There were so many. The ring, the fight with Cooper, the moment she handed kryptonite to her best friend.

She'd fled Chad's place disoriented, the high leaking out and taking with it her consciousness.

She hadn't awoken until after midnight, parked half on the driveway and half on Mary's manicured lawn. Katie had thrown up twice in the bushes before using her key to get into the house. She'd just wanted water and a toilet. She'd never once thought about the consequences of what she'd done.

Mary had been awake, frantically searching drawer after drawer.

I've lost it, she'd said. *Help me look, Katie. It was my mother's.*

Katie hadn't known, when she took the ring, that it meant so much. She thought it was costume junk, the ugliest thing in Mary's box of treasures. But it had been so much more, and as Mary told her about London and the bombings and how her mom slipped her wedding ring on young Mary's finger before she was shipped to America, Katie knew she could never face her employer again.

She'd quit. Right then, with no notice, with no visible remorse. She left Mary to her search, to scouring for a ring she knew would never be found. An hour later, Katie was on the road to Jacksonville with twenty unanswered calls on her cell phone and the knowledge that she had almost killed one best friend and ruined the other.

Oh, to be given one do-over in life.

"I can't do this," she whispered, her fingers tight around the steering wheel.

"Yes, you can," Asher said, rubbing at the rocks in her shoulders.

They'd gone to lunch at his parents' with at least fifteen other people. She couldn't eat. Not just because it was weird, uncomfortable, and way too crowded, but also because she'd told Asher she would come here and tell the truth. She'd made a promise she knew she couldn't keep.

"She'll hate me." That was only part of her hesitation. The other part, the deeper part, was that she couldn't offer more than an apology. She couldn't even give her hope that the ring might be found. Katie had stolen a piece of this woman's history, her past, her connection to her mother. "Sorry" was so inadequate; it was insulting.

"Probably." Asher's reply only made her sink further into the seat. "But that's her choice to make. Your choice is to face up to what you did. Consequences are part of that." He shifted uncomfortably in the passenger seat, and she wondered if he was thinking of Jillian and how after all this time, she still had never apologized for her lies.

Katie reached for the handle before she could talk herself out of going. She wanted his respect, and they could never move forward with this lie hanging between them. Asher deserved to be with someone who was brave.

"Do you want me to come?" he asked when she'd slipped one leg out of the car.

"No. Just don't go anywhere. I may need you to bail me out of jail." The words were offered teasingly, but they both knew an arrest was a real possibility. She didn't know the actual value of the ring but felt certain it exceeded the threshold for a misdemeanor charge. If Mary wanted to press charges, she could. The statute of limitations didn't apply if the theft was not reported.

She slammed the door shut. Her hands were shaking, her knees practically knocking as she walked the uneven sidewalk to the front door. Memories attacked her from all sides: Cooper standing behind a mower, running a towel over his head, winking at her and making comments about what he'd do to her later.

She'd actually thought they were compliments, the crude ways he talked to her. They meant she was attractive and sexy, but in truth, they only made her feel cheap, though she'd never realized it until Asher. He was the first one to treat her like a whole person, not just body parts that looked good in a short skirt.

Katie lifted her hand to knock, pushing back at the pressing thoughts. She needed to pray. Asher had even offered to do it with her. But she felt helpless to ask God to intervene. Why would He? She'd done this. She'd dug this terrible hole of deception. He had no reason to come to her rescue.

The door moved and Katie fought every instinct to run away. She thought of Slim and the way he'd held the ring between his fingers. He knew she was desperate, knew she'd take anything he offered.

Mary Blanchard appeared in the doorway, using her walker for support. A musty smell of neglect pulsed from the open foyer. "Katie?" She said the name with affection and surprise.

"Hi, Mary." They stood there, staring at each other. Mary was confused, Katie could tell that right away. She probably hadn't even known Katie had come back to Fairfield. "Do you have a minute to talk?"

The woman beamed as if having company was a luxury. And it probably was. She had no family left. Her husband had died ten years ago, and they'd lost their only son in a car accident when he was in his thirties. Hers was a life of tragedy, yet she was always faithful about going to church, every Sunday, arthritis or not.

"Come in, girlie. It's been what, years?" Her voice shook a little, as did her chin. She backed away slowly, carefully moving her walker around in the tight area.

"Yes, ma'am. Four years."

"You're still so pretty. Always thought that. So did that man of yours, if I recall."

Katie smiled. She always liked that about Mary. The woman didn't use much of a filter, but everything she'd say came out sounding sweet and funny because, well, she was barely five feet, with white hair and bright blue eyes.

She followed Mary into the living room, where the smell of sour chicken stock and urine was more fragrant than the plug-in fresheners put there to mask it. Indignation rose in Katie's chest. Her caretaker should be cleaning. It was part of the job, and Mary paid better than most.

"Do you have someone helping you still?" she asked while picking up the morning's newspaper from the couch.

"Oh yes. Lovely girl. She drives me to the beauty parlor and to church."

And obviously did nothing else.

Mary eased into her recliner, the one six inches higher than the rest of the furniture so she could get in and out without assistance. "I've wondered about you," she said after settling.

"I've wondered about you too. I'm sorry I left like I did. It was wrong." Katie pushed at invisible wrinkles in her dress.

"You were so upset." Mary's chin shook again as if remembering was zapping all her energy. "I didn't know what I'd done to make you so angry."

A lump crushed Katie's throat. She tried to swallow it, but it only pressed further, stinging her eyes with pain. "I was angry at myself. Not you. I'd done something terrible." She stopped when the first tear fell.

"Oh, darling, we all do terrible things."

She shouldn't cry. It was unfair to Mary. She deserved to be punished, not consoled.

"Not this," Katie whispered.

Her former employer watched her with misplaced compassion. She needed to just say it. Rip off the Band-Aid and face the horror of what she'd done.

"You didn't lose your mother's ring. I stole it. The day before I left. I stole it while you were napping. Then I sold it for drugs." She wanted to add that she didn't know its real value, but wouldn't let herself. It was an excuse to try and minimize the crime.

The air pulsed with silence. Mary hadn't reacted, or moved, even. Katie wiped her eyes, wrung her hands. She had no more words left that were any good.

Mary stared at the TV but didn't seem to be focused on it. "My mother gave it to me on the platform, right as the train was pulling up. She was crying because I think she knew she wouldn't survive the war. It didn't fit my finger, so she slid it on my thumb, told me to keep it close to my heart and she'd always be there." A tear slipped down her aged cheek. "I was going to give it to my son. But then the Lord took him too."

Breathing had become an afterthought, and the pain in Katie's chest was like an iron fist crushing her heart. She wanted to squeeze her eyes shut so she couldn't see the tears. Press her hands to her ears so she couldn't hear the heart-wrenching ache in Mary's voice. She'd done this. She'd caused this pain.

"I searched for that ring for months. Even hired movers to shift around furniture. I prayed a thousand prayers. Retraced my steps a thousand times. Until finally I came to the conclusion it had been thrown out somehow. That I had been so careless, I'd let it slip off the counter and into the wastebasket."

"I'm so sorry, Mary." *So empty. So little. So completely unworthy.* Katie hung her head, wanting to grab the phone and call the cops herself.

"After I came to America, my mom's cousin took me in. She was older and very devout. She'd encourage me to memorize scripture every week. Said we never knew when one day our freedoms would be taken away and we'd need His word in our hearts."

Katie didn't know how to respond. Didn't know if the trauma her confession inflicted had knocked Mary back in time, pulled her from her usual lucidity. But her former employer turned glassy eyes to her, and she knew the woman wasn't lost. Her words were intentional.

"'Therefore, as the elect of God, holy and beloved, put on tender mercies, kindness, humility, meekness, longsuffering; bearing with one another, and forgiving one another, if anyone has a complaint against another; even as Christ forgave you, so you also *must do.*'"

The silence lingered again, but a chill ran through Katie as vivid and real as if she'd been standing in snow.

"My heart is heavy with many feelings about what you did," Mary continued.

Katie could probably name them all. Disappointment. Betrayal. Confusion. Anger.

"But I'm not above God, and if He can forgive, so can I." She put out her hand, and it was the final snap to Katie's resolve. With sobs flowing deep in her chest, she knelt next to Mary's chair; held her wrinkled, cold hand; and cried like she never had before. The tender woman stroked her hair, making the sobs thicker, deeper. Katie had nothing to offer back to her, nothing but true remorse. Somehow that seemed to be enough.

When the sobs ceased and Katie could once again breathe without hiccups, she sat back on her heels. "I want to pay you for it. I know it's priceless and no amount of money could be enough, but I still want to give you something."

Mary watched her with an affection that made no sense considering the circumstances. "I don't want your money, but I would love your companionship. What if you came to work for me again? Three hours, three days a week. My young girl is sweet and gentle, but she's not much on conversation."

Katie laughed through her tears. Mary wanted her back? She would dare to trust her again?

"Does that work for you?" Mary's words held the gentle touch of a mother, and for the first time Katie truly understood the why the prodigal son fell to his knees and wept before his father.

"It's more than I ever hoped for." Mary had not only forgiven her, she'd invited her back into her life. Given her a second chance that would not be abused this time.

Katie stood, her body limp as if every ounce of energy had been poured onto the carpeted floor. She bit her lip, feeling as if she needed to say more before leaving. "If I could take it back, I would."

"I know, girlie. That's how sin is. We always want to take it back after it stings us." She smiled. "Would you mind bringing me my remote before you go?"

Katie walked to the end table, pulled out the DVR remote with instructions taped around every corner, and handed it to her.

"Does nine a.m. tomorrow sound okay?"

Katie squeezed her shoulder. "Absolutely."

CHAPTER 39

Mary had asked for her companionship, but after twenty minutes inside that house Katie insisted on cleaning, something Mary's new "caretaker" obviously didn't do. She started in the bathroom, scrubbing tile and grout and scraping lime from the shower door. It was gross, tedious, rough work, and yet Katie had never felt more alive. That hard, pressing burden was gone.

She dragged herself into her house on exhausted legs, wanting a shower so badly she could feel the water on her skin already. Her dad's truck was parked out front. Odd for a Monday, but then again, her parents' schedule had been unpredictable lately.

"Mom?" Katie peeked into her mom's makeshift bedroom and then the office. Both empty. She listened for the television or conversation. Silence.

The living room held nothing but some newspapers and a fat cat; the kitchen, only the unwashed breakfast dishes.

It was easily pushing ninety-five degrees outside, but Katie pulled open the back door anyway. With her walker, there were only so many places her mother could be, and a sick dread started to fester in her mind.

Her father's hunched back and a small stream of smoke brought immediate relief, even though seeing her dad puff on a cigarette still bothered her.

He must have heard the door and did a quick glance behind him. "Oh, Katie, you're home."

She sat down next to him. "I didn't see Mom."

He took an extra long drag, held it in, and blew out the smoke as though it brought a relief she couldn't understand. "She's at the hospital."

The dread came slamming back. "For more tests?"

Another drag. "That idiot cat knocked into her cane. She hit the wall first. Then the floor. She had her phone in her pocket and called me after she came to. Doc says she sprained her wrist pretty bad and has a concussion. They're going to keep her overnight."

Why wasn't she using the walker? Why hadn't they called her? Why wouldn't they move from this deathtrap of a house?

Katie clenched her hands, not saying any of those things out loud. Her dad would take them as criticism, and since he'd just lit up another cigarette two seconds after extinguishing the old one, she had a feeling he wasn't in a space to hear her opinions right now.

So she did something she never thought she'd ever have the courage to do. She wrapped her arms around her father and hugged him. "I love you, Dad. I'm so sorry you're having to go through this."

His cigarette hand dropped, his shoulders sagged, and then her gruff, closed-off hulk of a father cried. There was no sound. Just a dipped head and the tremble of his body.

She'd been so eager to see them move that she'd never stopped to think about what doing so meant. It meant the end of their dreams. It meant accepting that this disease would rob them of their life together. It meant questioning their mortality, and Katie knew those thoughts were void of any hope without Christ. She'd been there, living among them, and never once considered how much they were hurting too.

She lay her head on his shoulder. "We'll get through this. You, me, and Mom. You'll see."

His hand touched hers and stayed there, holding on, sharing the load until he regained his composure. He smashed the second cigarette and stood. "I'm gonna pack some things and head back up there."

"If you wait until I shower, I'll ride with you."

Her dad rubbed the back of his neck, his mouth set in a line that told her she wasn't going to like his answer. "Let's just let her sleep, and maybe you can come up tomorrow."

Katie took a breath, released it slowly. "Is she really still that angry at me?"

Hating confrontation the way he did, her dad walked toward the back door and swung open the screen.

She followed him. "Dad, I need us to talk about this. I want to fix things."

"There's nothing to fix, Katie. Stay here and I'll call when it's a good time to come."

"It's never a good time."

Her dad pressed two fingers to his temples. "I don't want to fight with you."

"I don't either. Heck, I don't even know what we're fighting about. I just want to go with you so I can see Mom."

"Fine." He dropped his hands and let out a furious sigh, as though she'd cornered him. "You can't go with me 'cause Cooper's there. He stayed while I came here to pick up some clothes. We were on a job, and the boy dropped everything to come help me. I know you two are circling the ring right now, and I won't have that in your mother's condition."

Katie pushed away the hurt. She'd wanted this, had chosen to cut people out of her life. She'd just never expected them to linger in the shadows.

"Don't look at me like that," her dad said.

"Like what?"

"Like I slapped you."

She examined her knees, which still ached from scrubbing Mary's floors.

"This isn't to hurt you. He's a decent kid, and he's been like family to us these last couple of years."

Unlike her. "Okay."

Silence stretched between them until her dad fidgeted under the weight. She knew what would happen next. He'd mumble something about time and hurry away before the tension suffocated them both. She backed away, giving him the out he obviously wanted.

"Listen. I was thinking about what you said. I think I'd like to talk to this Realtor myself."

Katie froze, searched her father's face for sarcasm. "You're going to sell?"

He ran a hand over the faded paint on the wall. "I said I'd talk to him."

In other words, *don't push*. Her father didn't rush. Not in life and especially not in decision-making. But the mere fact that he was even willing to have a conversation unraveled the knots in Katie's shoulders. She'd found peace with Mary. And now her parents were one step closer to getting safe and settled. Her two biggest goals were right in front of her, close enough to grab and tuck into the finished pile.

His fingers stopped when they hit chipping paint. "This place is going to need some serious work."

"We'll manage."

"I'll get some guys from work to come out. It will go quicker."

He said guys, but they both knew he meant Cooper.

"There's that face again."

"Sorry. I just wish it didn't have to be him, you know. There are other people who can help us." Asher, for one.

"It's going to level out. You'll see. Eventually the pain will disappear and you and Cooper can find a middle ground. Took me and my ex-wife ten years, but it happens." He patted her arm. "Go find that business card."

Katie watched her dad ascend their stairs, a deep sense of unrest unfolding within her.

He's a decent kid. He's been like family. You'll find a middle ground.

She couldn't think that way. Couldn't feel that way. Cooper had to stay the enemy.

𝕏

Her dad spent most of the afternoon at the hospital while Katie used her nervous energy to finish another set of shelves in the walk-in master closet. She checked the eBay sales, packaged up boxes, and made a list of what still needed to be sorted and organized. Then she made a list of everything that needed maintenance or repair.

Three pages. Well, at least it wasn't four.

A knock at the door sent her rushing in that direction, so ready to see the one person who could make all her tension go away.

"You said bring tools." Asher held up a duffel bag and sported a bright smile that was like sunbeams through dark, ugly rain clouds.

She palmed his face and kissed him, quickly and lightly, before stepping back. "You're my hero."

He dropped the bag, gathered her close with his solid arms, and made it clear a hero deserved a far better greeting. She didn't mind. She felt stronger in his arms, as though he could transfer all his goodness just by touching her. Protect her from the doubt in her mind and the gnawing conscience that'd worked its way into the recesses of her heart.

"Much better," he muttered against her lips.

She eased away, her pages of chores held tightly in her hand. "I made a list," she said, handing it to him.

His gaze brushed over the words, his hands flipping through pages. "You want this done today?"

"What? No. Just the stuff I starred. It's in the master bathroom. Dad would feel weird if he knew you were in there."

Asher dropped his arms, the pages skittering against his work jeans. "I think he's going to figure it out when he comes home and his toilet and sink no longer leak."

"Yeah, but it will be done, so who cares?"

His eyes swept over her face, her trembling hands, and the nervous way she kept shifting her weight from one foot to the other. "So, how long will your mom be in the hospital?"

"Just overnight, I think."

He picked up the tool bag, followed her to the stairs. "You didn't want to go?"

Yes. Desperately. "No. Mom doesn't do well when she feels helpless."

"A family trait, huh?" Warmth enveloped her hand and stopped her ascent. He touched her cheek, seeing inside her the way no one had ever tried to before. "Don't take it personally. People are sometimes the meanest when they don't want to need you but do."

She knew he was talking about her mother, but the little voice kept screeching.

You messed him up pretty bad, kid.

Cooper's only loved two people in his life. You and Chad. In one night he lost both of you.

No! She had to make it stop. That horrible pressing guilt was back, seizing her.

"Hey." Asher's hand tightened, pulling her from the words knocking around in her head. "You're obviously upset. Let's just put this 'honey-do' list in a drawer, pick up some flowers, and go. Trust me, I'm a pro at hospital visits. My dad used to take me all the time."

She sighed, wishing life could be that simple. "I'll go tomorrow. Tonight, I just need to check things off my list."

CHAPTER 40

There were no more secrets to uncover, yet Asher couldn't stifle his unease. He told himself he was inviting trouble by prying. That Katie's increased distance over the last two weeks had everything to do with the sale of the house and nothing to do with her pulling away from him.

Yet this was their first date since the restaurant, and she'd been staring silently at the pond for the last five minutes.

He took her hand, suddenly needing contact, and squeezed. She met his eyes, offered the same apologetic smile he'd seen since they'd walked out there. The one that said she knew she was being too quiet.

"I finished the house yesterday. The attic and shed are all that's left. I'm still in awe. Although now we can see just how run-down every room is."

"I thought Wade already had buyers."

"Oh, he does, but Dad wants top dollar. Says a little sweat will go a long way. I think the number range haunts him in his sleep."

"I can help, you know. I have plenty of vacation time. Let me take a week and come be your slave."

When she didn't respond, he looked at her, the way the sun was dropping in the sky at her back, the way her eyes stayed warm and soft on his. The worry returned. She had yet to talk about her plans for after the house sold.

She squeezed his hand tighter. "If it were up to me, I promise you'd be over there every day. But my dad is funny about trust. And honestly, I'm tired of fighting with him about it."

"I didn't realize it had become an argument."

She shrugged. "It is what it is."

He scooted in closer and tucked her between his legs, her back against his stomach. She melted against him and pulled his arms tighter around her. Her hair was freshly washed and smelled like lemons and honey. The scent drew him in closer. He wanted that smell forever, wanted moment after moment with her in this spot watching the water ripple in the breeze.

"Have you decided what you're going to do after the house sells?"

"No, but I still have time to figure all that out."

Nature squawked around them: insects buzzed, a frog croaked from the mud, two birds sang a melody back and forth.

He loved every sound. "You know, I never thought I'd be this happy again. And then you pulled in next door with your hundred-pound bag and made everything better. I want you to stay, Katie. Next door or not, I'm not ready to stop being with you." It was so much less than he wanted to say. He wanted to tell her he'd fallen in love with her. Fully, completely, and in a way that was unlike anything he'd felt before. Even with Jillian. They'd been perfectly matched on the outside, yet his soul had never felt this kind of peace. Not with her.

He waited for Katie to say something beyond the kiss to his hand and the sigh that made the hair stand up on the back of his neck. He knew what it felt like to be pushed. To be forced into a commitment he wasn't ready for. And he didn't want to do the same to her. Yet twice now, he'd shown his hand. He'd said *I love you* in every possible way but one.

"I wish I could read your mind right now," he said, stuffing down his frustration.

"I'm not so sure you'd like what you found in there."

"Try me."

"Do you ever stop to wonder if people are inherently bad? Or if selfishness ever really goes away?"

Asher searched for the right words. She'd told him her past. It was dark and ugly. But what he'd failed to get her to see was that *she* wasn't. Not anymore.

"I believe all of us are rotten, which is why we need Christ."

"But you were hurt by Christians. They lied. They put their own interests above your pain. They disappointed you enough to drive you from the church. So how do you know if you can really trust people when even those who try fail you?"

"You don't, I guess."

She went back to her quiet brooding, and the rigid muscles in her back said he'd somehow missed it: her question inside a question. He filtered back through the conversation, searching for the deeper meaning.

"Are you afraid of getting hurt?" Asher asked.

She unwrapped herself from his arms and spun around so they were facing each other. "No, I'm afraid of hurting you." There was a desperation in the way she said it, like she had no control over her actions. It irritated him. They were beating this horse to a slow, painful death.

"I thought we were past this. I've told you I don't care about who you used to be. I see you now, that's it."

"But what if people never really change? All this time, I've felt like a victim of circumstance. I've rationalized it a million ways. If Cooper hadn't found me the job at Mary's, then I never would have stolen the ring. If Cooper hadn't yelled at me that night or had just let us stay at the club, then I never would have gone to Chad's. If Cooper had just remembered there were spare keys in the bedroom, then maybe Chad would never have taken that nearly fatal hit. But what I never let myself see, until now, is that *I* made all those choices. I did."

"And you've apologized for them. Multiple times." Her cycle was continuing, that horrible march from regret to self-loathing to self-doubt. She still couldn't grasp that she'd been forgiven. "Katie, at some point, you're going to have to forgive yourself too."

"I just wanted him to be the bad guy. And here he is, helping my parents. He stood by Laila when Chad left. Kept my secret for years, and probably would have for longer if I hadn't come back." She paused, her eyes focusing on a spot behind him. "He went after me when I left. I never knew. I truly thought he'd be relieved to see me go."

A stabbing pain hit Asher in the chest, and for a span of a few seconds, he felt an ache that went past his bones to a place unseen and unfixable. "Are you still in love with him?"

Her eyes returned to his, with a flicker of surprise. "No."

His stomach settled and he exhaled deeply, only then realizing he'd been holding his breath. "Okay. Good."

Lines deepened around her mouth. "No. It's not good. It's what makes me so much more rotten. I've never been in love with anyone. I try to be. I pretend like I am. But there's always an escape plan, an out if I need it. That day I left, it was the easiest decision I ever made."

Fear rocked into him. He'd finally heard her. He'd brought her out here to declare his love, his intentions, his hopes and dreams for their future. And she couldn't even get her mind around the idea of caring about someone on a deeper level.

"You had a chance to leave a few weeks back and you didn't," he reminded her.

She studied her hands. "I know. I still can't figure out why."

Though she hadn't stopped frowning, relief edged out the doubts that had clouded his mind for a few moments. He touched her chin, tilted it up.

"My dad would say that people never fully understand love until they experience grace. You may be surprised by the decisions you're capable of making now. Surprised even more by what you can feel."

"Guilt. That seems to be my default emotion." She allowed him to gather her close. Allowed him a moment of full clarity as he attempted to kiss away her shame.

Her lips lingered on his, her voice not much more than a raspy moan. "You're so good. If I hurt you, I couldn't stand it."

"You're not the only tough one, Katie. I'm not naïve. If I wanted easy, I could have it. I want you. The old. The new. All of it."

Finally a smile came through the storms that had lingered on her face all afternoon. She shifted closer, straddled his lap, and ran soft fingers through the hair above his ear. "Are you saying I'm difficult?"

"I'm saying you're worth it." He kissed her then, and not the careful caress of before. This one was more demanding, dangerous. One where bodies collided and hands explored. One that would escalate into the shedding of clothes if he wasn't so determined to keep them from becoming too physical.

He gripped her waist and pushed, the act of stopping almost as painful as a punch in the gut. His eyes locked on to her. "Tell me you're going to stay."

She planted a kiss on the sensitive skin beneath his earlobe and whispered, "I'll consider it," before dismounting from his lap.

He used the much-needed pause to get himself back under control.

She stretched out her legs. "There's an apartment coming available in the Commons. My dad brought me an application."

"And you're just now telling me?"

She shrugged. "You're hot when you get a little demanding."

Yes, this girl was the opposite of easy. She was also everything he wanted, down to the crinkle on her nose as she brushed a centipede off their blanket.

He tackled her, pinned her with tickling fingers that made her snort through her nose and howl at him to stop. He'd wait. Tell her he loved her at a better time. When she wasn't too afraid to hear it, and more importantly, when she had forgiven herself enough to believe him.

CHAPTER 41

Katie hugged the cardboard box and stared at the black door leading into Joe's. Her two previous attempts had failed. The first time she'd come, Laila wasn't working. The second time, Katie had chickened out. This time she had nowhere to run. Cooper was at her house; his truck had pulled in just as her car drove away. She'd been anticipating his arrival for weeks, but somehow seeing his truck made her stomach ache.

The rage had been easier to deal with than this new compassion. Her lingering bitterness had allowed her to forget the times when he'd been sincere, even vulnerable with her. Allowed her to brush aside his horrible past and how he'd spent most of his childhood abandoned and rejected. It allowed her to forget the gritty emotion in his voice when he'd called her his family.

She shook her head as if it would reset her memory, and adjusted the box so she could pull open the door.

The lights were dim compared to the blazing summer sun, and it took Katie a moment to register Laila behind the bar, wiping and stacking glasses.

"We don't open until five," Laila said, absently but with just enough heat to let Katie know she'd seen her.

"I was hoping you'd have a minute."

The box was heavy in her arms. Full of more than just childhood memories, it represented a chapter closing in her life. A final good-bye to the past.

Katie set the container on the bar and took the stool directly in front of her old best friend. "I cleaned out the attic this week. Mom had put some things up there that belonged to you."

Laila still hadn't made eye contact. She finished drying a tumbler and set it on a shelf underneath a row of liquor bottles. Her eyes were puffy and red like she'd spent most the night crying. She'd never been good at hiding emotion. Her skin was too pale, her eyes too light, her heart too fragile. Unlike Katie, when Laila felt anything, she felt everything.

"So, you're still here," Laila finally said, lifting a flap of the cardboard.

"You told me to be different."

Laila rolled her eyes. "You've never listened to me before."

"Well, I should have. You were the only who warned me I looked like a green lizard in my formal gown, and I'll be haunted by those pictures forever."

"That's still the ugliest dress I've ever seen in my life." Laila's lip lifted and then fell back into a frown as if she'd caught herself smiling and wouldn't allow it.

The motion sapped the humor back out of the room, and a heavy silence took its place.

Laila opened the final flap and pulled out a tiny red bear with a pacifier in its mouth. There was no stopping the smile this time. "You found Binky?" Her eyes lifted, making contact with Katie's for the first time, and both girls just stared.

"Mom found him behind my old TV a few months after I left. She was clearing out my room—partially to hurt me, I think—but, thankfully, packed most of it up."

Laila tucked the bear into the corner of her left arm and rummaged through the box again. Out came their senior yearbook, the vase that held the first flowers Chad ever sent her, the friendship necklaces they'd both worn for years, and a framed eight-by-ten photo of her and Chad at the beach on their wedding day.

"How do you have all this?" she whispered, her eyes swelling again.

Katie swallowed. "You brought it over the first time you left him." It'd been the slap Chad needed to get sober. His sobriety had lasted six months. The second time Laila left, it lasted until the night Katie knocked on their door, high and desperate.

Laila set the wedding photo back in the box.

"Will you tell me what happened?" Katie knew she had no right to ask. If she'd stayed in town, she'd have known the outcome.

"Why do you care?"

Was it always going to be like this? Katie begging everyone to believe that she actually had a soul now? "Because I do. I loved Chad too. He was like my brother." She didn't need to explain that to Laila. They'd all been family.

"Well, you suck as a sister."

Katie's back tensed and she pushed down the fire in her gut. "I still care. Please, Laila, tell me what happened."

Laila crossed her arms and stared up at the ceiling. The gesture made the tip of her braid touch her lower back and reminded Katie of when they used to stand in the rain and try to catch water droplets in their mouths. Years of memories existed between them, and despite Katie's attempt to forget, they were woven into every inch of her heart.

Laila walked back to the box. "After he was released from the hospital, he only lasted a week before finding a source. But the cops were watching him, and they busted him during the exchange. He got probation and community service, but it cost him his job. Then school, 'cause he quit trying."

She picked up the necklace, brushed her thumb over the etched *Best Friends* in the silver.

"I left him two more times before accepting that he was never going to change. Not permanently. The drugs held too much power over him. This last time he used, I packed up his stuff and changed the locks. Cooper was the only thing that kept him from busting down the door. Chad took off for Atlanta after that, and I filed for divorce."

Katie's stomach rolled. "Did he sign the papers?" Even when he was strung out, she couldn't fathom Chad agreeing to let Laila go.

"No. But in Georgia, it doesn't matter if he consents or not. The divorce was final last winter."

Divorced. She couldn't get her mind around it. Laila and Chad had been in love since the third grade. They'd been each other's first everything. Theirs was the fairy tale that transcended logical thought. It was how Katie knew she'd never been in love. They had always been her standard.

Laila leaned a hip against the counter, still rolling the chain between her fingers. "When Cooper finally told me the truth, I was so furious. First at you, then at him for waiting four years to tell me. I'd just started speaking to him again that night we went to your house. I didn't know we were ambushing you, by the way. Another secret he'd kept from me."

"He knew it would hurt me more if you were there."

Laila sighed. "Maybe, but I think it runs deeper for him."

Silence drove into the space between them again. It gnawed at Katie, worked its way under her skin. She stood, leaned over to peer into the box. "There's more in here. A few of your shirts, two pairs of shoes, a jacket—"

Laila slammed a hand on the counter. "I don't care about any of that stuff."

Katie went still. Laila had never been aggressive. She was meek and relentlessly forgiving. "Sorry."

"I don't want your apology."

Katie wrapped a fist around the keys in her pocket. "I'll leave, then." She hadn't come here to upset Laila.

"I don't want that either." Laila paced behind the counter, fingering the end of her braid while she walked.

"What *do* you want?" Katie couldn't stifle the anticipation in her voice. The distant hope that Laila, like Mary, would find a way to forgive.

"I want to stop feeling so angry all the time. At you. At Chad. But most of all, I just want this nagging spark of hope to go away. The one that says 'If Katie got clean, if Katie came home, then maybe Chad will too.'" A tear slipped down her cheek, and her voice cracked. "'Cause I can't live with that hope anymore. It hurts too much."

"Laila." Katie moved toward her friend on instinct.

Laila backed away. "Don't." One hand wiped away the tears while the other hugged her stomach.

It was the deepest form of rejection, being told she wasn't allowed to share in her friend's pain. So Katie stood there and waited for Laila to calm. Waited for her to wipe her cheeks and put on a brave face that she had never worn with Katie.

"So you brought me shoes, huh?" Laila asked, returning to the box. "I really hope they're the cute peep-toe beige heels I lost."

Katie reached in, pushed aside the stack of folded clothes, and revealed hideous clogs. "Sorry, my mom chose to save these instead. We should burn them with my green dress."

A laugh burst from Laila's throat as she grabbed the bright yellow shoes. "I totally forgot about my primary color phase. I had red and blue too."

Katie pulled the blue pair from the box, and Laila almost squealed in delight.

"I didn't find the red pair, but I'm guessing they never made it back from the beach blowout our senior year." She smiled, and Laila smiled back. It was soft and genuine, and for the first time since she'd crossed the Fairfield city line, Katie felt as if her heart might become whole again.

The door burst open. "Hey, Laila, I need Joe's cordless drill. Mine can't get—" Cooper froze when he saw the two of them standing there, each holding a pair of bright, ugly clogs.

It was as if time stopped and reversed but messed up everything in the process. The three of them had spent hours together at Joe's, laughing, teasing, planning their next big party. But there was no humor or camaraderie now, only a stifling tension that threatened to detonate at any moment.

CHAPTER 42

L aila threw the shoes down as if merely holding them had been a betrayal. "I'll grab his toolbox." Her voice was quick and apologetic, and she and Cooper exchanged a look that reminded Katie she was no longer a part of their group.

Cooper watched her with those stormy, angry eyes of his. He wore faded work jeans and a T-shirt with two holes in the sleeve. He crossed his arms, making every inch of him appear tense and locked up.

This was usually when Katie would flee, or when she'd throw a defensive comment at him to try to make the prickling against her skin go away. But this time she didn't turn away. She met his eyes and set down the shoes. "Hey." It came out soft, and could even have been interpreted as happy to see him.

A simple olive branch, but the impact on him tore at her insides. For a quick second, the wall crumbled, and Katie saw what her conscience had been screaming at her since the gas station. Before her stood a broken, bitter man. He wasn't her enemy. He was hurting. He'd spent his life being rejected, and she had basically done the same thing.

She took a step closer. "Thank you for helping my dad."

"I'm not doing it for you." Cooper backed up a step and put his hand on the doorknob. An escape from her, it seemed. He'd been so forceful before, so determined to push through her shields, that his retreat made no sense. Except his face had gone slightly pale and his breathing was more shallow than when he'd entered.

"I know."

"Do you?"

Laila returned carrying a heavy metal toolbox. Cooper met her halfway, took it from her limp hold, and whispered something in her ear. He didn't bother with another glance at Katie before storming back out of the bar.

Whatever ground Katie had made with her old friend was lost with the slam of the door. Laila furiously started loading the box back up while Katie watched, having no idea what to do or say.

"Four years he waited to come through that door and see you standing there. Four years." Laila picked up the box in a swift motion and dropped it behind the counter. "And just now I saw it on his face. That split second when he thought you were back." She gripped the bar with both hands. "But you're not back, Katie, are you? This walk down memory lane isn't to restore the past, is it? It's the final breakup."

Katie closed her eyes and prayed for the exact right words. "Yes, in a way, it's the final good-bye to the girl who left four years ago. But it's also a new chance for the girl who came home. Laila, I know our friendship will never be what it was, but I really do want to build something new. You've changed. I've changed. Who knows what that looks like now?"

Laila went back to wiping glasses. "I haven't forgiven you."

"Okay." The truth hurt, but it was fair. Katie pulled her keys from her pocket and inched toward the door.

"Wait." Laila made a defeated sound. Looked away from her. "Maybe with a little more time, I might get there."

Katie's throat burned, a sensation that had become far too familiar. "Thank you."

Laila didn't wait to see her cry. She simply abandoned her row of spotted glassware and disappeared to the back.

Time. It meant staying. It meant proving she'd really changed. It meant being a better person far longer than just for a season. And strangely, Katie felt up to the task.

The sunlight burned her stinging eyes when she exited Joe's, but her lungs felt ready to burst. This was what Asher had been saying all this time. Feeling something hurt, but it also felt so amazingly real. The rush of emotion was staggering. She wanted to laugh and cry. She wanted to run to Asher, throw her arms around him, and thank him for opening her eyes. For showing her a world that didn't have to be gray, but alive with color and light.

She walked toward her car, and another flash of color halted her steps. Cooper's bright blue truck, the one she'd picked out down to the color of the leather, remained unmoving. He was leaning against the bed, head down, hands deep in his pockets. His profile exposed slumped shoulders, and periodically he'd kick a loose piece of gravel.

He must have sensed her approach, because every muscle in his body went taut. "I won't do this here," he said to his shoes. "If you've got something to say to me, we do it on my terms this time."

Her mind warred with her instincts. She and Cooper had never been civil. Even when they were together, their relationship held a certain simmering hostility, because neither was capable of being the salvation they both craved. She'd fail him. He'd fail her. That was the cycle.

"I won't go to The Point." The space was too tight there. Too crowded. It would be too easy to get sucked into the vortex of the past.

He kicked another patch of gravel, more aggressively this time. She knew him well, even after years apart. The Point had always been their spot. A place to forgive and to pretend that, for a moment, they were happy together. But it never lasted.

He straightened and turned, rested his forearm against the passenger window. "You afraid I'll make you forget about your new boy toy?" His voice was low and deceptively easygoing. But Katie recognized the flash of annoyance, the jealousy in the bite in his words.

She could spout back how Asher was more than some random guy. He'd become her best friend, her greatest ally, and the only person she completely trusted. He'd shown her what healthy looked like.

But Cooper wasn't interested in hearing any of that. He just wanted to make her feel small, the way she'd made him feel by not coming back to him.

"I just wanted to say I'm sorry."

He pushed off the truck sharply. "I told you I'm not doing this here."

She didn't retreat when he approached her, his eyes as fierce as a lion's.

"Where, then?" Because she wanted this done. Over. She wanted to move on and not have to fear seeing his blue truck around town, or in her parents' driveway, or at the store. She was done hiding. Done pretending.

"Our place." His choice of words was as calculated as their delivery. Cooper's house had never been Katie's, not officially. But she'd picked out the furniture, the window coverings, and the bedding. She'd been right there next to him when, with one signature, he'd gone from renter to owner.

She rolled through the potential consequences. They'd be secluded. If Cooper lost his temper again, she'd have very little hope of escape or help. But the list of benefits was longer. No one in town would talk about their argument, they could make peace, and maybe this final apology would be the key to being free of that horrible night. Besides, Katie wasn't weak. She knew how to defend herself, and she'd taken down men bigger than Cooper.

She had to make a choice: run or face her past. And she was done running.

"Fine," she said.

She hated that his eyebrow rose and his mouth twitched up as if she had just handed him the white flag. This wasn't a surrender. It was a means to an end.

He stepped backward without turning around, opened the passenger door, and gestured for her to get in.

She didn't move. "I'll meet you there."

"You sure? Last time we had a date, I waited for an hour."

"I never said I'd come last time. And this isn't a date."

He slammed the door and dipped his chin. There was a dare in his eyes that brought that old fight-or-flight feeling to the surface. The challenge that had pushed her to prove to the world that she was untouchable, uncaring, and unshaken.

Katie forced her shoulders to relax. She wouldn't slip into old patterns. Not with him. Not anymore.

One apology, and she'd be done with him for good.

CHAPTER 43

Asher studied the pile of crushed tile in his bathroom and wondered if he'd finally taken on a job too big for him. Powdery grout stuck to his clothes, his hair, his old work boots. It made the air a puff of dust that would have sent him hacking if not for the surgical mask he wore.

He swung his mallet again, and more tile fell from the wall. He needed a distraction and a physical outlet. Or at least something that would take the edge off the fact that Cooper was next door, helping Katie's father, worming his way back into her life.

The mallet made another shattering impact. She actually felt guilty over that guy. After all he did to her and said to her, she still cared that she'd hurt him. Well, if there was any doubt Katie was different, this pretty much confirmed it. He just wished he could beat away that tiny voice that said *nice guys always finish last*.

He brushed his forearm against his head, wiping away sweat. Only one wall to go. He raised his arms, but stopped when he heard what sounded like a faint knock. He strained to listen and heard the sound again, louder this time.

A smile cut his earlier scowl. Katie.

He threw down his tools, tossed his mask, and headed toward the front door, cringing as white residue left a trail through his house.

But the person behind the door wasn't his pretty girlfriend. It was her father.

"Mr. Stone? Is everything okay?" In two years, the man had never set foot on Asher's property, let alone ventured to actually knock on his door.

Katie's father tugged on his neck. "Yeah, it's fine. Um, listen, Cooper had to run and get a new drill, but that was over thirty minutes ago, and he's not answering his phone. Maureen, well, she's pretty sensitive to the heat, and with the AC shut down, it's getting pretty hot in the house."

"You need a drill?" Asher had two of them.

"Actually, well, I was wondering, do you happen to know anything about condensers? Katie said you fixed her car and could do just about anything. Cooper was almost finished; he just needed . . ." His eyebrows pinched together as he took in the sight of Asher covered in demolition dust. "Oh well, never mind. You're busy."

"Not at all. I'll grab my bag and be right over." Asher's smile didn't begin to express the elation welling in his chest. Mr. Stone coming to him was huge. More than huge. It was an acknowledgment that he and Katie were together.

"You sure? I don't want to put you out or anything."

"It's not putting me out at all." The firm conviction in his voice was enough to make Mr. Stone stop twitching and finally nod.

"Well, okay then."

In less than a minute, Asher had grabbed his tools and closed the front door. They descended the steps together, two men who just months ago barely exchanged hellos.

"So, I never thanked you for fixing the front steps," Mr. Stone said as they began walking.

Asher could hear the awkwardness in his tone. Katie had said her dad was a prideful man. He hated needing help, and hated even more that his wife's disease had forced him to rely on people.

"That's what neighbors are for. I have no doubt you'd do the same if I needed something."

Her dad nodded. "Yeah, I guess. Although there doesn't seem to be much you can't do. That kitchen out back is quite a sight."

"Thank you. It was fun to build."

"So, where did you learn how to do all this stuff?" His tone was becoming less forced, more relaxed.

"My dad isn't much of a handyman, so if we needed help, people from the church would come over and fix things for him. I paid attention, asking questions. When I was sixteen, I started working summers with different contractors, learning all the different trades. Carpentry is still my favorite."

"But you do computer stuff for a living?"

Asher rejoiced internally. Katie had been talking about him to her parents. Better still, her father had actually been listening.

"I guess I like to sweat on my own terms."

The man chuckled. "Yeah. I can't say I blame you."

They rounded the side of the house, where the air conditioning unit sat in disarray. Asher dropped his bag and inspected the work Cooper had already finished. It wasn't bad. He'd have done it slightly differently, but overall, the install was semiprofessional.

"I should be able to get this up and running in the next twenty minutes. If you want to take Mrs. Stone somewhere and get her out of the house until it cools, feel free."

Mr. Stone scratched his head and glanced toward the driveway. "Well, if Cooper comes back, I don't want things to get uncomfortable."

"We're grown men. We can be civil."

"I suppose that's true. At least I know you can be." Her dad pushed his hands into faded pockets. "I know I haven't exactly been the friendliest person."

"Trust takes time, Mr. Stone. I get that."

"It's Hank, by the way." The side of his mouth lifted in what Asher could assume was the closest thing to a smile he'd get from the man. "Maureen and I will pick up some ice cream while we're out. You have a certain type you like?"

The subtle invitation was more than a polite gesture. It was an invitation into their lives. "Anything with chocolate works for me."

Hank nodded. "Chocolate it is. I guess I'll pick up some strawberry for Katiebug as well."

His girl liked strawberry. Asher would have to catalogue that for later. Right now, he had a job to do.

CHAPTER 44

Katie took the long way to Cooper's house, the one that went around the park and passed by Fairfield Fellowship. She wasn't sure why she felt the need to drive past the building, but seeing it did give her a renewed sense of purpose. This would be closure. An end to a very dark chapter in her life.

She shut her car door and managed to take only a few steps before her hands began to tremble. Her stomach ached and her heart pounded against her rib cage so hard it hurt.

It was only a house: one story, with beige siding, a bright red door, and two hanging plants that Cooper had somehow managed to keep alive. Yet, as the door swung open and Cooper stood there, one arm holding the screen ajar, his back pressed against the doorjamb, Katie couldn't move.

She was only a few feet away, standing on grass that needed a good mow, yet her legs had gone numb.

"You coming in?" he called from the door.

She needed a minute. No, a year would be good. Maybe even four more.

The screen snapped shut behind him, and Cooper walked out to join her on the lawn. "You know, I stood right in this spot when I watched you drive away. I'd been seconds from getting to the car when you peeled out of the driveway."

Cooper lowered his head, his eyes fixed on the ground. He plowed one hand through his hair and exhaled, long and slow. "How could you do it?" His eyes found hers. "How could you leave when you knew an atomic bomb hit our world?"

The million-dollar question. The one that hung in silence from everyone's lips. Her parents, Laila, Joe. None of them could understand. Even Katie now questioned how she could leave without feeling anything. But even that was a lie. She felt everything that night: disgust, terror, regret, self-loathing, desperation.

She'd spent her life searching for numb, and she could usually manufacture the indifference. And when she couldn't, she'd drink or take a hit until the lack of feeling returned. But that night, she'd known her life was too broken to repair, too broken to ignore. So she ran away.

Now it was her turn to study the grass. There were weeds intermixed with the Bermuda. Evil interlaced with good—the story of her life.

"I was afraid." She could hardly believe she said the words, and to Cooper of all people. The one man who could and would use them against her the minute he needed some ammunition.

Arms encircled her. Familiar arms. And a familiar smell when her head rested against his chest. "That's all I've been waiting to hear." His hand caressed her head, and his grip tightened. "Let's talk inside," he whispered.

She nodded and he let her go. She followed him down the sidewalk, through the door, and into the living room that hadn't changed, even down to the picture of the two of them on the wall behind his recliner.

"You didn't take it down."

He followed her gaze to the portrait. "I guess I always knew you'd come back."

She eyed all the other things he'd kept. The fluffy blue pillows he'd said he hated, the shelf of movies she'd put in alphabetical order, the stack of books she never read but insisted she would.

But then the other things hit her like a flash of reality. The patched spot where he'd slammed his fist into the drywall; the corner chair where he'd stood over her, screaming that she was a worthless piece of trash that couldn't even keep a job; the opening to the kitchen where she'd slapped him after he implied Piper would be better in the sack.

She backed toward the door. This wasn't her life anymore, and she didn't have to apologize for it. Stealing the ring was wrong, handing drugs to Chad was unforgivable, leaving Laila in the hospital without a word or help was something she'd regret her whole life. But walking out on Cooper? Leaving this toxic whirlpool behind? It was the smartest thing she'd ever done.

"I have to go." She didn't bother waiting but was out the door so fast it made her suck in air. Clean air. Hopeful air.

"Katie." His hand on her arm stopped her halfway to her car.

She spun around and pulled away. His face was shrouded in brokenness, but this time she realized his pain wasn't hers to fix. What he needed, she couldn't give to him.

"I'm sorry, Cooper. I'm sorry I hurt you, but it's over. It was over four years ago. You've been hanging on to a memory that isn't real."

"It is real." His voice was higher, tighter, laced with anger and hurt and vulnerability. "From the moment I met you, I loved you. Then you gave me Chad and Laila and made this place a home. The only home I've ever had, Katie. I saved it because without that hope, I'm alone. I'm so damn tired of being alone. You said you were afraid, but I've shown you I can be trusted. I'm here. I stayed and held your family together. And I know if you would just stop hiding, you'd see it."

He thought he loved her. Even now, she could feel the conviction pouring off him. But this wasn't love. Love was allowing her to watch the pond for ten minutes without pushing her to speak. Love was fixing her front steps despite having been treated like a leper by her father. Love was waiting for her to say yes before taking their relationship further. Love was accepting her past, yet pushing her to seek out a better future.

Asher had shown her love. Not just with his words, but in every interaction.

"You're not hearing me, Cooper. I *was* afraid. I'm not now. I don't need to be numb anymore. I'm not hiding. I'm wonderfully alive for the first time in my life." She took his lifeless hands in her own. "You'll have your family one day, but it's not me."

Cooper stood on the grass, unmoving, as she drove away, but the guilt was gone. She was finally free, and not because she'd made her last apology and said her last good-bye. No, she was free because somewhere in that house, looking at the ghosts lingering from the past, she'd finally forgiven herself.

⋎

Asher had just tightened the last bolt when he heard the crunch of gravel, followed by tire squealing and two slamming doors.

"You followed me?" The voice was unmistakably Katie's, and a chill shot down his spine.

"Did you think I would let our conversation end that way?" The hard male voice echoed through air, followed by a string of expletives he hadn't heard since college. "Did you really throw out 'You'll have a family one day' and walk away? Like I'm some stray dog you picked up and dropped off at the pound?"

Katie yelled something back, but Asher was too angry to make out her words, too ready to end Cooper's intrusion into her life once and for all.

They were in each other's faces, both shouting, when he cleared the corner.

"You showing up here is getting real old." The edge in his voice surprised him. He wasn't a fighter. Just the opposite; he was usually the one calming volatile situations.

Cooper's hands were squeezing Katie's biceps, and suddenly Asher knew this would be the last time the man ever touched her.

"Are you kidding me?" Katie's ex shoved her away with a curse and extended a hand in Asher's direction. "What? Do you have him collared and trained to beg too?"

Asher lifted his phone. "You have two seconds to leave or I'm calling the cops. We'll get a restraining order if we have to."

"A restraining order? *She* cornered me. *She* begged to talk. *She* came to *my* house and fell into my arms. It's not my fault your girlfriend is already getting tired of you."

Katie cut Asher off before he could shut Cooper up with his ready hand. Had he ever thrown a punch? No. Not ever. But something inside told him if he did, he wouldn't stop.

He tried to push past Katie, but she blocked him again, holding on to his shirt with an iron fist. "Asher. This isn't you. This isn't us."

She spun around to face the monster she used to date but kept her hands locked on to Asher's hips, using herself as a shield in front of him. It made him sick. His sides cramped, and his skin was so tight it felt as if it would split at any moment.

"Go home, Cooper," she demanded.

"You know what, babe, you're right. You're not my family. You're not good enough to be. You're just a self-centered user who betrays every person who's been stupid enough to care."

Asher punched in 911, held the screen so Cooper could see it. "I'm not bluffing."

"Fine. I'll leave." He cleared his throat and stared straight at Katie as he spoke. "Come find me when she rips your heart out, choirboy. I'll buy you a beer." He pointed a finger at her. "You stay away from me."

"Gladly." Her voice could have cut through steel, and the caustic tone took Asher back to high school. To the hard edge of the girl he'd never known.

Cooper gave them both the one-finger salute as his truck snaked out of the driveway. Tires spun, dust flew in all directions, and finally he was gone.

Katie's body deflated and she let go of her grip on Asher.

Cooper's words became a gathering storm in his mind, and his gut twisted. "You went to his house?" Why had he thought he would be different? She'd made it perfectly clear she didn't fall in love.

"He wouldn't talk at Joe's, and I wanted closure." Her answer was delivered as such a simple fact that his blood pulsed in his ears.

"Yeah, it looks like you got it."

She recoiled from his biting sarcasm, and her eyes flashed with a temper he'd never seen directed at him. "I did get closure. If he didn't, well, that's his problem."

"Is it my problem too, then? Because I'm not okay with you going anywhere near Cooper by yourself. He's dangerous. Did you see him just now? He was one snap away from losing it."

"I can handle myself."

Asher couldn't stop the burst of emotion. "It's not about you. It's about me. How did you think I'd feel about you going over there?" He'd deal with the "fell into my arms" comment once he could breathe again.

Her eyes registered surprise but her voice came out clear and calm. "I don't know. I never considered you."

A bullet would have hurt less.

"Of course you didn't."

CHAPTER 45

Asher walked away from her.

"Hey, where are you going?"

"Home. Tell your dad I'm wasn't in the mood for ice cream."

Ice cream? What was he talking about?

His stride was way too long for her to keep up without running, so she ran until she could grab his swinging arm. "Asher. Will you stop?"

"Why? Why does it matter? Twice now I've laid it out there. I've told you I care about you. I've told you I want you to stay, that I see a future for us. But you've given nothing back. I thought patience would help you open up, but I'm just a fool. Your dad's going to sell the house, and you're going to disappear. And I know why now. Because you'll never consider me."

Katie finally understood his reaction. "That's not what I meant."

"But it's true. Did you even think of me once today? Because you're all I thought about. All I ever think about. Because I'm the idiot who fell in love with someone who refuses to love me back."

Her hand flew to her throat. He loved her. She'd known it. He'd shown her in a million different ways, but hearing it from him, even laced with disappointment, sent a flood of warmth through her heart.

Asher blinked like he'd just woken up. "Crap. I hadn't planned to tell you that way." His head hung as if there was no more fight left in him. He placed his hands on his hips and exhaled a long breath.

She stepped forward, touched his cheek, urged him to look at her. His eyes were glassy and sad.

"I love you," he said again, but this time with no anger attached. "I'm sorry if it's too soon, or if that scares you. But I can't help how I feel. And I can't keep wondering if you feel even a little of what I do."

"I feel everything you do." The words came automatically. She loved him. And it wasn't just a new feeling. She'd loved him for a long time. Far longer than she'd ever realized.

His reaction was immediate. His eyes closed, his head fell back as if the world had just slipped off his shoulders. She'd hurt him by keeping her feelings from him. Never again.

She tucked his warm hand in hers and squeezed. "That first night we talked, you gave me hope. You told me to take it one task at a time. And I did. Every day I woke up and I thought, I can do this, because I knew you were next door. I knew you believed in me, that you saw a person I hadn't even become yet." She kissed his knuckles, pressed his hand to her heart.

"You were patient and kind and selfless. And when it mattered, when it got ugly and you could have walked away, you stayed. You made me stronger, forced me to face my fears. I was wrong the other day when I said I'd never fallen in love. Because I've fallen more than once. Asher, I've fallen in love with you over and over again."

Her throat stung and her eyes filled with tears she didn't even bother fighting. "When I said I didn't consider you, it was because I see Cooper as my past. An ugly, dark period of time when I was angry and destructive. You're beautiful and bright and my future. I just wanted to close that door, so I could move forward. For good."

He gathered her close, inhaled her hair, caressed her neck. "There is no separation between the two. If you want us to work, you have to include me, even in the parts that aren't so pretty. I've been in a relationship with walls, and masks, and false smiles. I called it love, but it wasn't. What we have—real, honest truth, painful or not—that's love."

She pressed her forehead against his chest. "I'm sorry I went there without you. I'm still not used to relying on someone."

"Well, get used to it, because next door or not, I'm not going anywhere."

She gazed up at him, a tear falling from her eyelashes. "You promise?"

"I promise."

His thumb rubbed a spot on her cheek, his palm still firmly against the back of her neck. A rush of heat flooded her, and her hands tangled in his hair, pulling, begging for him to come closer.

He lightly brushed his lips over hers, and everything inside her tightened. His gentle touch deepened, his embrace tense enough to mirror everything she was feeling. Her body begged for more. Urged her to feel and explore and take. She'd had many experiences, but he was the first to truly know her. They were connected already in so many ways that physically was the only step left.

But if Asher was right and this type of love only came after knowing Christ, then she'd have to trust that He knew best when it came to sexual intimacy. She wanted that closeness with Asher. That heat and passion and abandonment, but only when they could have it without regret or shame.

Asher broke away from her. "I think your parents just pulled in."

They had. She'd heard the rumble of her dad's engine but hadn't wanted to stop. "I know."

They were still locked together, their mouths only inches apart.

"We should go over there," he said.

"I know."

He tried to let go, but she held on tighter. "You're not moving."

"That's because I don't want to."

"Well, your dad and mom are watching us now."

"Good."

He pulled her arms from around his waist. "Come on. I just finally made some headway with your dad. I don't want to lose it."

She peeked back toward her parents, but they'd already gone inside. "What type of headway?"

He wrapped an arm around her shoulder and pulled her along as he walked back to her house. "I fixed the air conditioner. Right before the Cooper showdown. Your dad actually came over and asked for my help."

Warmth spread through her body like she'd just downed hot chocolate. "That's a huge step for him."

"And for us." Asher met her grin with an equal one. "I didn't like the idea that your parents resented me. Family is important."

"They resented me, not you. They thought you were going to be another thing I quit, so there was no point in getting to know you. His coming to you means he's starting to trust me again." She choked on the last few words. Maybe in time he'd trust her enough to let her share her faith with him too.

"What about your mom?"

She inched closer to their front steps. "Some personalities never really mesh. But I do think we're making progress." She climbed up two of the steps and turned, placing her hands on Asher's shoulders. She was actually eye-to-eye with him. "One day at a time, right? Find purpose in each one."

"I can't believe you still remember what I said that first night."

"Remember? Those words have carried me through all the tough days since."

"If I'd known you were going to quote me, I would have been more profound. I should have given you scripture or something from one of Dad's sermons."

She leaned forward and lightly kissed his lips. "You gave me a part of you, even before I knew you had. That's why your words mattered.

Sometimes people need more than a verse and a prayer; they need to know someone cares."

His hand slipped to the nape of her neck. "I love you," he said, right before his lips met hers.

If she heard those words a thousand times she would never tire of them.

The front door slammed behind her. "Good night! You two kiss more than teenagers in a backseat. Now get in here. The ice cream is melting."

Katie grinned at her mother. "At least it's the ice cream and not you anymore, although I do hear water can be detrimental to your type."

Her mom rolled her eyes, but Katie didn't miss the way the corners of her mouth twitched. It'd been a long time since they'd been able to tease each other without bitter truth laced through each word.

Katie took Asher's hand and pulled him along, passing her mother, who firmly grasped her walker.

"It was mighty nice of you to drop everything like you did to help us," she said.

Asher let go of Katie's hand. "Anytime. I was happy to do it."

Her mom fidgeted under his kind stare. She wasn't used to people simply helping because they could. He laid a hand on her white-knuckled grip. "It won't always be this hard." His words were laced with compassion and understanding.

Her mom turned away without responding. But her body language said more than words ever could. Her lip trembled, and her eyes welled up with tears that were as uncommon for her as they were for Katie. Once again, Asher's simple statement became important and meaningful.

They left her mom on the porch and walked down the same hall that had felt so hopeless just a few months ago. The air inside was fresh, the house organized and cleaned. This was her new beginning. Right here, hand in hand with her hope from next door.

CHAPTER 46

A month later, Katie's parents signed two sets of documents. One to sell her childhood home. The other to purchase a small handicap-accessible house in Fairfield Community, where her mother could receive all the care she needed.

She had also signed her own document—a six-month lease on a one-bedroom apartment downtown. Ironically, it was within walking distance of Joe's, a proximity she planned to fully exploit.

Though still cold, Laila thawed a little each time they spoke, and Katie knew why. Laila needed to know she was staying. She needed to feel that Katie cared. And she needed time, which for once, Katie felt capable of giving.

"Second load just took off."

Katie spun around to face Asher as he walked into her empty bedroom. He'd been a champion this week. Packing all day, moving furniture, running for takeout. If she had a million years, she could never say thank you enough.

"I'm so relieved for my parents, but I can't help but feel a little sad."

"That's understandable. You did grow up here."

"Yeah, but I have very few positive memories."

"I'm guessing the ones you do have are pretty great, though."

She eyed the bare walls, thought of all the nights she'd spent with Laila and Chad in this very spot. "They are."

Asher picked up a sheet of packing paper and balled it up. "This place definitely needs a good vacuuming. I think your dust bunnies had babies."

She smacked his arm. "I'll get to it tomorrow." Still feeling nostalgic, she walked the perimeter of the room, stopping at her window. "Chad would climb through this window every time Laila spent the night."

Asher peered through the glass. "How?"

"There used to be an oak tree right outside. Dad cut it down after he caught me sneaking out my sophomore year. That's when I memorized the squeak patterns on the stairs. Turns out that escaping through the front door is actually easier than scaling two stories."

He shook his head. "My parents have no idea how easy I made things for them in high school."

She laughed, and an old memory snapped in her mind. She pulled Asher over to the closet. "Can you see past the top shelf?"

He lifted up on his tiptoes, allowing his eyes to reach past the white wood. "Yes. Barely."

"There should be a quote carved into the wall."

He squinted at the scratch marks. "You couldn't just do black marker?"

"Too cliché."

He scooted closer, lifted himself higher. "'I would not wish any companion in the world but you,'" he read.

"William Shakespeare."

"And you said you weren't good in school."

"I wasn't. That was Chad's quote. He did it one night while Laila and I were asleep. The next day, she woke to a note that told her where to find it." Sadness echoed through her, and the air in the room suddenly felt heavy.

She backed away from the closet, wrapped both arms around her waist.

"His addiction is not your fault."

"I know. But his overdose was."

"Katie." Asher cupped her face, forced her to look at him, although she didn't want to. "You didn't make him take the drugs. That was his choice. His decision."

A tear fell. She'd stopped fighting them while she was alone with him. He loved seeing her raw emotions, and she loved that he did. "He was my family. So was Laila. And I let them both down. I want to fix it. I want to find him and make him see what he's losing."

"Would that have worked with you?"

"No."

"Exactly. He has to find his own way home. Faith is a journey. It doesn't have a stop and start date. It grows with time. Sometimes it falters and stumbles, but every misstep can be used to shape us. Pray that God puts people in Chad's life the way He did in yours."

Reverend Snow.

She exhaled. "You're right. I just still feel so responsible."

He wrapped her tight. "Forgiving yourself is the hardest thing to do. It took me a year after my breakup with Jillian to finally let go of the shame."

"How did you do it?"

"Time. Prayer. Lots of hammers." He chuckled. "And you, of course."

She buried her face in his chest, welcomed the strength of his arms. "I know you're right. I'm just not there yet."

"Well, maybe this will help." He released her and pulled a small padded envelope from his back pocket. It was orange, with labels covering the surface. *Certified. Insured. Fragile.* The end had been cut open and was frayed. Slowly, he stuck two fingers in and pulled out a ring.

She could only stare. Rose gold. Flower design. An emerald shining in the center. "How?" Her breath faltered, and while she desperately wanted to touch the ring, her arms were numb and unmovable.

"I tracked it down. When I explained the situation to the representative at eBay and gave her all the dates and the seller's information, she contacted the buyer privately. He agreed to sell it back to me."

Her eyes bounced from the ring to him and back to the ring. "When did you . . ."

"It's been a while. I went back to the pawnshop and got as much information as she was willing to give me—which was all public record anyway, but getting her help cut my research time. Then it was just a matter of persistence. It arrived this morning."

He stretched out his hand and placed the ring in her palm.

The light metal was cool and delicate. She closed her fist around the object that had represented all of her failures. Months before, she thought finding this ring would give her absolution and peace, but now she knew that could only come from the One so much greater than jewelry. God didn't have to give her this tangible blessing, but He had anyway. And now she'd be able to give Mary back the piece of her mother that Katie had so callously taken away.

She slid a finger through the hole and let the gem sparkle in the light. "I prayed for a miracle." But she never really believed she was worthy to receive it.

He brushed a thumb across her cheek. "Looks like God gave you one."

She stared at the man in front of her—the same man who had shown her the beauty of true love—and covered his hand with hers.

"Actually, He gave me two."

Love is patient, love is kind. It does not envy, it does not boast, it is not proud. It does not dishonor others, it is not self-seeking, it is not easily angered, it keeps no record of wrongs.

1 Corinthians 13:4–5, (NIV)

ACKNOWLEDGMENTS

There are some books that you just feel called to write. Books that inspire you to grow and to reflect on how far God has carried you. This is that book for me, and I'm so grateful to all who have helped me on this incredible journey.

To the Waterfall Press editors and staff: thank you for loving this book as much as I do. For encouraging me and for giving me the freedom to be creative and true to my voice. It's been a pleasure working with all of you.

To my fabulous agent, Jessica Kirkland, for challenging me to dig deep and find the right story to tell. For never accepting anything other than my best, and for setting an example of hard work and dedication. You are an inspiration to me.

To Nicole Deese, for the million texts and chapter excerpts you read. For always telling me the truth, even when I don't want to hear it. For being a beacon of faith and for making me love writing every day because I get to share my crazy stories with you. And for being the kind of friend who sustains time and distance and makes life so much more enjoyable to live.

To my sister, Angel, for always reading my first draft and encouraging me every time you do. For your wisdom and friendship, and for being the best sister a girl could have.

To my amazing writing critique partners—Connilyn Cossette, Dana Red, Lori Wright, and Laurie Westlake—your talent inspires me to demand more from each page. Thank you for your steadfast commitment and for reminding me every week who gets all the glory.

To my wonderful readers—you make writing fun. Your continual encouragement, e-mails, and reviews pick me up on the hard days and bring me unending joy.

And finally, to my amazing husband and children—for all the sacrifices you make, allowing me to pour my heart and soul into every word. I love you more than you'll ever know.

ABOUT THE AUTHOR

Photo © 2015 Karen Graham

Tammy L. Gray lives in the Dallas area with her family. They love all things Texas, including the erratic weather patterns. She writes modern Christian romances with true-to-life characters and culturally relevant plotlines. She believes that hope and healing can be found through high-quality fiction that inspires and provokes change. Writing has given her a platform to combine her passion with her ministry.

86428396R00195

Made in the USA
San Bernardino, CA
28 August 2018